# SCOTT COVE

H J Pettersen

ISBN 978-1-956696-86-8 (paperback)
ISBN 978-1-956696-87-5 (hardcover)
ISBN 978-1-956696-88-2 (digital)



Rushmore Press LLC
1 800 460 9188
www.rushmorepress.com

Printed in the United States of America

# FOREWORD

Thank you always to Kat, my perfect partner and wife. And a heartfelt thanks to Mrs. Etta Overton for making a place in her home for a kid that could not make the last ferry to the island when he turned out for sports.

# CHAPTER 1

Logan bounded down the steps of Charley's house. The early morning air had a touch of crispness as summer was coming to an end. He headed to the marina to find Dad, who was trying to get the new king crab boat ready to head to Alaska in a few weeks.

The crab boat was sitting quietly in its slip at the small marina. *Dad must be at home working in the garage,* Logan thought. He trotted up the hill toward home, happy that his first year of high school would start in a few days, and more importantly, his fifteenth birthday would soon follow.

As he cleared the two steps to the back door and opened the creaky screen door, he saw Mom cutting up vegetables at the kitchen sink. "Hi, Mom, where's Dad?" Logan asked in one breath. "He wasn't at the boat when I stopped by."

"Dad's down to Grandpa's cabin to start tearing apart Big Kanute. Now that Grandpa is gone, Kanute needs to go."

"No, Mom! I want Kanute for myself."

"That poor old rotten boat? It hasn't been able to hold water out for years."

"But Mom! I can fix it this winter, then use it for fishing."

"No. Your dad and I have decided it's unsafe." She looked over her shoulder at her slender son and smiled. "But he does want you to help him take it apart."

Logan slumped into the chair by the table, crushed by the thought that the boat he had spent so many years fishing with Grandpa on was now going to be destroyed.

"Do you know what Dad plans on doing with all the parts he's taking off Big Kanute?"

"No. You might ask Dad when you get there," Mother said, now watching her youngest out of the corner of her eye.

"Now it's a bright sunny day, so hop on your bicycle and get going. You might have fun taking all the equipment off Big Kanute."

Logan stood up and picked up the cookie jar, feeling its heaviness. He took the lid off and grabbed three cookies in his almost man-size hands. "I'll go, but it kills me to destroy a good boat. See you for lunch."

Mom heard his light step on the back porch of the two-story house on 19th street as he cleared the steps in one stride. Logan grabbed his fender-less bike leaned up against the front yard fence. He threw a leg over the seat and pushed off, pedaling as fast as he could for Grandpa's shack six blocks away on Q Avenue.

He thought if he hurried, he might be able to convince Dad not to destroy Kanute. He was sure he could replace a few planks and make a seaworthy boat out of her.

Logan continued to race across Main street, pulling up on the turned-up handlebars to jump the high curb then pumping the pedals toward Dad and Big Kanute.

Why was this turning into the most critical moment of his life? His biggest dream was to own his fishing boat and now, a month shy of fifteen, he felt ready to take on the task of repairing Big Kanute.

Besides, he had worked with Dad every winter rebuilding boats when he wasn't in school. Surely, that gave him the skill to do the work needed on Big Kanute.

Cruising into the sloped yard of the little house his grandfather had lived in for over forty years, he saw Dad's tired rusted-out Dodge Coupe hitched up to a just-as-rusty single-axle trailer backed up next to Kanute.

Dad, with a sledgehammer in one hand, a crowbar in the other, and a big smile on his face, was walking toward the boat. He was a big man, but not tall. Logan had a couple of inches on him at six feet.

They both had a great sense of humor and got along okay, as long as it was going Dad's way. Logan was sure Dad considered him "free labor" or for a better description "a rented mule."

"Dad, you don't really want to destroy old Kanute, do you? She was Grandpa's boat."

"Logan, we have been over this too many times," Dad said gruffly. "You and I both know she's in bad shape. All the seams leak and look at the plywood roof. It's separating. Even the keel bolts have rotted out.

"There are a lot of better boats around. Now put your gloves on and go up on the cabin. You can start pulling those portholes out. Be careful not to break the glass."

Logan knew it was hopeless to push his Dad when he used that tone of voice. He grabbed his gloves and tools and climbed the ladder up to Kanute's bulwarks. Unscrewing and carefully working the portholes out, he grumbled under his breath, quiet enough that Dad couldn't hear. "You don't understand. I can't go North unless I have a boat of my own. Mother won't let me work on the fishing boats unless I'm with you, and now that you've sold the gillnet boats and bought the king crab boat, that leaves me high and dry on the beach. Or would that be up to a creek without a paddle?

Logan continued muttering. "You're leaving for westward Alaska in a month, and here I sit." He knew his dad wouldn't be home until next summer, and then he would work on the boat and gear. *Caramba! I need a boat,* he thought.

Hanging himself over the edge of the boat, he called, "Hey Dad. What about all the hardware we're pulling off Kanute? What'll you do with that?"

"Put it in the garage, for now, I guess. Don't have time to do anything else. Are you going to work or ask questions all day? Now do what I ask!"

Logan could tell Dad was frustrated. He still had lots of work to do yet on his boat before heading to the abundant crabbing grounds in the Bering Sea.

"Yes, sir. But I want first shot at buying all the hardware off Kanute, including the old Union Putt-Putt engine. Ok?"

A plan was already growing in Logan's young fertile mind.

"We'll see. Now, would you get the rag out and get to work for the last time? I want to get home on time for dinner. When you finish with the portholes, all the rotten wood goes in the trailer. We'll haul it to the dump then load the hardware to go home."

*It seems like half our house is for storing Grandpa's stuff since all his fishing gear is in the basement already.*

"Do you promise me a chance to buy the hardware?"

Dad's voice got gruffer. "Logan, if you don't get to work, I *will* promise you a swift kick."

Logan knew when Dad used that stern tone of voice, everyone cleared out. They did what he asked, and he wasn't kidding about the swift kick.

Father and son worked all morning under a cloudless sky, and the work was hot and dirty.

Mom showed up with lunch at noon and she was a welcome sight. "How are you two doing?"

Henry smiled at his pretty wife. "Thought I was going to have to smack young noisy there. He wouldn't shut up and go to work. Sometimes, Mother, I wonder if he is my son. Are you sure you didn't find him under a cabbage leaf somewhere?"

"Oh no, he's your son, all right. That you better believe. Grandpa always said the apple doesn't fall far from the tree."

Logan had barely started chewing the last bite of his bologna sandwich when Dad stood up, signaling it was time to get back to work.

Mom wished them a pleasant afternoon and left for home. They finished throwing the rotten pieces of wood from the boat cabin, and what Dad had pulled off the hull, into the trailer.

All loaded up, they headed for the dump. The rust-red Dodge complained as the transmission bumped into first gear. The trip was quiet, even with the noise of the rattly old steel trailer they were towing.

Logan started to say something, but Dad hushed him. This whole thing was not to Logan's liking.

A deep shadow had already covered Big Kanute when they got back from the dump, and the day had slipped away on them.

They lifted the little two-cylinder Union engine into the trailer along with the shaft, rudder, and brass trolling gurdy drum. Logan considered this the crown jewel of the old boat. The remaining small marine hardware finished filling the trailer bed. After tying the mast, boom, and sails on top, they headed home with the Dodge transmission complaining again as they put her into first gear.

The full trailer turned into a sizable pile in the middle of the garage floor. Dad took his hat off and wiped his brow, signaling it was time to knock off for the day.

Mom came out to tell them dinner was ready as Dad was putting his hat back on.

Soon, Logan had bolted his dinner down and headed to the garage. He wanted to get things organized.

Ellen cleared the table as Henry sat in his chair. "What will you do with all that old junk out there? I know your son has his heart set on being the proud owner of it all someday."

Henry gave a big smile. "You're right, Mother. I'll be putting a new inflatable life raft on the crab boat. The old lifeboat on top of the house is too big and cumbersome. Our boy doesn't know it yet, but I want to swap my lifeboat and all Kanute's gear for his skiff."

Mother frowned and shook her head. "That will be hard for him. He sails that little boat every day unless he is helping you or in school. I remember when he built it, across the alley in Burnt's shed."

"He and Burnt can build a good boat out of the lifeboat and Big Kanute's gear. They'll both be up to the challenge. I know they enjoyed putting the skiff together. I'll talk to Burnt in a few days or so, then Logan and I will have the conversation."

"Thank you, Dad," Ellen said, patting Henry's shoulder. "It's killing that boy with you going to Alaska and not taking him along. The boat and equipment will keep him busy until you get back next summer."

# CHAPTER 2

It was hard being almost fifteen.

Logan had started fishing with his dad when he was at the tender age of eight. Every summer, he was out of school early, then back to school late in the fall. There wasn't much time for kid stuff. And fishing was dangerous work. There was no playing around while working on the boats or fishing nets.

At the end of last season, Dad had sold his salmon fishing boats and bought an Alaska King Crab boat. Now, he would be leaving for the Aleutian Chain in Alaska next month.

The King Crab rush was starting, and this year, 1964, was forecasted to have a big season.

Dad was figuring on making enough money to support the family by catching lots of crab, and Mother knew he would be gone a long time.

It was getting dark as Logan walked out the back door to their dilapidated two-car garage behind the house. Its faded yellow paint was peeling and cracked, and the shingled roof looked tired and worn.

As he stepped inside, it was completely dark. Out of habit, he reached next to the door frame and found the light switch. One rotation of the knob and a loud click powered the lonesome light bulb above the dirty plank workbench.

Parts and pieces from Big Kanute had been stacked and piled everywhere when they unloaded the trailer. Logan was looking forward to organizing everything.

Little Kanute, the seven-foot skiff Grandpa used to get himself ashore when Big Kanute was on anchor, was leaned up against the far wall.

Logan remembered all the times he and Grandpa had rowed the old dinghy, Grandpa's big arms pushing on the oars. Then Logan would take over the rowing as Grandpa encouraged him.

Logan shook his head, knowing those times were long gone. He had been quiet during dinner, but then he was quiet most of the time, keeping his thoughts to himself. Logan didn't have much to say unless it was to Grandpa or Dad, mostly talking boats, and now, even that would be gone soon.

Getting back to the task at hand, Logan noticed the two-cylinder Union Marine engine sitting out in front of all the gear. It had a reverse gear mounted on the back of the bell housing. That little motor had run great when they pulled Big Kanute out of the water a few years ago. Logan loved to listen to the small engine run. It would sound like putt-de, putt, putt. Or was it putt, putt, de putt? It has been a while since he had last heard it run. They all affectionately called it "Putt-Putt."

Grandpa had rigged sails on Big Kanute with a gaffed main and a small jib forward. Logan needed to find the right size boat for the mast and sails. They were still in good shape and ready to go.

He started moving a few things from the floor to empty spots on the shelves. Each piece brought back memories, and he was determined to put all of them on another boat.

As the week moved on, Logan got most of the gear sorted and organized as best he could.

His favorite item was the little Putt-Putt Union engine. He would roll over the small motor with the hand crank every day to make sure there was lubrication in the cylinders to prevent it from seizing up. Someday, he would put her back to work.

Logan's big dream was here, and he wasn't going to let go of it.

Sitting there next to Putt-Putt, he heard the garage door swing open. It was Dad. "How you are doing, son?"

"I'm good, Dad. I keep thinking about Grandpa and all his stories, morning, noon, and night. What a great man he was."

"Yes, he was. We all miss him very much." Dad paused and waited until Logan looked up. "You still want all this junk of his?"

"Yeah! You bet I do. I only need a boat to put it in."

"Well, I got a deal for you. I was going to ask you earlier before Grandpa passed on."

Dad looked sad. Grandpa's loss still showed on his face.

"Logan, would you consider swapping your skiff for the lifeboat sitting on the crab boat? I'm going to pull the lifeboat off the boat. The darn thing is too big, heavy, and clumsy to get into the water safely. With it nested on top of the house, I'm not sure how it would launch in rough seas anyway."

"My skiff?" Logan felt panic crawling up his backside. "Dad, I don't know. Burnt and I put it together."

Dad continued. "I have a new inflatable raft we loaded the other day and hung on the galley bulkhead. That will take care of anything that comes up for my crew and me.

"To make the deal a fair one, I'll throw in this pile of gear from Big Kanute, including little Kanute there. That'll give you something to make it to shore in."

"Wow, Dad! That's quite a deal. That includes the engine and trolling power reel, right?"

"Yep. Everything on the shelves and in this pile on the floor." Dad waved his arms to include the unsorted collection. "It's all yours, lock stock and barrel. I don't want anything. Now, don't forget to keep the sails and rigging from your sailboat."

Dad paused. "All I want is the skiff and oars to put on top of the crab boat wheelhouse."

"When could we bring the lifeboat home?" Logan asked, his mind already working on designing his new boat. "Then I can get started putting her together right away."

Logan's whole life had just turned on a dime. This was a chance to make his dream come true.

His new boat, Dad's old lifeboat, would be big enough to go out in the San Juan Islands and live on her for the summer.

He could fish the kelp patches for rock and lingcod. Then when the tide went out, he could dig a few clams, and pick a few oysters on the same low tide, just like Dad and Grandpa had taught him.

Logan was smiling from ear to ear. "I need to go and talk to Burnt. He could give me advice about putting it together, now that he's retired from the big tugs. Wow, Dad! I can't wait to get started."

He didn't tell his dad what his actual plans were. For now, he would outfit the lifeboat, knowing all of Big Kanute's gear would fit, and the boat would become his fishing boat.

It was even big enough to take him north, if need be, to make money.

Once he got to Alaska, he could hand-troll salmon and earn enough to buy a bigger trolling boat.

This burning desire wasn't new, but now it had a way to come true. All he wanted to do was to fish Alaskan waters. He had listened to everyone talking about it his whole life. He made a promise to himself that he would do whatever it took to make this happen.

Dad borrowed a single-axle boat trailer to haul the lifeboat home. Tomorrow would be Saturday, and they would get an early start.

Getting up early the next day, Dad already had the boat trailer hitched up to his old '50 Dodge Coupe. Man, what a beater it was. The car was covered in rust and the old flathead-six engine literally ate oil.

A plume of blue smoke belched from the engine as Dad started it up.

Logan didn't care. He was a proud new boat owner today.

Dad told Logan to row his skiff from its mooring at the little marina over to the crab boat.

Once his skiff was by the crab boat, they wrestled the lifeboat off the top of the wheelhouse using the davit winch. Then, they lifted it over the gunwales and lowered it into the water.

Logan transferred the sails from his skiff to the lifeboat for the ride home. Then the little skiff was hoisted to the top of the wheelhouse and mounted in its new cradle.

Logan took a minute to say goodbye to his boat. He and their long-time neighbor Burnt Jensen had built her strong and she would serve Dad well.

He was excited to show Burnt the lifeboat and knew he would understand this was for Big Kanute's gear. He wouldn't tell Burnt this was his ticket to go north, yet.

The morning air was still fresh. The few clouds would soon move on and let the sun warm things up. Logan wasn't worried about the coolness. He was figuring on rowing his new boat as fast as he could.

Dad untied the lifeboat and gave it a shove to get him started for the ramp. Logan slid the big oars into their oarlocks.

*These are huge compared to the skiff.* At twelve-foot, one oar was as long as his old boat, and he was pulling on two of them.

Logan soon realized that the whole boat was huge. She had high sides, with seats across from gunnel to gunnel called thwarts. "Now, this was a real boat!" he announced to the world. "Not a little work-skiff with a tiller on the stern."

He settled in, pulling on the oars together, finding the rhythm to rowing, and feeling the muscles in his back and arms work.

After clearing the breakwater, Logan had to control his urge to head for open water and not ever look back. That would be the next step in his "big dream." *That won't work.* There was too much to do to get the boat ready for open water. Besides, if he left now, Dad would hunt him down and kill him. Yep, it would be murder at sea. Only the crabs would know what happened when the body hit the bottom of Guemes Channel with heavy boom chain wrapped around it. *Leaving now would not be a good idea.* Logan's mind came back to the present, steadily pulling on the oars.

He was to pull in at the nearest boat ramp which was between the old shake mill and the pulp mill, just around the corner from the marina.

As Logan rowed past the pulp mill, his mind went to wandering. He was pulling into Ketchikan, Alaska, back from a long fishing trip out in the Straits.

Ever since he was a little boy, he had listened to stories of the fishing fleet heading north, and soon, it would be his turn.

Logan was a fisherman's son, and there was never much money to do things, so he daydreamed a lot. The second-best escape was reading books from the library.

Now that he owned a real boat and had the genuine gear to complete her, he was anxious to start work.

Dad was standing at the bottom of the ramp with the trailer backed in the water to the top of the tires. He had hip boots on, ready to wade in and guide the lifeboat onto the rails on the trailer. Shortly, the boat was resting nicely on the borrowed trailer. Dad smiled as he started winching her the rest of the way.

"Did you have a good trip?"

"Did I! If you weren't waiting for me, I would have kept going." They both laughed.

With the bow held tight by the winch, Dad fired up the old Dodge, and out of the water she came.

The sand was soft here next to the tide flats, especially at low water. Logan hoped they didn't get the old Dodge stuck because Dad would be hopping mad for sure, and no one wanted to see that.

They stopped at the top of the ramp to lash the boat to the trailer. "All fast?" asked Dad. Logan nodded, yes. They jumped into the Dodge and headed home.

In a matter of minutes, they were backing into the backyard.

Logan had set up all the blocking the day before, making it easy to back the trailer up and finish blocking the boat. Then Dad pulled the trailer out from under her.

She sat, straight and level, with her keel set on blocks and the sides supported by bracing timbers.

"Good job, Logan."

"Thanks again, Dad. More than anything, thanks for bringing her home."

# CHAPTER 3

Logan was proud to have his new-to-him boat in the back yard. He had set up the blocks next to the garage where he could work on her all winter.

Dad took the trailer back to its owner, and Logan immediately started the task of cleaning her, deciding what he had to do next.

First, he scrubbed down the outside, then unloaded the miscellaneous junk inside. He gave her a good sweeping and finally a thorough scrubbing on the inside.

By the time he had completed the cleaning job, it was dark. Dinner time had come and gone. Mother had fixed him a plate and left it covered in the fridge.

As Logan was eating his cold dinner, Dad came in and sat in his chair at the kitchen table. "What do you think, Logan, you still okay with the trade?"

"You bet I am, but I do have one problem, though. I've been working on boats for the last six summers, and we rebuilt boats in the winter. Those were all wood, but this one is steel. I don't know how to put the stuffing box and cutlass bearings in her. Will I need to do some welding?"

Dad thought for a minute. Logan could see his eyes light up. "You remember the power install conversion in our little Lucky II Bristol Bay boat?"

Logan did remember. He knew all the stories of the wooden boats. Initially, commercial fishermen could only use sails. Then, a new fisheries law came into effect. They were allowed to use motors in their open sailboats for gillnetting in Bristol Bay, Alaska.

Dad continued, "You remember the big cannery outfit, Columbia River Packers, out of Astoria? They had a bunch of these boats. Every one of them was the same, right to the last steamed plank." He smiled, watching Logan's face as he was thinking, staring at the plate of food in front of him.

"It's been a long day. You must be tired. Well, son, they were having the same problem, getting the shaft through the stern with a stuffing box and installing a stern bearing. Is a light going on for you now?"

"Oh, wow, you're right. I can make a template, then build one out of steel to bed and bolt to the stern just like the wood boats did. So how about that long strip of steel like the stern horn timber?"

"Cut a chunk out to fit the shaft through. Make sure you use heavy material, quarter-inch steel, or better, to make that adapter. Don't forget you need to bed the engine first, then align the shaft."

"You're right, Dad. I'll go to my room right now and make some drawings. That'll be a lot of fun."

Logan was proud of his dad. He was smart this way, being Grandpa's son and raised around boats. And now he is teaching his son.

Being a fisherman's son was hard at times. Logan's dad would work long hours in all kinds of weather, and the pay wasn't much. The family never had extra money for fun things. Usually, they just had barely enough to keep them fed.

Logan's dad knew what he was doing. He had given Logan a challenge and a project, and he knew this was the best thing he could do before heading north. Logan would need to think and solve problems on his own.

School was starting next week, and Logan had already started football practice. He kept thinking he would rather be working on his boat. He had all the parts laid out, waiting to install, and time was slipping away. Dad would be leaving in three weeks and every spare minute Logan had was spent readying the crab boat for her trip north.

It still hurt to think of his dad and crew leaving without him. Dads and sons had always made the fishing season together. This year, it had all changed for Logan and he knew he shouldn't dwell on it.

The three weeks flew by, and it was time for Dad to go north. *There must be a calling they had to answer.* Logan knew his dad had it, and he could feel it in himself as well. It was like an itch he needed to scratch. He, too, would be packing up someday and heading north like so many others before him.

Dad kept feeding advice to Logan. "Don't forget the lifeboat has a steel hull. Ground her good and hang plenty of zincs on the bottom. If you don't, she'll waste away right out from underneath you.

"What are you going to name her, 'Tin Tub'?" he said, followed by one of his big belly laughs.

Logan had thought long and hard on this subject. "Think about it, Dad. When we were fishing all those summers, going to different places, people always asked us, 'Where you headed?'"

"Yeah, you're right. So, are you going to call her 'Heading North' like I am doing with the crab boat?"

"No, you can name your boat that. I'll name mine, 'Points North.' That's the direction I want to go. Dad, I still wish I could go with you."

"Yeah, I do too. Makes me sad. You watch out for Mom and Sis. Next summer, we'll work on the boat here in town together. Alright?"

"That's a long time away, you know."

It was time to take Dad to the dock. The crab boat was ready to go, fully loaded with grub and gear.

All their friends came down to the Port Dock to see him and his crew off.

Logan was sad, and the ugly truth was it hurt inside, like when Grandpa passed. He wondered if that feeling would ever go away.

All the crew gave their families hugs and shared tears on that overcast day. Yes, it was a gloomy day. The only thing missing was rain.

Once onboard, the excitement mounted with everyone waving and shouting back and forth.

Two crew members untied lines and pulled them aboard, and the boat slipped away from the dock.

The crab boat made a traditional circle in front of the Port Dock like the rest of the fishing fleet did when heading north.

Logan stood on the dock holding his bicycle, watching the crab boat getting smaller in the distance.

The smoke from her stack became thinner the farther away she went. Then she slipped around the point on Guemes Island and was out of sight.

Logan was feeling sorry for himself. The finality of being left behind was almost killing him.

Pondering his future, he caught sight of an enormous tug northbound up Rosario Straits. It was chugging puffs of black smoke as it towed a heavily loaded barge.

Ever since he could remember, the tugs had been coming out of Seattle, hauling machinery and supplies, heading for Alaska up the inside passage.

Logan's dream machine started up again. He was dreaming and wishing he was going north on that tugboat right now.

"There's a thought. . ." he said to the universe, his eyes following the slow progress of the tug.

He remembered one of the stories Burnt Jensen had told him. During WWII, Burnt was a deckhand on the old Miki-Miki wooden tugs. They hauled goods and equipment to Alaska on barges. The tug crew always made sure each barge had an emergency tow line dragging behind it with a buoy ball on the end of the line.

From time to time, salmon trollers would tie the buoyed line to their bow and get a free tow to wherever the barge was going.

Logan's face broke out into a huge smile. "Hey, why not? That sounds like a great idea!"

The dream machine kicked into a higher gear. That would be fun to do. Logan needed to know which tugs and barges were going to Alaska and which ones weren't.

*Guess the bigger the tug, the farther they're going.*

Burnt could tell Logan how that worked.

With a final look over the water, Logan turned his bike and headed toward home. He planned to visit with Burnt first thing and talk about his idea.

Burnt could keep a secret, but if he didn't, Logan knew he would be dead in the water.

# CHAPTER 4

School was not a favorite activity for Logan. He would rather be out fishing and making money. Still, the subject was not up for debate. Logan would go to school to make his mother happy and finish the task. To Logan, any kind of work was better than being held prisoner in the classroom. Not to mention being around a bunch of kids he didn't have anything in common with.

Classroom days were spent staring out the window, daydreaming about being in rough seas and fishing King Crab with his dad.

The picture was so detailed in his mind. He could see himself hanging onto the rocking boat with one hand and working gear with the other, catching crabs, lots of them.

Then Logan and his dad would deliver to the buyer, selling their catch and getting a pile of money for their payday.

Logan knew that was the life for him—not sitting in school listening to some old duffer standing in front of the class, droning on about things he could care less about.

He did have one good friend in school, and that was Charley. Now girls were another thing. Logan didn't think a girl would give him the time of day if she had to. That was his guess anyway, and that was fine with him.

Besides, girls always wanted it their way and that didn't work for him. What he thought about was someone who wanted to share the relationship 50/50. Not that he wanted a girl or a commitment. No thanks. Right now, his life was too busy with his boat. Girls demanded all your time, he thought, and that wouldn't work.

On top of all that, he hadn't found a girl who liked to catch fish the way he did. Wow, now that would be a real girl.

Logan decided he'd need to keep an eye peeled. She had to be out there. Most likely, that would be up north. They probably knew about fishing and fishing people up there.

Mid-October rolled around, and he was halfway through football season. The rainy season was hard on the team. The rain never let up and all the football practices were mud baths.

When it wasn't raining in the early morning, they had frost to deal with. Come to think of it, the weather was depressing.

Carrie, his younger sister and a sixth-grader, loved school, and, as usual, got straight A's.

Logan's grades, in the ninth grade, were lousy at best, and he didn't care. The coach kept warning him to keep his studies up, but Logan couldn't find the time.

Dad had been gone for six weeks now.

Points North looked forlorn in Logan's backyard, covered with two tarps to keep the rain out.

In the back of his mind, she kept gnawing away at him. He knew he should be working on the engine bed project, but his birthday came and went, and life carried on. Nothing was going on in the girl department either, even though he was fifteen now.

Now Charley was sixteen and already dating someone. He loved cars and girls and it looked like having a car was paying off for him. Logan was happy for Charley, but he still had no interest in getting a girlfriend.

The two friends would hang out together at school. Charley would treat Logan like a younger brother, but with respect.

Soon, it was the end of October, and freshman football was winding down.

Logan started getting ready for the wrestling season. He liked wrestling because what happened out on the mats depended entirely on him, not a team. And because he had worked all summer on the fish boats, the hard, manual labor made him strong and agile for his age. His older neighbor, Burnt, always told Logan he was harder than nails.

After the Saturday evening movies, he and Charley pulled up in front of Logan's house. He noticed the preacher's car parked out front.

Logan slid out of the car, glancing back at Charley. "This might not be good," he said. Logan noticed a couple of other cars next to his mom's car. He recognized them as friends from Mom's church.

Logan referred to it as Mom's church because he didn't want anything to do with it.

He walked toward the house, waving goodbye to Charley. The closer he got, the more worry crept into his mind. *All right, no alarm, I've seen them here before.*

Logan walked around the house and stepped onto the porch. He could hear a lot of sobbing and crying going on in the kitchen.

"Oh man, this is not good," he muttered as he opened the door to the kitchen.

Logan could see Carrie and Mom standing in the middle of the floor, crying hard, their arms wrapped around one another.

Mom's friends were sitting in the front room, mumbling to themselves. The Reverend Benson and his wife were together in the dining room.

Logan walked up to his mother, preparing for the worst.

Mom saw him, turned, and hugged him, sobbing. "There was a huge storm. Your dad, crew, and boat are gone. They went out and never came back. That's what the Coast Guard said." Mom started crying harder.

"All they could find were some crab pot buoys tied to a dinghy. They . . . they think it came from your dad's boat."

Logan knew it was his boat. He had tied the buoys to it, and he knew Dad had used it for storage. "Mom, is the crab boat gone for sure? Would they know that for sure?"

Logan couldn't believe what he was hearing. "Do they know it sunk?" He kept questioning and repeating himself.

"Yes. The Coast Guard said there were two other boats close by that got a call. They said it sounded like your dad to them, and it was just a short call for help."

"The next morning, the boat was not where he said they were. They all searched, and there was nothing found."

Logan could hardly understand his mom through her sobs. "They said the seas were huge, and the winds were gale force."

He couldn't say anything. The lump of pain growing in his chest was just like when Grandpa died.

Everything was too close-in for him standing in the kitchen. He couldn't breathe with all these people in the house.

Logan needed to get out of there now and fast.

"Mom, I'm sorry, I need some air. Excuse me, please." Logan went out the back door and stood in the fresh air of the backyard.

There she was, the little lifeboat, sitting silently, waiting for him. The dim light from the back porch reflected off the tarps covering her in the near darkness.

Logan called out to the lifeboat, "I bet you could have saved them. Dad had that brand-new inflatable life raft. It was right there hanging on the galley bulkhead. Why couldn't they get into it? Why didn't he use the new raft? Why wasn't there time to get it into the water?"

The little lifeboat sat silent. Frost was starting to form on the tarps from the chilly dampness of the evening.

These questions raced through Logan's mind, even though he knew the lifeboat was too clubby like Dad had said. They would have had to chop it loose and hope for the best.

Logan knew the Aleutian waters of Alaska were too cold to survive for long. He gave a great sigh, feeling his whole life shifting under his feet.

"I guess it's you and me, old girl, wherever we're heading. Damn! This is killing Mom and Sister."

Logan knew he couldn't go back into the house. He didn't want to be around the preacher, a self-righteous know-it-all, and his mob.

One time, the Reverend felt he had to chew on Logan because Logan had a habit of talking during the sermon.

The Reverend short-stopped Logan on his way out of the church to set him straight for being disrespectful.

Logan informed him it came from working on the boats as a fisherman's son. Down on the docks, he had to be like that. Logan then told the Reverend to take a hike and called him and the rest of his flock "a collection of holy rollers and busybodies." He had no time for any of them.

Returning to the present, Logan's mind turned to his mom. *This whole thing is stupid. I'll go into the house for Mom and not make a mess of it, but if any of them try to tell me how to think or even suggest how I should act, there will be a problem.*

Logan stood on the back porch looking through the window in the kitchen door. He could see everyone gathered around, praying for Mom and Sister.

Not wanted to interrupt the praying, Logan sat on the stairs that went up to an apartment above, watching through the window into the kitchen and living room.

After a while, when they got tired of praying, Mom's church friends started leaving through the front door.

The Reverend and his wife came out onto the back porch. "Logan, my boy, you should be in there with your mother and sister in their time of need, not sitting out here, sulking."

"I'll be in there with my mother as soon as you folks clear out."

Logan could see the Reverend thinking the situation over. He frowned, turned to his wife, and guided her down the steps then toward the street.

Dad had decided to get some religion in his life awhile back. Logan thought he must have felt guilty about something. Dad decided to kick Logan out of the family because Logan had refused to attend the church and told Logan to sleep in the basement from that day forward. Logan never trusted the church or the people in it.

Logan waited until everyone left then went through the kitchen to find his mom. Both Mom and Sis were sitting in the living room. Mom was calmer now with everyone gone. Of course, they hadn't missed the conversation on the back porch.

"I'm sorry you had to see that, Mother. I apologize," Logan said. He walked over to the old wood rocker and sat down.

"Yes, this is quite a shock for all of us," Mother said, standing up and heading toward her bedroom, just off the living room. "I would like to go lay down for a while."

Logan turned to his sister, genuinely concerned. "Sis, how are you doing? Are you holding up?"

"Logan, why couldn't you come in while everyone was here?"

"You know my feelings about those people. Dad kicked me out of the family because of them."

"You were getting along with Dad when he left for Alaska. What happened?"

"He needed my help when he had a lot of work to get done on the boat. That's when he would get friendly. Sis, you know how he would run hot and cold. If he needed something, he would be your best friend."

Logan gave a heavy sigh, "Damn, Sis, I guess you wouldn't see it. He was always kind to you and Mom. I always felt like a rented mule around here. That was exactly how he treated me when others weren't looking.

"I'm sorry, Sis, but the whole thing angers me. I didn't get a chance to say goodbye to him. None of us did."

"Logan, could you please watch your language? Mom doesn't like it, and neither do I. Don't you realize you're becoming some kind of tough guy?"

"I wonder why! First Grandpa, now Dad, and then the church folks hovering around. I want to take a long break from this place. Most of all, leave the tear-jerking drama in my dust."

Logan's younger sister stared at him, not saying a word.

"This coming summer, I hope I can take my boat out for a long trip. That would work for me, a very long trip. For now, I have another thought. It's still Saturday night. Think I'll go find Charley."

Logan left the family house and headed downtown. He found Charley driving up and down Main Street in his old Chevy. Logan jumped in as Charley slowed to a stop.

They rode along together, and Logan wasn't talking. Charley asked what was up. Logan agonized then filled him in on what was going on, with the loss of his dad and the crab boat.

Charley drove around town and listened to his young friend. He finally asked, "How do you feel inside?"

"One-word, Charley, *mad*." Charley nodded, understanding.

Things were quiet until it was time for Logan to get out at his house in the drizzling rain.

# CHAPTER 5

Logan slipped quietly into the house, holding the screen door to keep it from banging. In the dark, he felt his way to the basement stairs. Once down the stairs, he found the string for the bare light bulb over the washing machine.

Logan reached for the sleeping bag and air mattress stuffed into a shelf next to his bed. He planned on going out to Points North, hoping that would help keep the back of his mind from buzzing over the loss of his dad.

In the black night of the backyard, the drizzling rain created rivulets that ran off the tarp and down the blocks holding Points North off the ground. Dodging puddles in the unmowed grass, he climbed under the tarp and into the boat.

She felt friendly and dry inside.

What Logan liked most was the quiet solitude she provided as he settled down for the night. Stretched out on top of his sleeping bag and air mattress, he enjoyed listening to the rain lightly tapping the tarp covering the boat.

There was a coolness to the air to go with the total darkness inside the hull. He felt safe here. He had to find a way to quiet his mind. So many feelings were trying to come through. Concentrating on the sounds around him, he could feel his anger slow. Things weren't churning in his gut and mind as bad as when he first laid down.

Logan slipped into the sleeping bag and the rain lulled him into the deep sleep he desperately needed.

It was Sunday, and sure enough, Mother came looking for him. She was not one to give up and after last night, she figured he needed to seek forgiveness for his actions with the good Reverend.

This was not where Logan was at in his thinking. There was still an ember of mad glowing deep within him, and it wasn't going out anytime soon.

"Are you in there?" she asked, tapping on the hull of the lifeboat.

"Hi, Mom." Logan popped his head out of the tarp.

"Good morning, son. Why don't you come to church this morning with your sister and me?"

"No thanks, Mom, thank you anyway. Don't think the church is for me today. God stopped by last night, and we had a nice visit. I squared up with him, ok?"

He took a long pause as his mother gave him "the look." "Don't need the church to do that today. It was all done before I fell asleep. Thanks anyway for the offer."

"Come along with us, and it'll do you some good. We need to be thankful for what we have even with the loss of your father."

"Mom, the only reason I would do it would be out of respect for you. Once I get there and see the holier-than-thou-bunch, you'll see me wanting to tell them to stuff it."

He paused again. *This is not good. I should think before blurting things out.* "No, Mother. I'll be out in the garage working on my gear for the boat."

Mom shook her head. "This is sad. You don't want any help, and you can't see the good it could do you. Rather than letting the anger build and boil over inside you the way it is."

"No, Mother. I don't want any help. That would be because I don't need any help. Thank you very much, anyway. You go have a good time with your friends."

"We will pray for you anyway, like it or not," she said with a smile.

Pausing for a moment, Logan started to reflect on what his smart mouth had just rattled off.

"Ok, hold on, Mom. You win, maybe it would be a good idea to keep you and Sis company today.

"Thank you, Logan."

Logan couldn't help himself. He asked, "Why would I need to get all duded-up to go to church?"

Mother was not in the mood for a long explanation. "Because that is what you do when you go to church."

After a bath and with a clean set of church duds on, Logan was ready to roll. The ride was quiet except when Logan asked, "Why so early? We're only going to church, right?"

"I thought you would like to go to Sunday school today. You could call it a bonus, and don't forget to pray for your father, please.

"You might say hi to Katie Garrick too. She's asked about you the last two times we were in church. She's a nice girl, and it might do you some good to visit with her. You never know, you might have something in common."

Sister spoke up from the back seat, "Yeah, Logan, she's a free girl after breaking up with Jessie."

"Oh, right. Katie's two years ahead of me and has a driver's license. What would she want with a guy like me? No car, no money, no interest in dating, and besides, I have a boat to build. And there's one more thing for my 'No' list . . ."

"Oh yeah, what would that be?" Sis piped up again.

"No time. On second thought, if rumor has it right, when Jessie and Katie split up, it was his boat that got in the way of the boyfriend-girlfriend stuff."

"All right, you two, we're here. I'll see you both where we normally sit right after Sunday school. Logan, no slipping out the back door. I expect you to be there."

"Mother, why would you think I would do that?" He gave his mother a warm smile.

He knew how much the loss of Dad had hurt her, and he knew he had to be there, whether he liked it or not.

Being a freshman in high school now, he was to be with the other high school students. He wasn't all that excited about being there, but here he was.

As Logan walked into the classroom, he saw an empty chair in the back row off to the side. It was where he liked to be—not to bother anyone and no one to bother him. He made that clear with his body language. When someone new walked through the door, he would not look up to acknowledge them.

Logan felt someone slide into the chair next to him.

Before he could look up, he could smell beautiful perfume.

*Wonder who that is?*

"Hey Logan, it's been a while. How have you been?"

*Ah, should have guessed.*

"I'm good, Katie, how about you?"

Logan took a quick scan across the room and saw Jessie and Katie's younger sister, Millie, sitting together.

He wondered if he was being set up. He could be drug into the boy-girl drama crap as Katie's ex-boyfriend was with her younger sister. Now perhaps, Katie could have a younger boy to be with also. That would be a jealousy payback.

Logan realized he needed to quit being a pessimist. Not all things were bad or going to turn out rotten.

He turned and was locked into Katie's deep blue eyes. He politely smiled as if to ask, "Yes, what can I do for you?"

She returned the eye contact, followed by the biggest welcoming smile she had.

It didn't faze Logan the least. Everyone knew she was a demanding girl and he had seen it firsthand in church and Sunday school for many years.

Yep, this girl had to have it her way or the highway.

Now the highway would be just excellent for Logan. He had too much going on in his life for now.

Logan had to figure out how he was going to get Points North outfitted by spring.

Girls cost too much money and time. And he certainly didn't have much of either.

"I'm sorry to hear about the loss of your father."

"Yea, word travels fast in the church circle, doesn't it?"

"That's because we all care about you and your family."

"Thank you for your concern. We'll be ok. Dad was going up to a dangerous place, and we all knew the risk."

"Yes, that is a terrible place. Have you been there?"

"No, I haven't, but I will someday."

"Why would you do that?"

"People have been going there forever. Dad's number came up somewhere. It could be heaven or the other place, you don't know. But his name did come up on a list, as we all know now.

"Besides, he is in a better place, right? Isn't that what they always say around here?" Logan said, gazing across the room and seeing the classroom fill up.

The Sunday school teacher started clearing his throat to get the class to quiet down.

Logan thought, *What am I doing here? There is nothing here I need or want.*

Katie looked to the front of the classroom also. She didn't go up front where she usually sat.

Logan thought she might have moved a little closer to him as his arm brushed hers. He could feel her body heat radiate in the small sphere they had created by sitting so close.

*Shoot, there is that blasted perfume again.* It lingered in the air with its sweet essence that put Logan in a trance.

Time raced by faster than it ever had as the teacher droned on. Before he knew it, Sunday school was over. They all rose and prayed together, and that was it.

He needed to find Mom and Sis. Somehow, Katie must have felt the heat as well, as she leaned toward Logan. Logan shook his head to clear his mind as they turned to go out.

Wouldn't you know it Jessie and Millie were walking past.

The first was Jessie. He smiled, "Hi, Katie, Logan."

Looking straight at Logan, he grinned. "I heard you got a boat. Lifeboat hull, isn't it?"

"Yea, it's an old one. We tore Grandpa's old Kanute boat up and kept all the hardware. That will help a lot to put it together."

Jessie didn't even glance at Katie as Millie stood close and held his hand.

*It must be over for them. Man, they were "the" couple of the century. I thought Katie was picking out a ring set. Guess I don't have a clue, and the truth is I don't want one.*

Jessie asked, "Would you mind if I come by some time and take a look at your boat? I would like to hear your plans for her."

"Sure, that sounds great. You know where I live, right?"

Jessie nodded yes. "Ok, I'll give you a shout next week."

"You got a deal."

Katie moved fast and put her hand on the inside of Logan's arm.

Logan could tell she intended to show that they were an item now.

*Yes, she could find an underclassman to Jessie.*

It didn't faze Jessie one bit. Now, on the other hand, Millie squeezed Jessie's arm to say, "Let's move on now."

*Woo wee, no doubt about it. There was still tension between the two sisters.*

Logan wasn't going to peel Katie's heated grip from his arm, and she wasn't letting go either.

That hand stayed there on Logan's arm as they reached the pew where Mother was sitting with Sister tucked in close beside her.

Logan dropped Katie's hand and sat next to his mother. Katie followed him into the pew. *Guess she's figuring on staying here.*

Halfway through the sermon, Katie took Logan's hand and ignored the look her father gave her, sitting a row across from them.

After the sermon, they walked out, and Katie pulled Logan aside. As she turned him to face her, he saw her face surrounded by blond hair, sky-blue eyes looking up at him.

*She is beautiful. Bossy, but beautiful.*

"Logan, I would like to see more of you if you would have the time."

"Great. Sure. Most of my time is chewed up with working on the boat, though."

"That's fine. Could I come by while you work on it? Maybe I could help you. I helped Jessie paint on his dory. He named it Dragonfly."

"Ok. Not much painting going on with it being winter. I have a lot of cleaning and rebuilding to do."

"That sounds like fun. I'll give you a call before I come over. My mom will loan me her car. Then we could go to the A&W and have a root beer when you have finished for the day."

"Maybe. I don't know if I have time for that, but we'll see."

She squeezed his hand as she walked away. Logan's eyes followed her.

*What did I do? Guess I'd better ride it out. I hope the drama doesn't turn out like one of those soap operas on TV that Sister likes to watch.*

"Hi, Mom, ready to go? I want to get back to work on the boat."

Walking out to the car, Mother commented, "You seemed to be enjoying yourself."

"Oh no, we're not going there, Mother," Logan responded quickly as he got in the passenger's side. "She was the one who wanted to sit with us."

Mother smiled, "Logan, you never know. You might become good friends. I don't think it would hurt you to know a nice girl from church."

"I got a boat to put together. I'm not spending a lot of time talking about a bunch of nothing."

Sister had to add her two bits from the back seat. "Yea, Logan, I could see you and Katie out on a double date with Jessie and Millie."

She started to giggle, picturing the happy couples. The boys could talk about boats, and the girls could talk about family and church.

"One word, boring," Logan replied. She went back to giggling.

They weren't home ten minutes, and Logan was already out in the garage working on boat gear.

* * *

The week was quiet at school and at home.

That is until Thursday, when it all started going downhill fast for Logan. It was bound to happen sooner or later, Grandpa would say.

Logan was set up for failure walking around with the chip he had on his shoulder. He knew he was daring anyone to knock it off and Logan knew someone would try. He knew it would feel good venting all his pent-up anger. Whatever the price, he didn't care, even if they kicked him out of school. That would give him an excellent excuse to go north and leave all this hyped-up drama behind him.

Word was going around that a junior bully at the high school was pushing around the freshman kids. The junior was aching to find a new victim to boss around by flexing his muscle on the underlings.

Logan decided to do something about that and found him in a car in the parking lot with his buddies, having a smoke during lunch break. Logan asked him about the talk he was spreading about a Black Friday on first-year students. Before he could answer, Logan informed the junior that he would not be pushing first-year students around anymore, or he would have to answer to Logan.

That didn't go over very well with the junior. He said, "Yea, what would a lightweight freshman like you do about it?"

Logan's reply was short and to the point, "How about we cancel the Black Friday and have us a real live Red Thursday here and now?"

The junior sneered and laughed in Logan's face. He did it in front of all his buddies to let them know what a big man he was and how stupid this freshman was for even thinking such a thing.

The junior threw his cigarette butt on the pavement and opened the driver's door.

Six or more of the larger freshmen were circling the group of juniors sitting in the car. They wanted to keep the fight even between the one running his mouth and the one defending all the freshmen.

There would be no backing down even though the school rules were firm about absolutely no fighting.

Logan wanted to fight the junior here and now, whether he liked it or not. Besides, he knew this could be his ticket out of here.

Logan stood and waited. The junior couldn't stand the pressure, turning redder by the minute. Suddenly, the junior yelled, grabbed the front of Logan's shirt, pulled his other hand back and slapped Logan hard on the cheek.

Logan just smiled. Now it was his turn. He launched a haymaker as his knuckled right fist flew across the junior's face before the bully could gather himself up from slapping Logan.

The junior went down hard on the parking lot gravel. Blood spurted out his nose and mouth as he groaned with disbelief at what had happened to him.

*Too bad,* Logan thought, *this will ruin the new Van Heusen shirt you're wearing.*

The junior rolled over on his back with his nose lying flat across his face, and none of his buddies wanted any part of Logan. They just stared at him thinking he was crazy, and to tell the truth, they weren't far from the truth.

Logan was crazy with anger and frustration from losing his dad. He had refused to tell anyone that. And now he had found a way to let it out in the parking lot. Too bad it turned out to be on an unsuspecting smart-ass junior.

The other juniors scraped up their bloody, sobbing, mess of a friend and headed to the nurse's office, then to the hospital for x-rays and resetting his nose.

Logan was escorted to the principal's office by two male teachers. Even they were careful to keep their distance and hands off him.

It was plain to see Logan wouldn't be right until he calmed down. He didn't taunt them, but he made it clear that they were not to touch him. They could get the same treatment the junior did.

Once in the principal's office, Logan knew the outcome wasn't going to be pretty. He was ready for it and didn't care. Once out of here, he was going to pack up and head north. That was where he belonged anyway.

The conversation was short. The principal decided he was going to punish Logan for fighting with swats with a 36" wooden paddle.

"That won't do any good," Logan hollered. "You will not use that paddle on me. Because I'll take it away from you and give you the same treatment if you touch me."

No doubt about it, that made the principal hopping mad. The principal paused to think over the situation. He knew things could go too far too fast.

He needed to call the police and have Logan hauled off. The Principal could see Logan's deep-rooted anger and that he could care less if he had to go to jail for doing significant damage to him.

As they stood toe to toe, the staff could hear the yelling all the way out to the front office and down the hallway.

Logan heard the office door slam open and hit the wall. He shot a glance over to see if it was reinforcements for the principal.

No, it was Coach Edwards, the varsity wrestling coach. This man was big, all the way through, at 280 pounds, six foot four inches, and not an ounce of fat. There was only solid muscle standing in front of them. He was an ex-marine that fought in the Korean War. Logan could see he would be mean if he had to be.

Logan thought, *No, I won't be taking him on any time soon.* The look on the coach's face told Logan to shut up and sit down.

Logan turned to a chair in front of the principal's desk and sat down.

The coach was a real man's man and didn't have to threaten him with a paddle. Only the weak used paddles or other sadistic devices to shore up their shortcomings.

Grandpa was right when he said only cowards and bullies use sticks. He called them equalizers for what they were missing in their life.

Coach asked the principal, "Have you talked to any of the witnesses?"

Principal's reply was flat. "Didn't need to, he put a student in the hospital."

"I have talked to the others that were there." The coach watched the principal's reaction.

Coach continued, "The junior picked the fight and swung first. Once it started, Logan here stopped the whole thing with one swing."

Coach kept talking, "I know Logan, and I have him in JV wrestling. Yes, I have even kicked him out of freshman matches for unnecessary roughness. And yes, he does have an anger problem.

"I can explain it to you, and I'd like to work it out if you could give me some time. Now can we discuss this in private?"

The principal nodded. Coach looked over to Logan and said, "Logan, you go on over to the gym and suit up for wrestling practice. We'll talk there."

Everyone in school knew Logan was unforgiving and could be mean.

On occasion, the older boys would take him to the dances with them. They would call him "good backup."

Now it all was coming home. Logan was not proud of what he had done. He would rather have a quiet life in the background. He never wanted to bother anyone and wanted no one bothering him.

He couldn't figure out why he was always so angry.

Logan had his eyes glued to the floor as he came out of the principal's office. It was between classes, and the hallways were teeming with students. He knew they were staring at him, and he didn't want to look back. What could he say?

He heard Katie's voice as he walked by her wall locker. "Logan. Hey, Logan!"

No answer. He had nothing to say to her.

"Logan! You headed to the gym?"

"Yea."

"Let me walk with you," Katie said as she slammed her wall locker door shut.

He looked up to find her beautiful smiling blue eyes and golden hair tied into two ponytails, one laying on each shoulder. *This girl is beautiful.*

"Ok, I just don't want to talk about what happened."

"All right, that's fine. Could you walk me to my next class?"

"Yeah, I can do that." She gave him a pretty smile. He gave her a tight-lipped smile back. That was all he could gather up for now.

There was so much going on in his head right then. There wasn't any room for someone else to add to it.

"What time do you get out of wrestling practice?"

"How would you know I am going there for practice?"

"I have my mom's car. I could pick you up, and we could talk while I drive you home."

"Katie, I'm ok. You don't have to give me a ride. But I guess we're all wrapped up by six."

"Good. I'll be there."

"Well, whatever you want. When I come out, I'll walk down the hill for home. You know where I live, right?"

"Yes, I do. Here's my class," she said, stopping. "I'll see you then. I hope you have a good turn out with all that's gone on today."

"Thanks."

Logan gave another slight smile to say goodbye, and his heart was a little lighter.

# CHAPTER 6

Following the coach's orders, Logan walked to the gym, not knowing what was in store for him. Once at the gym and changed into his wrestling gear, he went straight to the wrestling practice room and waited for the coach to arrive.

The room wasn't huge by any standard, but it had wall-to-wall mats on the floor and no windows. There were even mats hanging on the walls.

Logan automatically started warming up for turnout like he always did, doing push-ups, sit-ups, and running in place. He was trying to burn off some of the adrenalin-charged anger, fueling the mad he had on.

It wasn't twenty minutes later when the coach came in and sat down on the bench by the door. He called Logan over to sit on the seat across from him. Logan quickly did what Coach asked, sitting on the other bench four feet from the coach, ready to listen.

Coach started, "Rough day, huh?"

"You might say that" Logan answered without attitude or making a face. He used his best respectful deadpan look, with his eyes glued to his wrestling coach, waiting.

"Sorry to hear about your dad."

"Guess we got to go sometime, Coach." Logan looked to the floor when he answered him. He would rather not talk about his loss. Things were still confusing. Logan wanted time to sort it out by himself. God already knows Katie wanted to wedge herself in there, wanted or not.

"I understand. It's hard to lose someone you love."

"My mom and sister will be okay. At home, we don't talk much. It could be because I don't go to their church. We don't have much to talk about."

"You talk with your actions. On the mats, you tell me you're tough, don't you?"

"Coach, you know I am. You've kicked me out of matches for unnecessary roughness.

"What are your plans when they kick you out of school? You do realize the way you're going that will happen soon enough?"

"I want to go north to Alaska. Once I get my boat put together, I'm out of here, with or without school." He paused. "Sir, it just doesn't much matter. All due respect."

"You know the juvenile hall is the next stop if you keep fighting?"

"Yeah, that wouldn't surprise me. All I want is to be left alone, so I can get my boat fixed up and get out of here. If the courts want to throw me in juvie, then so be it. Guess the boat will be there when I get back."

Logan paused, thinking. *The old man always said if I took the trouble to land up in jail, he wouldn't take the trouble to get me out. And I believed him. It told me my worth. Well, hell, guess it's looking like a one-way ticket, huh?*

"What are you going to do, Logan? How about you find a girlfriend? That might keep you out of trouble."

"That, Coach, I don't think is possible. I have looked but didn't find any takers. Besides, they always want it their way."

He stopped running his mouth to think for a second. *Well, there might be a chance with Katie. Second thought, she's not my type. Too much church and drama.*

"I'm headed north, Coach. Then all this crap goes away. Having someone in a relationship is a long way out. There might be a place for it when I get more peace in my life. Though that's not likely to happen in this school, town, or the Evergreen State of Washington."

Coach continued, "If you get kicked out of another match, they won't let you wrestle anymore for the year. You realize that, don't you?"

"Coach, I don't want anything at this school. All I want to do is fix my boat, put her in the water, and not look back."

Coach could see he wasn't getting anywhere. "Okay, what do you have to do to this boat?" He waited patiently for Logan. It was his turn to talk. "Go ahead, fill me in, tell me about her."

"She is an 18-foot steel lifeboat hull. Dad swapped it with me for my boat before he went north. Now I need to put in all the boat gear Dad and I salvaged from Grandpa's old boat. I have the engine, shaft, propeller, and all the running gear to install. The boat will need a small cabin built to keep me out of the weather. Also, I need to hook up the power troll reel to fish with and then rig the mast and sails."

"Sounds like you have everything to do the job?"

"Not quite, I need some steelwork to set the tail shaft in the stern log and plywood for the cabin. Most of all, I need better wood tools, and a welder would get things rolling in the right direction. "All I have is a hammer, a hand saw, and a few nails. Dad had all the other tools on the crab boat when she went down."

Logan was on a roll. The coach could see the thing Logan loved most in the world was "his boat."

"I can't find a job. I've looked high and low for one. People stare at you and shake their head when you ask them for a job. They don't even bother saying no to you."

Logan had been staring at the floor. He looked up as he finished telling the coach how things were going in his life.

"Yeah, I remember how that was," Coach said. "It's tough trying to find a job around this town. You need to know someone. Most of all, you have got to hang in there, Logan, don't quit trying."

Coach gave a deep sigh. "I need to check around on a few things. Could you keep from getting into a fight for the next week?"

"Yeah, I guess so."

"Logan, I'm dead serious. You need to stay out of trouble. There could be a possibility that I can work something out. No more fighting, can you do that?"

"All right, I promise not to get into any fights on the school grounds."

"Oh no, you don't. You don't need to fight anywhere anymore. Are we clear on that?"

"Yes, sir, I can do that."

"We'll focus on getting that boat work done by spring. Most of this is up to other people as I need their permission. There is no guessing on doing this. Others need your trust when giving their approval.

"Now, no guessing. I want your word, man to man. Do we have a deal?"

"Yes, sir, you have my word on it. We have a deal."

"Logan, another request. Could you do us both a favor and not take your anger and aggression out on the mats here? You know you'll lose by losing your head. Think things over. Wrestle smart like we're teaching you. Control. You need to keep control of your thoughts in that Scandinavian head of yours to wrestle smart. If you want that boat done, you need to keep your head and work smart. Now let's go to work.

"And, by the way, you owe detention time for fighting. It might do you good to check out a couple of boatbuilding books in the library and take them to detention with you. It could come in handy."

Turned out that afternoon was one of the best practices for Logan. The other team members had a lot of comments about him beating up the mouthy junior.

Logan played it down as best he could. He felt ashamed of what he had done the more he thought about it.

As he stepped out of the boy's locker room into the dark, damp cold fall in their small northwest fishing town he thought maybe he could explain it to Katie if she wanted to listen to him.

He walked along, eyes on the sidewalk, thinking about what had gone on all through the day.

*The coach was right. It was a busy day.*

Now, he had to live with the results of his actions. The old man would always say, "you own it." He was right. He created it, and it was all his.

Logan walked along, lost in his thoughts as a car pulled up alongside the curb. A familiar voice called out. "Hey, sailor, you want a ride?"

The passenger window was rolled down and Katie leaned forward to see him in the half-dark on the sidewalk.

"Come on, get in, and I'll give you a ride home."

Logan slid into the passenger seat. "Thanks for the ride. You didn't have to do this, you know."

"I wanted to. My mom is great for loaning me the car. She thinks I'm at the library studying. You're a bonus on the way home. How was your talk with the coach?"

"He was ok. It seems I shook some people up. He said he would help me get things sorted out."

At the stop sign, Katie looked over to him, worried. "Are they going to kick you out of school for fighting? That's what everyone is saying. Other than the darn bully had it coming."

She drove on slowly, waiting for Logan to talk.

"No, they're not kicking me out. Well, that's what the coach said. But I can't get into another fight on or off the school grounds."

"Can you do that?"

"I will give it my best try. If I fail, there is always Alaska waiting for me. Right now, I need to face my mom. I'm sure the school called her."

"What will you tell her, Logan?"

"The truth. That's always worked with Mom. It might not make what I did right, but it will be the truth."

Reflecting on what to expect, he continued. "Then, the lecture will come and the grounding. Mom knows that won't hurt me. All I want to do is to go out to the garage and work on my boat gear."

"That sounds reasonable. Do you think I can come for visitation during your incarceration?" She giggled.

As they approached Logan's house, he could see the lights on in the house. Mom was standing at the kitchen window, fixing dinner. She was deep in thought and didn't look up.

Logan gave a big sigh saying more to himself than Katie, "She doesn't deserve this."

Katie sat behind the steering wheel with the reflecting headlights showing her honest concern for Logan and his family. Saying nothing was the best thing she could do now.

"Thanks for the ride, Katie. Maybe I'll see you at school tomorrow. Oh, yea, I have a couple of weeks of detention to do for fighting today."

He reached over and gave her hand on the steering wheel a squeeze. "Thanks again."

"Do you have first lunch?"

He nodded as he slid out the passenger door.

"Good, I'll see you then." She gave a big heart-melting smile. "You won't be getting into any fights with me sitting beside you."

He smiled back. "If you say so. Goodnight Katie, see you tomorrow." He closed the door as she drove away in the dark.

Logan walked through the back-porch door as Mom looked up from the kitchen counter. "Hi, Mom."

Sis came into the kitchen from the living room. "Who dropped you off? That wasn't Charley's car. If I didn't know better, that was Katie Garrick's mother's car."

"You should get a job with the town cops," Logan said, trying to be light-hearted. "You know all the cars and who they belong to in town."

"It was Katie. I knew it."

"Could you leave us? Mom and I need to talk without interruption. Please."

"It's about you beating up on the junior in the parking lot, isn't it?"

Mom said, "That's enough. You go back to your homework. Logan and I need to talk."

Sis started to say something but looked at her mother and decided better. She returned to the living room to finish her homework.

"The school called. I'm sure you know that. What do you have to say for yourself?"

"The truth is all I can say," Logan replied. Mother never yelled. She was a kind and respectful listener. When it was time, she would let you know what she had on her mind.

They talked for twenty minutes as Logan explained everything, including his meeting with the coach.

Logan's mother said she knew that part as the coach had called her at work and explained what he had in mind. Worst of all, he had said that her son was headed down a dangerous path if he didn't make some changes soon.

Logan and his mother agreed that he would be grounded for the next two weeks. School, then home after wrestling turn-out, and yes, he could have friends over. Katie and Charley would be welcome guests if they wanted to come by.

Mother smiled. "You don't think I missed your ride when you came home tonight, do you?"

"No, Mother, you don't miss anything."

The more he thought about it, the more ashamed he was for what he had done.

* * *

By the end of the week, Logan had found the junior alone in the hallway at his locker. Logan took the chance to apologize for breaking his nose.

The junior said it was "ok." He had it coming.

The next afternoon, Coach Edwards pulled Logan into his office. He had sat down with Principal Cameron and cut a deal. The coach was also the shop teacher at the high school. He had the experience of working in a boatyard in the summers when he was going to teacher's college.

Principal Cameron agreed to have Logan bring in his lifeboat to work on during and after class. He was to let the others help him so that they could learn with him.

Logan couldn't believe this turn of events. He could see Points North coming alive.

The first thing he had to do is dig up a boat trailer and some way to tow it to the high school shop.

That turned out to be simpler than he thought. Mother suggested that Charley drive the old Dodge, and Logan could borrow the same trailer his dad had.

Charley, Logan, Katie, and Mom loaded Points North on the trailer Sunday evening.

Early Monday morning, Charley and Logan towed her up to the high school auto and woodshop.

The coach was there with the doors open, as they backed the trailer in, then blocked up the boat's stern.

Logan picked up the bow with the shop engine hoist, and Charley pulled the trailer out from under her.

After blocking the rest of the hull up, they returned the trailer and Logan thanked the owner repeatedly. Then Mom's old Dodge went right back in front of the house. The boys jumped into Charley's Chevy and headed back to the school in time for their first class.

Logan thought this was one of the happiest days of his life as he walked into the classroom.

After school, Charley and Logan started hauling the gear to be put on the boat at the start of the next semester.

The coach helped Logan arrange his classes so he could get all the required courses out of the way by lunch. Then he could spend the rest of his day in the shop working on Points North and then keep working on the boat until they locked up or kicked him out. Whichever came first, usually, it was for both.

The coach informed him that once his grades improved, they would see about a key. Then he could come in early in the morning and stay working later in the afternoon.

"The rules are strict", the coach reminded him. "Do not screw this opportunity up."

Logan smiled. "No sweat, I know this is my one shot, and I'm keeping it."

Katie stopped by to visit and see how he was doing on restriction at home. When he could, Charley would be there also.

The three of them had found a good friendship and enjoyed the time they spent together in the garage.

Even at lunchtime, the three would share lunch like old friends.

No one was putting the moves on anyone, and that was the way Logan wanted it—only good friends for now.

A lot of the gear for the boat was still at home, like the engine, shaft, propeller, and rudder, as they would be prepared in the garage.

It was good planning where his time was so short at the school shop. He would bring the parts to the school shop only when it was time for them to be mounted on the boat.

The best help of all next to Charley and the coach was his neighbor Burnt. He was more of an adviser than anything else, and his advice came in handy. When Logan got stumped with a problem, Burnt would have the correct answer for him.

Coach still made him turn out for wrestling. He could feel his anger slipping away more every day. At the same time, his wrestling was improving. Logan found he no longer needed to wrestle mad. He wrestled smarter using the skills and tools taught to him by the coach.

In shop class, Coach would have Logan help him while he was teaching. And a lot was going on. First, Logan had to build the engine beds. Both beds had to be sawed on the band saw because of all the compound angles needed. The school had an old cast iron eighteen-inch band saw. It was perfect for the job. It turned out to be the most used tool for everything.

# CHAPTER 7

Logan was standing at the door every morning when the janitor, Mike, arrived and let him into the shop. Then Mike would go down to the line of school buses, check the oil levels and warm all the buses up before the bus drivers arrived to take them out on their routes.

One day, Mike invited Logan to come along. "You ever make engine checks then crank them up, Logan?"

"Yeah, on my dad's boats. He made me the engineer, and that was one of my jobs. Well, one of the many jobs anyway. I guess he trusted me."

"I can see that. Now, how about you let me teach you the routine. Here, we need to check a few more things, like lights and stuff. Most of all, get them good and warm."

Logan learned that Mike would be running late once a week and other times there was more work than he had time to do. Mike had all his chores to do and couldn't make all the checks on the buses.

And this was where Logan came in. Mike had shown him how to make all the checks, even explaining how to fuel the buses if needed during the warmup.

Fueling the buses included pulling them up to the fuel pump and putting them back in their parking spot.

When the principal found out a student was driving the busses around in the back parking lot, he flipped, especially since it was Logan, who was still on his watch list.

Mike had a lot of explaining to do. He spent a long time in the principal's office to explain why he could use the help.

The coach walked in and joined in the conversation. He was more than happy to explain the benefits of more responsibility for Logan as an excellent learning opportunity.

The principal finally relented, laying down strict rules where Mike had to approve each morning's chores.

Logan enjoyed working with the "big machinery," as he called it. He especially liked starting the diesel engines and listening to the big old rigs rumble.

Points North was coming along. The next job was getting Mom to let him load the boat engine in Dad's rusty flat-bed trailer. That turned out to be easy, and she was happy to drive him, the motor, and the trailer up to the school on a cold dark winter morning.

Logan and Coach unloaded the engine and reverse gear from the trailer, then Mom and Logan took the trailer off the car at home. Mom headed to work, and Logan ran back up to school.

After lunch, Coach explained to Logan and the class how to fit the engine beds and then make the lineup for the propeller shaft.

The trick was to use blue chalk to fit the beds. Coach called this a dry fit. It had to be perfect if Logan wanted to distribute the engine weight evenly throughout the hull.

Logan had to slow himself down like he did when he was wrestling. There was no hurrying on this job.

He hung the engine in the engine hoist and rubbed the blue chalk on the bed timbers in the boat. Then he set the little motor onto the bed timbers, making sure it settled in tightly.

Next, he lifted the engine with the hoist and planed down any spots where the blue chalk had rubbed on as these were the high spots.

He repeated the process many times, setting the engine, lifting it, planing the high spots, and resetting the engine.

In and out, it went for the fourth time. Finally, it was right. The next day, Logan drilled holes in the bed and the students bolted the engine through the bed timbers to the backing plates outside the hull.

Things were improving at home for Logan. Mom was getting used to the idea of Dad not coming home ever again, and Sister was forever busy with her homework.

Now Logan needed to get the cabin and frames laid out and built in the garage. When Points North returned to the backyard, the cabin would be bedded and bolted on the forward part of the hull.

Burnt helped where he could and was still the perfect source of information.

Mom also helped out where she could. Logan's project still took cold hard cash to get done and there wasn't much of that to go around. Christmas vacation was coming up, and Logan needed to find a job fast for boat money.

Over lunch, Cameron Hayes, a school friend, said he needed someone to help him cut cordwood. He and his dad had found enough people to make up an order of twenty cords of cut, split, and stacked cordwood. And, it needed to be done before Christmas.

"What does it pay?" asked Logan.

"Ten bucks a cord to you, and you can sleep on the floor in my bedroom. Mom said she would feed my help. Dad will supply the chainsaw and tractor. I can cut the wood off of the back of our farm."

"Wow, that sounds great! When can we start?"

The two boys had cut wood together last spring to make extra money. They worked hard and fast, producing better than one cord a day. Logan knew this job would need to be done faster.

The boys started the first day of Christmas vacation. Logan caught the 6AM ferry to the island and while standing on the dock, he couldn't help but notice the blackness of the winter morning. The cold seemed to be biting into him. He was looking forward to working up a sweat with steam rolling off his backside.

Cameron, a couple of years older than Logan, pulled up in the farm truck they would use to haul the cordwood. The boys had spent a lot of time fishing together in Cameron's boat and camping in the woods.

"Last night, Dad and I got all the equipment we'll need. Also, he showed me what trees we, or should I say you, are to fall. One more thing, Dad said you could sharpen the saw because you do a better job of it than either of us."

Logan smiled. They both knew a neighbor had given Logan an old Titan chainsaw when he was ten years old. That raggedy old jag-toothed beast was a cranky one. She bucked, kicked, and snorted a lot, but Logan was so proud of it. Logan and the saw became the best of friends after he spent two full weeks cutting up beach logs for an older friend that needed firewood for the winter.

Both Cameron and Logan wanted to get the twenty-cord done in five days. They would need to fill the order at four cord a day. It was a tall order, but they thought they could do it by starting early and finishing late.

Cameron fired up the tractor, and Logan followed him, walking out to the forest with the saw over his shoulder. Logan stopped to sharpen and gas up the chainsaw. By the time he was ready, Cameron had all the trees marked for him to cut.

He started falling them all in the same direction as fast as he could.

Logan's dad had taught him how to fall and limb trees before he got his saw. Early on, Dad would log in the winter and fish in the summer. After school and on the weekends, Logan was there helping and learning whatever he could. All that was before Dad bought old boats to rebuild in the winter with Logan's help. Then all summer long, they used the boats to commercially fish.

Now, Logan made sure to keep a couple of trees felled and limbed ahead of the tractor.

Cameron backed the tractor up to the logs, and Logan hooked the chokers up. Then Cameron towed the logs to a cleared spot in the woods. There, Logan would buck up the logs to stove-sized woodblocks, then both boys would split them with a splitting maul and throw them into the old farm truck.

Finally, they stacked the wood tightly in the farm truck's flatbed, once again, by hand. Then it was ready to go to the customer for dumping out, and you guessed it, stacking once again.

Logan would stay to saw and split more blocks of wood while Cameron delivered the wood. The best part was the reward for all their hard labor when Cameron collected the money.

The five days went fast, as the boys worked 12 hours or more a day. With it being winter, they were in the farm truck before daylight every morning, and they returned to the ranch in the dark.

Logan would sharpen all the axes and mauls and sharpen and tune the saw every evening in the farm shop.

It was hard work, but well worth the money they earned.

On the afternoon of the fifth day, they threw off the last two cords and stacked them. After picking up Logan's bedroll at the house, Cameron dropped him off at the ferry dock with $200 cash in his pocket.

Not a dime of this was going anywhere but for the much-needed boat money.

# CHAPTER 8

"Logan," Mother said, getting his attention. "Tomorrow is Christmas Eve. I would like you to come with your sister and me to the services in memory of your father."

"I would be happy to, Mother. I was planning to be home for Christmas Eve. I knew you would want me to go to church with you and Sis. That's why Cameron and I worked so hard to get the wood cutting job done."

Mom looked pleased. "Thank you for that. I knew I could count on you. You're doing much better lately. What are your plans this evening?"

"Thanks, Mom. Think I'd like to visit with Charley unless he's found a girlfriend in the last five days. And tomorrow, I'd like to work in the garage until it is time to get cleaned up for church. I'm sure you'll let me know what time that is."

Mom smiled, "Oh yes, I will. You never know, church might do you some good."

Logan thought, *I'm not so sure how that works. I know my going to her church will help keep her happy, and this is the first Christmas without Dad around. Things were okay between Dad and me when he went north, and I'm glad of that.*

That evening, luck was on Logan's side, and he found Charley at home. Up to his same old stuff, he couldn't stop talking about cars or girls.

All Logan could think about was his boat sitting blocked up in the school shop. Soon, wrestling season will be over, and he could put all his time into Points North.

Logan had a definite goal. He wanted her finished and ready to go on the last day of school.

Coming home early that evening, he went straight to the garage. Inside, the single light bulb was dim over the bench and he felt the cold as he looked around. Tomorrow morning, he would build a fire in the potbelly stove in the corner. Dad had put it in the garage when they were working on their salmon nets in the winter. No more salmon nets would be here.

Logan smiled with pride as he looked over his current project, admiring the top cabin frame for Points North. It sat on four sawhorses in the middle of the small garage. *It has nice lines.*

Logan asked himself what his plan was when he got her done. He kept thinking of the northbound tug towing the huge barge in Rosario Straits the day Dad departed for Alaska.

*That would sure beat mowing lawns for the summer. I could get a job on a fishing boat in Alaska. I'm big enough, and Dad taught me how to work.*

*Guess I better call it a night. I'll put the sides of the cabin on the frame tomorrow. Soon, I want to bring Points North home and finish her in the backyard.*

The next day, Logan heard his younger sister Carrie come through the garage door. "It's time to get ready for church, Logan."

"Okay, let me damper down the stove, and I'll be right there."

"Logan, why don't you like our church?"

"I don't care for the people and how they think they can order you around. Most of all, Sis, I don't like how they won Dad over into the church, then he decided I was no longer a member of the family because I didn't think like him.

"I'm sure they're well-meaning, and that's fine for you and Mom. I don't need them in my life right now. Tonight, I'm doing this for you and Mom because I care about you both."

"Thank you, Logan, we appreciate it."

The service had a routine. Logan sat with Mother and Sis for the show they put on telling the story of Jesus. It was the same every year, how it came about with the angels, manger, the works.

Katie came by and sat with Logan. Her mom and sister were in the program.

Yep, same old story, the very same people, and the Rev. Benson himself. He cornered Logan on the way out the door. "Where have you been, Logan? We've missed you."

Logan looked at him, no answer.

"You're always welcome here, anytime. Remember that, Logan."

All Logan could say was, "Thank you, sir."

It made him boil inside, thinking how they drove a wedge between him and his dad.

On the way home, Logan was deep in thought and trying not to say anything negative about the church. He changed out of his Sunday clothes and went out to the garage through the drizzling cold winter rain. He wanted to be to himself, not giving the cold and dark a thought.

He built a fire in the stove and started sanding on the cabin portholes. They needed a good cleaning, then fresh paint before he installed them. As he worked through the day, he dreamed about traveling through the waters of British Columbia. He could only imagine what he would see. Would it be rough at Cape Mudge like others talked?

What about Seymour Narrows and Johnston Straits? He had listened to the stories since he was old enough to remember what they were talking about.

*My mother may not like it, but this is where I'll be heading.* "Where the fishing is good, and the people are friendly."

* * *

Before Logan knew it, Christmas break was over, and he was back at school.

Points North was coming along on schedule. Logan figured he needed her home around the first of March to put the cabin on. Then, he would install her little white-gas cook stove and finish the inside.

He remembered he hadn't given much thought to fitting the mast, sails, and all the external hardware. There was so much to do and so little time to do it! He had to be ready to go on the last day of school.

Wrestling was okay, but he did it more to make Coach happy and Logan figured he owed Coach big-time with bailing him out of trouble from fighting and arranging to get his boat done.

Now that wrestling was out of the way, he had a boat to finish and take north.

Logan didn't realize he had kept his grades up, and other learning opportunities had come his way, unnoticed as he focused on getting the boat done. And with all he had learned in shop, plus helping Mike the janitor, he discovered a newfound confidence working on his boat and being around other people. It was a most welcome feeling. He felt an inner peace and was no longer filled with frustration.

Charley had put in a lot of time helping and teaching Logan. He had Logan do all the welding, so Logan could learn for himself, just as Charley's dad had taught him two years before.

Early one Saturday morning, Katie came bursting through the garage door. Logan was seated on the three-legged stool sanding on his white gas stove, getting it ready to paint.

"Where is he?" Katie blurted out.

Logan had no idea who she was talking about. "Where is who?"

"You know, where is Charley?"

"Charley? Why? Did he make you mad? Did he hurt you or something?" Logan knew Charley didn't have a mean bone in his body.

"No, he never hurt me, but if he doesn't do something soon, he will."

"Whoa there, Katie. We're friends and all but, don't you be taking me where I have no business to be."

"No, it is nothing like that, silly."

Logan could see she was cooling off. "Ok, tell Uncle Logan what he can do to put things right between you two."

"Why doesn't he ask me out on a date? I like Charley, he is a little shy, but I like him for who he is."

"Well, that is a nice starting place for a relationship. Do you need my help to kickstart this romance?"

"Logan, this is not a romance like you would fantasize in your head. I want to spend some time with him. You know what I mean."

"Not sure I know what you mean," Logan replied with a grin. "Come on, let's give old Charley a call and see if we can get him over here. Then you two can have this conversation one-on-one as they say."

Logan dialed Charley's number on the wall phone in the living room. Katie stood close to Logan's shoulder, not to miss anything said.

"Hello, yes Ma'am, it's Logan. Is Charley home? Ok, I'll wait." He turned, smiled, and nodded at Katie.

Logan turned and looked out the dining room window. "Hey, Charley, yea, everything is cool here, man. Well, except for one thing. Do you remember what we talked about the other night?"

Logan waited to let Charley talk. "Yep, you hit the nail on the head."

Another pause. "You best saddle up and get on over here pard and have that conversation with Katie. She's standing right here, hanging on every word."

"Ok, see you in a few." Logan turned to Katie as he hung up and smiled.

"As soon as he can get his pants on and brush his teeth, he'll be over. Let's go back out to the garage and wait for him."

It wasn't but a minute, and they could hear some fool burning rubber down the street.

"Well, there you are," Logan commented as Charley came gliding through the door. "Ok, folks. Why don't the two of you go for a long ride? You've both talked to me, now talk to each other. I want to come along, but I have boat work to get done here."

They both gave a sheepish grin.

As they went out the door, Logan shouted, "Good luck, you two."

*Whew, that's over. No more games, please. Hopefully, this is the start of a long relationship.*

* * *

Points North was finally ready to come home. The boys borrowed the neighbor's boat trailer one more time and used Logan's mom's Dodge to tow Points North. She was a whole new boat now with the engine shaft and propeller install completed. Logan was proud that he had done most of the work himself, and he almost busted with pride when they loaded Points North on the trailer.

Logan must have thanked Coach a hundred times for helping him so much and the coach could see Logan was on the right track now.

The new cabin was in the garage waiting to be mounted. Points North had become a "she." Grandpa said boats had girl names because the vessels protected the crew like a mother.

Now the work began at home. Logan would get a couple of hours in before school and then work until dark every night. It was slow, but the job was well done. Logan would feel safe in her.

Soon, the day to put her in the water would come, and Logan could hardly wait.

Finally, it was the middle of May, and school was winding down. Logan had finished the last coat of paint and now he could put the rigging up for fitting.

"Grandpa would be happy to know that all big Kanute's gear was well and alive on the new Points North," Logan said to Burnt, leaning over the backyard fence.

He still had to finish up the galley and the bunk forward.

Later that afternoon, as he was down inside the cabin, Mom had to holler to him to get his attention. "Logan, are you there?"

He popped his head out, "Hi Mom, how's it going?"

"Logan, we need to talk. I never see you anymore with all the time your boat is taking and school on top of that."

"I apologize for not coming in for dinner, Mom. What do you want to talk about?"

Mom paused, "I want to know what you're planning for the summer. Are you going to sail around the islands?"

Logan had already thought about what he would tell her. "Something like that. You say I'm too young to fish with anyone but Dad. So, I'm thinking of finding a job while I'm out in the islands sailing around with Points North here. How does that sound?"

"I'm not sure. You need a better plan than that. I need to know where you're going and where you will be," Mom said sternly.

By now, Logan was on his knees on the main deck, his arms crossed and leaning on the boat's guardrail.

Mother was standing next to the side of the boat, looking straight into his bright blue eyes, waiting for an answer. She continued, "Logan, that won't do. Like I said before, you need to keep me informed on what's going on."

"Okay, okay, Mom. I promise you'll be the first to know when I touch land. Will you accept collect phone charges?" He smiled with a big grin.

"Collect charges? Where are you going?"

"Well, Mother, I'm sure not hanging around Fidalgo Island. There isn't any work here. I've looked, you know that. Maybe in Friday Harbor, there might be a dock job or even a dishwashing job for me somewhere." He smiled and waited for her answer.

They continued to play this game. What Logan never did was try to outsmart Mom. She always had him cold. "Well, okay, you go have your adventure. Keep it in the San Juan Islands and call me once a week. I want to keep track of you. Is that clear young man?"

"Yes, Mother, crystal clear."

*Mom doesn't know it, but that is not the place where Points North and I are going.* The plan he was counting on was not to look back until September. He was done with this town. Come the sixth of June, the last day of school, it would be time to be moving on.

The Christmas money was going fast. Cameron had two more woodcutting jobs lined up and Logan was happy to help. Those two jobs and an additional stump digging job provided Logan another two hundred dollars to finish the boat for the trip north.

With the loss of Grandpa and then Dad, it made him feel like running as fast as he could.

He didn't understand why, but he just couldn't sit still.

New places were waiting for him to explore, and the time had come to launch his girl.

# CHAPTER 9

Points North was as ready as she could be for the big splash.

The first problem was no trailer. The owner sold it this spring, and that left Logan with a boat and no trailer. No one else had one to loan him either. It was a problem for a hardworking new boat owner. What's a boat without water?

Charley and Logan were discussing Logan's dilemma in Charley's garage.

Logan lit up like a light bulb when he spotted an old Model A-frame Charley's dad had stored in the corner.

The boys moved the frame to the middle of the garage and got excited as they examined it.

It had axles, wheels with working mechanical breaks, and a steering wheel. With a little work, they might be able to make it fit Points North.

"Charley, what if we tipped the steering wheel forward? Then we could make room for a piece of plywood down here by the brake pedal. I could stand on it while you towed the frame."

"If we don't get caught trying to sneak it by the cops," Charley said. "If they did find us, they would hang both of us right then and there on a streetlamp. Let's not even think of what my dad would do to me. Logan, he would skin me alive. Then I would be hung and skinned out twice on the same day. That would exceed my pain tolerance. I'm not so sure about this. I like my life the way it is, not to mention my hide."

Logan smiled, his mind still trying to make his idea work. "Think about it. We could use the old rope in our garage to tow it through the alleys."

"You mean tow it with my car? Oh no, you're nuts. Not on your life. You know it would be my driver's license that we would be throwing on the chopping block."

Logan joked, "My John Deere tractor is in the shop for a tune-up today, or we could use it. Besides, this will work. When we get back to the house, I'll rinse down the frame and set the steering wheel back where it belongs. Your dad will never know we used it."

"Oh, no. No saltwater in the wheel bearings, now I know you're crazy."

Logan pressed on, "No, Charley, no saltwater whatsoever. It will work. Hear me out, please."

Seeing that Charley was still listening, Logan kept talking to keep the idea on the front burner. "We can take her down to the cleared-out beach spot next to the old shake mill. That's a perfect spot to set her on the mud at low tide. She'll slide right off the trailer. Then we'll take the Model A-frame straight home and make it right again. Charley, I know this will work! Don't you agree with me? What do you think?" Logan leaned back, proud of his idea, and hoping Charley would agree.

Charley scratched the fuzz on his chin. "You might have a point," he said with a long pause. "Let's look at the frame. I'm still not convinced this hair-brained idea is going to work at all. If anything, we'll be in deep du-du if anything goes wrong. My gut is telling me, don't do this."

Charley was almost right. It took some doing to fit chocks to set the boat on the frame. The steering wheel was just right tipped up. Also, Logan dug up an old apple box to sit on for the trip from Charley's to his house to pick up the boat.

They debated the best route to take. Charley knew all the back streets, and Logan's backyard was only ten blocks away. Now the only hitch seemed to be crossing Commercial Avenue, the main street in town. They couldn't do it without the cops seeing them.

"The town cops patrol that main drag all the time," moaned Charley.

"Charley, we have to cross Commercial. There's no way around it."

Logan could see Charley was sweating it. He knew Charley was more worried about his dad catching them than any of the town cops.

"I would never see my driver's license until Dad goes to the Old Folks Home. And that would be because he needed a ride. Logan, that would mean no dating or anything. Darn you, Logan, you could care less."

Logan smiled. *Charley's right.* He was heading North and not looking back. He had to get this done any way he could.

To complicate matters more, Charley's dad was the city mechanic and knew all the cops. The odds were stacking up against the boys.

They decided to go ahead with their plan. Charley backed his car up to the Model A-frame and tied the thirty-foot rope between the not-so-sturdy-bumper of Charley's car and the center bar of the A-frame. Logan climbed aboard and sat on his apple box. All he had to do was hold the steering wheel and push on the brake pedal when needed.

Charley got in his car and slowly pushed the gas pedal as the rope tightened, and the frame started to move, its brakes dragging and letting out a squeal in protest. Luckily, neither Charley's mom nor dad was home. Logan had to stand, using all his muscles to turn the wheel, as the steering mechanism was stiff from old age. He pushed hard on the brakes to slow it down as Charley came to the end of the alley. Logan couldn't believe how exciting this was.

They were approaching Commercial Avenue now. Charley slowed only long enough to look both ways and hoped not to see a cop, then got excited and tromped on the gas.

"Too hard, Charley!" Logan shouted. They shot out of the alley as if out of a cannon, crossed the main street, and dove into another alley.

Logan didn't have time to look around. The old corkline he had used for a tow rope acted as a giant rubber band. Luckily, it had a lot of spring left in it and didn't break. Logan hung on as best he could as the A-frame whiplashed when Charley hit the gas.

If the rope had broken, Logan knew he would have been sitting there on the apple box in a bare car frame in the middle of the main street in town. What would he say to the police? He was positive Charley would not be anywhere around.

The final destination was only two blocks away. Charley let the car coast, seeing Logan in the rear-view mirror, a big grin across his face.

They crossed the last street, finally slowing to a stop in the alley next to Logan's garage.

They both got out of their vehicles and stood there. Then they jumped up and down with excitement as the adrenaline raced through their bodies. They had done it! And only fifteen minutes had passed. They finally untied the A-frame, pushing and steering it by hand into the backyard, and rolled it under Points North. Logan would lower her onto the trailer that night. Now it was time to get to school.

Charley wasn't too worried about his dad. He never went out to the garage during the week, so the coast should be clear for a couple of days.

Logan had the boat loaded that evening, strapped down, tight as she could be. Tomorrow morning, he would unstep the mast and lash it and the boom to the top deck, then stow the rudder on board. There should be no chance of damaging it on the way to the beach.

Points North looked good with her fresh coat of white paint on the hull, black guardrails and red bottom. Dad would call that "a little lipstick and perfume for the old girl."

Little Kanute wasn't loaded on board yet. They would lash it to the top of the cabin before they headed to be beach.

Logan checked the Tide Book. Wednesday, the next day, was the day for the best low water at 3:35 PM.

They needed to work on the next part of their plan. The boys figured to pull her down to the beach, steering the A-frame to get it into position to back down on the beach.

It was just steep enough to give the A-frame a push and let it coast to the water's edge, then chock the wheels and run out a long line to the back of Charley's old Chevy.

Logan would throw the anchor off the stern and set a wood block under her. The keel would land on the block and some makeshift braces on the sides would prevent her from falling over.

Then, Charley could drive away with the trailer, leaving Points North sitting on the beach, waiting for the tide to come in.

They both agreed it was a great plan. Easy as could be, especially after driving the A-frame across town.

The next morning, as they loaded Little Kanute, the boys looked at each other. They both saw that the apple box wouldn't work. The boat's bow was taking up all of the space on the model A-frame where the box needed to be.

Logan would need to stand while driving the towed boat. They figured he could hang on to Points North's bow with his right arm clamped to it to keep his balance, then stand on the piece of plywood for the ride to the beach and back to Charley's house. He would turn the wheel with his left hand, hit the break with his left foot while standing on his right foot. Sounded easy enough.

Once again, they shot across Commercial Street between alleys, headed for the beach. Charley tromped on it, and Logan thought they could have been "shot out of a cannon." Just like the last time.

They rolled full tilt down to Q Avenue, their plan coming together perfectly, even making good time as Charley swung the boat and A-frame around to back her down to the water's edge.

That is where their luck run out. Sargent Bo Dawson pulled up behind them and stopped right square in front of Charley's car.

He was smiling and shaking his head as he slid out of the cop car.

*Sgt. Bo is a nice man but tough*, thought Logan. He figured they had one big chewing coming.

Charley and Logan walked up and met the officer at the front bumper of Charley's car. They stood smiling as if this was a normal activity.

"Well, well. What are you boys up to today?"

Logan piped up, "Well, Officer, we're trying to make the tide and float Points North today."

"Yeah, I can see that. But the way you're going about it isn't entirely legal. Besides, you two are outright busting the law. I don't know where to start. Charley, what do 'ya think your dad would say, being that he works for the city and all?"

Charley dropped his smile, and his face turned a pasty white. *Oh no*, he thought, *here we go.*

Logan piped up again "Sgt. Bo, the whole thing is my fault. I talked Charley into doing it. He didn't want to do it. I had no one else, and the trailer we borrowed before wasn't available. Do you think we need to tell his dad?"

Before Sgt. Bo could answer, Logan kept the chatter up. Yes, it was a lot of double talk and Sgt. Bo could see that.

"You would be welcome to come home with me and tell my mom since dad's not here anymore," Logan said, scraping up anything he could get to take the heat off his good friend.

"Yeah, I heard about that. Too bad your dad was lost when the boat went down. Where you headed with this old lifeboat?"

*Now, this is good,* Logan thought. *We got him talking rather than chewing on us.*

"Well, sir, as soon as school is out, I plan on doing the San Juan Islands. That's as far as Mom will let me go. I'm hoping to find some work out there. Getting Points North here ready has taken up my whole winter, besides football and wrestling. She sure has been one heck of a project."

"So, you're trying to make low-water. Tell me what you got in mind."

They explained their idea in detail to Sgt. Bo. After considering all the planning the boys had done, the sergeant decided to help them push the trailer to the water's edge.

Logan set the wood keel block then tied the long rope to both the Model A chassis and Charley's car frame. Then, he ran down to the boat and threw the anchor out some twenty feet into the water behind Points North and made it fast to the stern cleat.

Logan gave the signal for Charley to pull easy. The trailer slid out from under Points North.

Sgt. Bo steadied her as Logan ran around, blocking up the hull. The blocks would keep her straight and upright until the tide came in and floated her.

They pulled little Kanute off the cabin top and laid it above the beach waterline upside down with the oars tucked inside. That would let Logan row out to her after the tide came in, and after Logan had returned the Model A-frame as he found it.

Sgt. Bo offered to escort the boys up to Charley's house. They were sure they'd get a lecture from him once they got home, but before they got back to Charley's house, the sergeant peeled off, and they didn't see him again.

Logan and Charley pushed the frame back into the garage, exactly where it was before, making sure there were no tracks to show it had moved. Logan reset the wheel, took off the plywood, and put the apple box back where he found it.

"Do you think Officer Bob will tell your dad?" Logan asked.

"No," Charley said. "He was getting a kick out of what we were up doing. He's a good cop."

"Thanks again, Charley. You sure have helped me out a bunch. I'd better keep an eye on things as the tide comes in. It happens faster than you'd think."

"Yeah, I got to run out to the service station. There're some things I need to get done. I'll drop you off at the boat."

As Logan got out of Charley's car, the tide was already halfway to the waterline on the hull of Points North. *What a beautiful boat she is.* Points North looked happy, waiting for the tide on this beautiful sunny spring afternoon.

Logan rolled Little Kanute right side up, grabbed the bowline, also called a painter, and started dragging it to the beach line. He pushed the little boat into the water and waded out far enough to climb in. Logan rowed to Points North, climbed aboard, and immediately checked the bilges. *Great, she's dry.*

Now he needed to step the mast before setting the guy wires. After all that, there was the rudder to hang.

Logan could feel her coming alive by the wiggle as he walked around her. The weight was coming off the support blocks as the tide came in.

He gave a pull on the line attached to the block she was held up with. All at once, it came free from the keel, and he watched the block float up to the surface.

*Hurray, this is it!* She was floating and her anchor held her fast. Logan was so excited he could hardly contain himself.

He hurriedly dug out the engine crank for his pride and joy, little Putt-Putt, gave it two cranks with the choke on, then took off the choke; one more crank, and she fired.

Putt-Putt had a beautiful sound all her own. It was the steady putt-putt, de-putt, he remembered so well when he went with Grandpa in Big Kanute.

He sat by the engine, watching the flywheel move steadily and smoothly, spinning around and around. He then gave a glance to watch the valve rods moving up and down. Memories of being on Big Kanute with Grandpa came flooding into his mind. Grandpa's laugh, listening to all his stories, and of course, advice, and the sound of the little engine, steadily running in the background. He so loved it then, and now it was in his boat, brought back to life.

Logan pulled the anchor and moved Little Kanute to the stern to tie him off. Logan pushed the tiller over to the port.

Without thinking, being almost in a trance, Logan reached down and engaged the clutch to put Putt-Putt in gear. Points North moved, slow at first, then gathering speed.

"We're moving!"

He glanced over the side rail to see the bright, calm water. The side water rippled away from the bow making a small but steady wake alongside Point North's hull.

Points North ran perfectly. Logan checked the bilge and tightened the shaft packing. No vibrations, this is good—no extra water in the bilge, better yet. He then looked over the side to see only sweet smooth water that gave back his reflection. The water opened with the bow and closed with the stern, lying behind them as they found it, leaving only a small trail of bubbles in the smooth glassy water, just as Points North's bow had found it.

The sun was going down fast, reminding Logan he didn't have much time to get her put away for the night.

Points North putted at low idle as he brought her in slowly toward a lone piling standing in ten feet of water. It was in front of where Grandpa's old cabin had been.

Logan pulled up to the piling, then backed down using the reverse gear. At the same time, he threw a line around the piling and made it fast, leaving just the right amount of slack.

He reached down to shut the magneto off as the little engine went quiet.

Logan pulled out a line with some fishing floats he had strung on it and tied it around the piling. The floats would float up and down with the tide on the piling and not hang up. Then he re-tied the bowline to the floating line, and Points North was secure for the night.

A voice floated over the water to Logan. He looked up toward the darkening beach. Points North was north of the marina where the fish boats and yachts would tie-up. There used to be a couple of old cabins just above the tideline. The thought warmed Logan's heart, remembering when Grandpa would call this area 'Little Chicago.'

Logan spoke to the emptiness, "I did it, Grandpa. Big Kanute has come home one more time."

"Logan let's go now," the voice said. "It's time for supper."

It was Mom. She was standing on the beach with a light sweater on to keep the evening chill off.

"Isn't she great, Mom? She runs smooth as can be, everything works."

He closed the little engine hatch cover and locked the cabin-top hatch. *She'll be okay here until tomorrow, right after school. Then, I'll be back.*

He rowed Little Kanute into shore where Mom was standing. Logan pulled the dinghy up above the tide line and rolled it over.

"Looks like you finally made it," she said. "Congratulations!"

Mom was happy to see him so pleased with the boat. He had accomplished the dream of putting Grandpa's boat parts in the lifeboat that belonged to his dad.

"Mom, you can do anything if you put your mind to it."

She smiled, "Yes, you can, and yes, you did."

# CHAPTER 10

The last day of school was tomorrow, and all was well. Logan headed to the beach to load the last of his gear. Points North would be all packed up and ready to leave. Logan had even packed his old chainsaw, hoping he could make some money along the way, cutting cordwood. That old chainsaw hadn't let him down yet.

Well, Logan almost made it out of there without a hitch.

The Imperial Small-Town-Marina Harbor Master showed up with a problem. He came hurrying down the beach while Logan was loading the last of his gear into the dinghy.

You could see the joy in the Harbor Master's face where he had caught Logan red-handed. Logan saw him coming and bet himself that the Harbormaster had been waiting in the bushes all day, sipping on his flask of Old Crow.

As before, Grandpa called this place Little Chicago where old shacks had once stood on pilings. The port had removed the cabins, and now only the pilings remained.

Logan had Points North tied off to one of the pilings. Leon, the Harbor Master, came to a stop, huffing, and puffing, out of air.

"Logan, these are port piles. You cannot tie to them without paying."

"It's only a little boat!"

"If you have a cigar box with a string on it, you got to pay the Port."

Logan thought quickly. "I'll be darned. I've never heard of that before. I should check with my classmate, beings his dad is one of the Port Commissioners."

The Harbormaster's demeanor quickly softened. *Yep, that worked.* "How long are you going to be here?"

"Until school lets out tomorrow, and I'm heading for the islands. You won't have to bother no more with me, I promise."

Leon scratched his balding head, dandruff flakes floating to the ground. "Well, okay. This one time, then that's it, no more favors."

Logan never did ask him for a favor. He only needed a little slack.

"Thank you so much, Mr. Stenhouse. I promise I'll clear out as soon as I can after school's out."

The next day, Mom and Sis came down to Little Chicago to say goodbye. There were few words spoken. Logan didn't have anything to say. He was too excited about the upcoming trip. Mother was different as she reminded Logan, multiple times, to call once a week or he would be in hot water.

With no ceremony or band playing, Logan shoved off after giving a quick hug and good-bye. Mom and Sis stood on the beach to watch him row out to Points North. He had to get going as low water was only three hours away and there was still time to ride the ebb out the channel.

Logan wanted to make Reef Point on the south tip of Cypress Island for the low-water slack tide. That was the best time to do some good cod-fishing. If luck was with him, he could catch enough for tonight's dinner and the next day. Then he would hook up with a towboat headed north.

Logan pulled himself up on Points North's deck and tied off the dink's painter, making it fast to Points North's stern. He jumped down to the deck, opened the small engine compartment, set the engine choke, and gave the engine a crank. Putt-Putt fired on the first crank and was soon warming up at a nice idle. Logan was so proud and excited he could almost burst.

He looked back to the beach as Mother and Sister gave him a final wave, took in the bowline, and cast off the troublesome Port piling.

As he came around the breakwater of the marina, he felt such a relief. Finally, he was on his way. Points North cleared the hilly rock lookout off to his left. The rocks and trees never looked better over his shoulder.

Once in the channel, Logan cranked up Little Putt-Putt to full-tilt cruising speed. She was making good time with the fair tide.

As he went past the Port dock, he remembered waving to his dad eight months earlier. Logan smiled as he recognized Charley leaned up against the hood of his old Chevy with Katie hanging on his arm. They waved as Logan went by.

Charley was the only one except Burnt that Logan had told what his entire plan was. He knew Logan was not coming back until fall and could be even later if he decided he was having too much fun.

Three hours later, Logan made Reef Point on the south end of Cypress Island, and the tide was slack. He and Cameron called this their favorite fishing hole. Logan knew he could catch a mess of cod here for some of Grandpa's cod stew and that would hold him over later this evening.

As expected, the fishing was outstanding, with a dozen little brown beauties in the boat within the hour.

After catching dinner, Logan started up Little Putt-Putt again and rode the flood up the west side of the island to Strawberry Bay. He studied his surroundings carefully to find a suitable anchoring spot for the night, looking for protection from the wind and swells from passing boats.

"This is where we'll anchor, girl. Our 'first night underway,' as Dad called it."

Logan pulled out the pocket watch Grandpa had given him. He called it a Big Ben. Didn't do you much good if you didn't wind it, which Logan had forgotten to do. The tides are hard to predict without a clock.

He was guessing it must be late afternoon when he sailed into Strawberry Bay, on the east side of Strawberry Island.

Using a sounding lead he had put together, with a knot every fathom, Logan measured three fathoms of water depth.

At six feet per fathom, that would be eighteen feet, and he wanted a scope of at least 3:1.

The scope is how much line from the boat to the anchor. If you didn't have enough anchor line out, and the wind and tide come up, you could drag anchor or, worse yet, wake up on the beach.

So, eighteen times three was fifty-four feet of anchor line needed. He may not have been good at reading, but he was particularly good at math. You needed that on the water.

Logan had already marked his anchor line every thirty feet by tying different colors of yarn around the line, and each marked length was called a shot.

He let out two shots of anchor line to set the anchor. Sixty feet, perfect.

Logan finished securing the boat and sails. Getting all the gear stowed was easy because there wasn't much there.

The cod he caught earlier needed to be filleted. Logan pulled the fish out of the fish bin, an old plastic tub he had found in the garage, and cleaned all of them.

Grandpa had taught him how to make the world's best cod stew. That would be codfish, of course, spuds, a whole onion, some water, salt, and pepper.

Logan threw in some parsley Mom had given him, then a bit of canned milk with a tablespoon or so of cornstarch dissolved in it. He was starving and was certainly ready to eat in thirty minutes. Finally, Logan put a small rice pot to cook on the tiny white-gas cookstove he installed this spring.

Logan was reliving Grandpa's dream with Big Kanute. Grandpa never did make it to Alaska. In Logan's heart, he was determined to make it, come hell or high water.

As dinner cooked, Logan watched the bright orange sun set to the west over Strawberry Island. There was not a breath of breeze or even a ripple in the water alongside Points North. The water was like a mirror. He could see his reflection when he looked over the side and smiled.

Soon, Logan was wolfing down two big bowls of codfish stew and rice. He thought he might have overeaten before bedtime.

Logan cleaned up the cramped galley area and crawled in his snug little one-person bunk.

Finally, his adventure had begun.

Laying in the bunk, Logan couldn't close his eyes. There was too much buzzing through his mind. The first thing he started to think about were the tugs going north.

Logan had gone over to Burnt Jensen's house to talk a couple of months ago. He tried recalling the conversation word for word as best he could. Burnt was a good friend of the family and trustworthy. Logan needed to tell him what he was planning to do. He could fill Logan in on how to determine which tugs and tows would be going to Alaska.

Logan didn't want to wake up in Vancouver, Canada. That was just north of the border, only fifty miles or so from home. He would be in deep trouble and everything he had done last winter would be for nothing.

Burnt laughed, "When we talked before, you were right. The bigger the tug and barge, the farther north they're going."

Logan asked, "Okay, which ones don't go all the way to Alaska?"

Burnt scratched his chin. "For starters, no gravel barges, and that goes for fuel barges too. Yaw, no empty freight barges, those will be coming back from up north. Then you would get a free tow to Seattle." He laughed and shook his head, picturing Logan's face if he pulled into Seattle.

"Almost everything headed north will be heavily laden, and they'll be steaming for Alaska. Remember this now, Logan. They will be full up to the gills and making the slowest of speed. For you and that tin tub of yours, the slower, the better."

Burnt quizzed Logan again, "Do you know why I say that?"

"Yes. When I pick up the emergency tow line buoy-ball, if I'm not careful, the ball could get hung up and trip Points North."

"Yaw, dats right. Then what would happen?"

"If I let her take too big of a shear, I won't be able to get her to steady up in time."

Burnt continued, "The odds of her rolling over are great. The rest of the story we would read in the newspaper." He laughed and kept talking. "Yaw, in the obituary section. Do you have a clear picture? It's tricky with your Points North being as small and light as it is. You know, the biggest problem I see is that you will be alone, and things go wrong in a hurry when you're alone."

Logan could feel the pit in the bottom of his stomach grow, listening to every word that came out of Burnt's mouth.

"Remember this too. You be careful when you make Cape Mudge. If it's flooding, the water boils when it comes out of there. It'll be dumping out all the water from Discovery Passage and Seymour Narrows. That will be the first of many dangerous places you'll find in Georgia Straits. It's the current coming down on your nose, with a strong wind on your stern. The tide and wind are working against each other, and that makes the swells very, very steep with no backside.

"Let me repeat that. There will be no backside to those swells. You and the tug and tow are bucking that blasted flood-tide current.

"You stay on your toes and be ready to cut loose if you need to. The wind could get you too broadside on the stern of the tow and smash you into it. There would only be a bunch of crumpled pieces of tin lying on the bottom if that happened. Yaw, I guess you could say nothing is free in life.

"Once you make it through that, you can ride the bull ebb out until she changes again. You be sure to run for cover, or you'll get hung back up in the flood. After all that, it's a free ride up to Johnstone Straits. Then keep an eye out for another free tow.

"I almost forgot, once you're inside of Cape Mudge, you'll be safe. Campbell River is a nice B.C. fishing and timber town. It's on your left if you need something and want to make a stop."

Logan thought about what Burnt was telling him. "What about when I hook up? Can I use the float dragging behind the barge?"

"Yaw, but don't get crossed up and put her in irons. We've already covered dat. Dat could roll the boat, and you'd be dead."

"How do I keep from doing that?"

"Pick up the buoy well forward of your beam and keep your little tin tub straight as an arrow, in line with the wake of the tow. You already know this is where being alone is the hard part. You need to steer the boat and handle the buoy at the same time. One last thing, Logan. If it doesn't feel right, it isn't right. You bail out right then and there. There'll be another tow coming along before you know it."

Logan nodded. "I'll keep her in a straight line and listen to my gut."

"You can figure on a tow leaving Seattle once a week for Anchorage. They time it out to be at Cape Mudge at the end of the flood tide or a little before. That's about thirty-six hours or so from Anacortes. If you come out of Tide Point on Cypress Island, you should be able to catch an easy ride."

Logan thanked Burnt for all the information and went home to think it over. Now, as Logan lay in his bunk, ready to make a move, he wished he had taken notes as they talked. At least when he got home, he did sit down and write out everything he could remember.

"Well, here we are, old girl, in Strawberry Bay, only two miles south of Tide Point, waiting."

With his tummy so full, and tired from the long day, Logan fell into a sound asleep, listening to the night noises in the bunk of his snug small tin tub.

# CHAPTER 11

Logan bolted straight up in his bunk. Out of nowhere, a foghorn was blasting right next to him. It was loud enough to scare the daylights out of him. He was sure it was right outside of his boat. The darned thing could be so close it could run him over in the dark and never see him.

Logan could hear the big engines' pounding followed by the loud squeal and swish of its giant propeller. Then came the ear-splitting blasts of the deafening foghorn again.

"Crap, I'm going to die on my first night out."

Logan started running all the possibilities through his head as he fought to get out of his sleeping bag and bunk.

*Did I drag anchor? Will we get run over our first night out? I already asked myself that, so knock it off and get out of this bunk!*

Finally, Logan cleared his bunk and bag. He staggered out on the deck, bleary-eyed, in his underwear. *This is one of the thickest fogs I've ever seen. I can't believe it.* No wonder his eyes were so blurry, it was the darned fog.

Looking up, he could see the moon breaking through the low-hanging thick fog bank. Again, the foghorn blasted, making him jump—one long blast followed by two short blasts. Dad had taught him that it was a tug with a tow.

It sounded like it was heading straight down on him and his little boat.

He could hear the big diesel engine again, boom, boom, boom. But where are the tug and tow? He strained to listen to make out the tug's location, still standing on the deck, a tight grip on the mast to steady himself.

Once more, there was the horn again. This time was different. It was louder.

He was thinking things out as fast and calmly as he could. The light came on. *Did we drag anchor and are now drifting loose in Rosario Straits?*

Logan crawled forward, groping around in the foggy dark except for an occasional sliver of moonlight. *There it is.* He found the anchor line and gave it a hard pull. It was still made fast to the bottom. *That's what we want.*

He needed to take a sounding to check the depth of water under him. As quickly as he could, he made a sounding with his home-made lead line. Two fathoms, and all was well. A big tug would be aground if he came into where Points North was.

Then the long and two short blasts of the foghorn again. This time it was fainter.

He could tell it was getting farther away. It was inbound on Rosario Straits on the west side of Cypress Island.

He remembered now, from fishing with his dad, that noise travels quickly over the water.

He thought of past times, remembering some terrifying nights when they didn't know if they were in or out of the shipping lanes.

Logan shivered from the cold and went below to put on his long johns. *For being the start of summer, it sure is chilly at night.*

The cod stew was still warm in the pot. Logan dished up a big bowl full and crawled back into his bunk for a midnight snack.

*Think I'll get a bit more sleep. Out here, you never know when a little extra rest might come in handy.*

Logan woke up to small waves slapping against the tin hull. It was loud inside Points North, like a handful of marbles rattling around in a soup can.

He got up and stuck his head out the cabin hatch cover.

The wind slapped him in the face as if saying, "Hey, it's blowing out here."

He hadn't figured on the wind coming straight out of the south. With dawn breaking and dim light in the sky, he could see the thick low cloud cover. *Might be 5 o'clock. Wish I'd wound that silly pocket watch. Better get dressed and pull the anchor.*

The little two-cylinder motor started right up, waiting for Logan to put her to work. Pulling on the anchor line by hand made him put his back into it. Grandpa had taught him, "Pull hard, come easy." This morning, he was pulling hard, then he pulled harder. Nope, never did come easy. Finally, the old club anchor broke the water, and they could get underway.

With Little Putt-Putt going putt, they passed the north end of Strawberry Island. Logan slowed to put up the jib, and that steadied the boat. Whitecaps danced on the tops of waves all around him and his little boat. As he looked across Rosario Straits to the west, he could see swells breaking all the way across. "This is a good wind," he told Points North. "Could be 25 or better, and this could last for a couple of days."

It was close to dawn now. Logan could see the outline of Blakley island and then the shape of Peavine Pass before Obstruction Island. He scanned the horizon to the north. It was still dark enough to make out the quick green light of the Lidia Shoal aid flashing, barely showing, but showing all the same.

Logan and Points North came around the corner of Tide Point in the early light. The automated marker, all the way out on the point, was flashing white.

Logan was guessing they had 25 to 35 knots of wind. "I need to put it in the log. Dad was always making me put the course, weather, and wind in the boat log." Making the turn at Tide Point, the land sheltered the little boat from the wind. The wind was still blowing over his head, but the water was calm.

Logan tucked into the shore as tight as he dared. He could see the long sandy beach in the dim light. Taking his time and making multiple soundings, he found three fathoms of water about a hundred feet off the shore. Logan dropped the anchor, again letting out plenty of scope on the anchor line. That done, he turned and dropped the jib to the deck on the bow.

As he shut down Little Putt-Putt, Points North swung around, pointing southwest into the light breeze. She was lying in the current with the dinghy streamed out on a line behind them.

At last, all was quiet. Logan thought he would have some of his world-famous cod stew and work on the boat. There was always plenty to do, readying her for the big trip north.

Everything was fine until the ebb started. Points North had laid in the tide fair. Then she took a heavy shear in the stream. Suddenly, the bow took off to port and the boat leaned hard to starboard, the current pushing her. Logan grabbed the tiller and straightened her out.

The shearing was a quirk, but Logan had to solve this problem if he and Points North were to be drug behind a huge barge at five or six knots.

*Could it be the three-quarter-inch bow stem with the extra steel sticking out was hooking the water?* Like Burnt had said, "If you get in irons, then most likely, you could be dead."

Points North was cranky on the anchor with the tide change. He tried setting the rudder at different angles. Then he tried more scope on the anchor. He even tied a reef in the mainsail. Nothing seemed to help much.

*Maybe a bridle rigged on the forward chocks would help steady her up.*

Logan tied the middle of a spare line to the anchor line and ran each end to the chocks on the port and starboard forward quarter. She steadied up much better. When the boat would start to sheer, the bridle checked her bow, and she responded and came back to her original heading.

The only other thing he could do was go back to town, drill a hole in the bow stem, and shackle a line at the waterline. *That wouldn't work, too many questions.* The bridle would have to work. Logan knew he would need to use it when he tied off to the barge. When the time came to hook the harness up to the tow, he would keep his fishing knife close at hand. He could always cut the line if it fouled.

Next was to find out if she could sail. After lunch, Logan pulled anchor and sailed her back and forth in the bight behind the spit. *That was good*, he thought. She came about and responded well when asked to make a maneuver.

The tide changed, and the flood started, so Logan sailed his boat north to Cypress Reef and Towhead Island.

As they passed the vast bight under Eagle Cliff, Logan remembered that he and Grandpa had seen a great battle between an eagle and a salmon there. The eagle finally won but it was hard work, with the salmon almost pulling the eagle underwater.

It was getting dark when he finally started the motor and dropped the sails. Logan thought the bight by Towhead Island might give him more cover from both flood and ebb currents. Twenty minutes later, the anchor was down and fast and as Points North settled down, Logan noted they were less than 50 feet off the beach. The anchor held good as she stemmed the tidal current stream without effort and Logan noticed the current was a lot less when lying in the back eddy.

He was happy. "Not bad for a beginner. We can live with this. Think I'll heat some cod stew and rice to get me through the night."

It looked like a pleasant evening with the skies west over Orcas Island brilliant red. "Red skies at night, sailors delight," Dad would always say. Then he would laugh and say, "Could be it won't blow like hell in the morning."

This little bight didn't have a name, so he named it in memory of his dad and grandpa.

Each day, Logan sailed farther north. By the fifth day, he had reached Peapod Rocks northeast of Doe Bay on Orcas Island, and the longer he was on the water, the more comfortable he was. The thought came to him that he could take off for Alaska with his putt-putt power.

That was a bad idea, he decided. He didn't have all the right charts or enough fuel for Little Putt-Putt.

And he was afraid of the Canadian Customs officers. Those people would ask too many questions, and then there would be trouble.

No, he and Points North would stick to the plan. If that didn't work out, his backup plan was still to take Points North to Friday Harbor and look for a job.

Logan reminded himself that this was his dream, and he could make it if the right tug and tow went by. "We'll stay and wait, Points

North, you and me. We're in it together until hell freezes over, or we run out of rice, whichever comes first."

The next day, Logan was hungry for lingcod. As he sailed around Peapod Rocks, he remembered Burnt had said a barge would leave Seattle once a week for Alaska. If his memory served him right, it was a week ago that he was startled awake in the dead of night by a tug blasting its horn. He couldn't forget that darn thing. It scared the bejeebers out of him.

*So, with all that figuring, there should be a tug and tow coming along sometime today. It's been a week to the day, so where is my free ride to Alaska?*

Logan searched for a large bed of bullwhip kelp and found one by a rock cliff. Dad had taught him that kelp grew in fourteen feet of water.

Logan sailed Points North up to the edge of the rock wall and dropped his jig to the bottom. They called it hand-jigging.

The tide turned to slack and his fishing improved. By the time the tide turned again, he had two 20-pounders in the boat.

Logan looked up to check his surroundings, glancing down the straits, and his heart started to race. He saw a north-bound tow, black smoke pouring out of her stack. The tug was huge and close enough already to see she was a real beauty, WWII era, built of wood. Odds were, she was one of the big single-screw diesel-powered tugs he had read about at the school library.

The barge had all kinds of freight on its deck, heavy equipment tied down in the center, refrigerated truck-trailers loaded on the outside and a row of house trailers on top of everything.

Logan shouted, "This is it! If we're going, we got to go now."

Logan knew it was almost too late in the day to go for it. He raced to pull the anchor, putting up the sails, and headed his little boat straight for the tug and barge. Points North made good speed with the fair tide and the wind on her back. Running as hard as he could, Logan knew he needed a plan, or it could be a big disaster.

So, here was his plan. Points North was sailing downstream to meet the tug. She would come about as she reached the tug, Putt-Putt up and running full tilt. He would drop both sails as he headed for the emergency towline buoy. Burnt had talked about that buoy a lot. It had to be there. What if it wasn't?

The downside was if he missed the tow, it would be almost dark. What then? If he rolled her over, no one would ever find him. Maybe a crab or two would, then the sand fleas would have their way.

Logan scolded himself. *Quit thinking like that.* He remembered Coach. 'Believe in yourself, you can do this.' Coach also said, 'No guts, no glory.' *Well, this is it. No guts, no glory.*

"The tow," as Burnt called it, looked to be making six knots, northbound in Rosario Straits. Logan could see they were abeam of Strawberry Island, bucking the ebb tide. There might be a couple of knot run-off, so Logan estimated he was doing eight knots southbound.

Six plus eight. Logan and the tug were closing at fourteen knots, faster than he was comfortable. *Who would have guessed our rate would be that?*

Logan planned on starting the motor before he passed the tug going in the opposite direction. Then he would cut her hard over to come in behind the barge. Logan took a second look at the tow. It was close behind the tug, only a couple of hundred yards between them. He will have act fast to make this work.

The pit of his stomach was churning, and his nerves were on edge.

The only thing that could help him was a backwash or eddy behind the barge. That would give him some breathing room behind the barge with less current.

*God, I hope I can catch that eddy.* Charley had been telling him about race cars. During a race, they would use the backdraft from the race car in front of them to reduce the wind drag.

*There should be a back eddy on the barge.* If it wasn't there, he knew the barge would plain and simple walk away from him.

As planned, Logan had Putt-Putt up and running, out of gear, as the tug passed. *This is happening way too fast!* He knew he could make this work. *Take a deep breath.* He pulled steady on the rudder. Points North headed for the port-quarter of the massive barge. With his other hand, he dropped the mainsail. He couldn't drop the jib sail. No time, things were moving too fast.

*The tug is moving way fast.* Points North was now forty feet off the port-side of the barge. He could hear the slap of the water breaking on the bow of the barge. The hiss of the swells, foam, and water running down the side of the barge grew louder. Daylight had faded, and it was hard to see. He could see the stern of the barge coming up like a freight train.

Logan double-checked his calculations. If he didn't do something quickly, the barge would blow on by him.

Logan pulled the tiller handle, hard over, as hard as he dared. He had a distinct fear it could snap in two. If it broke, he would be out in the Straits without a rudder, in the dark, in the shipping lanes. It couldn't get much worse than that.

*Why am I thinking all this?*

"Pay attention to detail, Logan. It may save your life." He remembered Burnt, again. Logan continued to pull the rudder hard to make the bow come to port. Points North was now heading straight at the black steel side of the barge.

Logan reached down for little Putt-Putt's throttle, threw it wide open, asking the little engine for everything it had to give.

*Woo-wee!* Points North's bow cleared the stern of the barge by inches. Suddenly, calm surrounded him. The back eddy was there, waiting. Logan didn't cut the throttle right away and a slingshot seemed to be throwing them across the stern of the barge, almost running over the floating polyline that tethered the emergency buoy.

*Holy smokes, this isn't going well.*

With the rudder still hard over, Points North came about quick. The buoy was on his starboard bow, floating in the wash of the barge's stern.

Logan fought the wash and slowly gained on it. "I think we have a chance here, girl." He needed to hook the buoy and tie it to the bow bridle, steer the boat and control its speed at the same time.

It was the longest ten minutes of his life.

At full throttle, Little Putt-Putt finally reached the buoy. Logan needed to get a loop on the line, and then he could let go if anything went hay-bale on him. Right now, that was looking more likely than not. Darkness was coming, and he hadn't thought to grab a flashlight.

Earlier, Logan had laid out a boat hook to pick up the tow line. He picked up the boat hook with his right hand and put the tiller in his left. If he could hook the buoy line and run it up to make a slack loop, he could loop it with his bowline.

He reached out over the side of the boat, extending the boat hook as far as he could. He missed! He shifted his feet for better balance and reached out again. This time, he caught the buoy line with the boat hook.

Points North veered toward the line. Logan corrected the tiller, straightening her out. He grabbed for a short piece of line and hurriedly tied off the tiller, then worked his way up the side of the boat. He pulled the buoy and line aboard as the little boat gained on the barge.

Logan put the bowline loop over the buoy, and Points North took a sheer, ripping the buoy out of Logan's hands. Things were going haywire in a matter of seconds.

The bowline hung up on the aft stay of the mainmast and the buoy jammed between the mainstay and the cabin, forcing Points North to take a heavy shear to port.

"Oh, no!" Logan cried out. Burnt had said, "Don't let it take a sheer," and that was just what she was doing. The boat headed away from the buoy with enough force to lay her over. Water started pouring in over the gunwale and through the scuppers.

The sheer force ripped the tie line off the tiller, throwing Logan to the center of the boat.

There was too much water in the boat now and not enough time to cut the buoy line clear from the mainstay. The only thing Logan could do was to try to steer the boat out of this watery grave and he only had thirty seconds to do it right, or the party was over.

Logan grabbed for the tiller. He pushed hard to bring the bow to starboard. Points North responded too fast, even with all the water in her, again whipping Logan off balance. He fought to feather her steering, taking a deep breath. Finally, she started to settle down. The water quickly drained off through the scuppers.

It was as if Points North smiled. She began to follow the barge straight and trim. Keeping the motor full throttle, Logan inched up closer to the barge, creating more slack in the buoy line. He lashed the tiller, this time to both sides of the boat.

*Why didn't I think of that sooner?*

Logan ran forward to the starboard mainstay and unfolded the buoy. It popped out from the bulwarks and flew back into the water, trailing behind the barge like it was supposed to.

The bowline slowly became taunt as Logan slowed the motor and loosened the lines on the tiller, slowly taking the tension off. As he shifted the engine out of gear, the boat seemed to relax. Finally, they were gliding along without a care.

Logan was so busy he hadn't noticed that darkness surrounded him. The barge's stern light was bright, and he had been close enough to use it to light his way. *I couldn't read a newspaper, but I could see what I needed to do.*

After a few deep breaths, he laid his big fishing knife next to the bowline—a precaution, in case he had to get loose. Cutting the line was the only option, if that happened.

Logan nestled the mainsail into its home, wrapped next to the boom, then pulled the hatch cover open in the center of the boat and stuck his head down below. He found twelve inches of water in the bilge. The water hadn't reached the generator or engine yet, and he gave a short prayer thanking God for the helping hand.

The water had to be pumped out right away. The extra weight made her ride too low in the water and harder to steer.

Logan started Little Putt-Putt again and clutched in the small Jabsco bilge pump he had installed on the front of the engine. He could hear the water pumping overboard as the flywheel turned the pump. He jumped up on deck and started pumping with his deck hand-pump.

Soon the water was low enough that he was no longer worried. He switched off the magneto and Little Putt-Putt went back to sleep.

*What a day!* Now, Points North was gliding along smooth and peaceful. And to imagine there was so much terror just a few moments ago.

The quiet of the night was suddenly overwhelming. The only sound was the rumble from the propeller as it turned in the current.

Logan realized he was starving. He remembered what Burnt had told him, "Thirty-six hours later, you'll be staring at Cape Mudge."

*That will be the next problem. I'll be ready this time. He said it could get real nasty with the tide one way and the wind the other, as if the last thirty minutes hadn't been terrifying.*

Logan warmed up some dinner and figured his position. Lawrence Point, on the northeast tip of Orcas Island, was way behind them.

"Lady, we're in for it now, no turning back, and I don't want to. Next stop, Alaska."

The enormity of Logan's trip stuck him. He thought about all the work he had done on Points North and Little Putt-putt, recalling the precautions he had taken to make his journey as safe as possible. His dad had always taught him, "Good preparations and planning help Lady Luck do a better job."

Fried cod and rice were on the dinner menu, and he threw in the last carrots he had on board. He devoured the food, realizing how hungry he was.

After he cleaned up the galley, he decided sleeping on the bow would be best. That put him next to the towline and the big fishing knife. If anything went wrong, he would cut the bowline. At least, then he would be free, not rolled over by this massive hunk of steel called a barge in front of him.

He looked to the lighthouse behind him. *That must be Pathos Island, the last lighthouse for the US. We must be in British Columbia now, all the way to Dixon Entrance.*

"Alaska, here we come!"

# CHAPTER 12

Other than tending the buoy line, there wasn't much to do, making it a long ride for Logan and Points North. He spent time going over Grandpa's old charts, figuring out where he was and remembering old times.

Logan remembered he needed to block the shaft from turning in the morning daylight. The water was going by the propeller and turning the tail shaft like it was running. He didn't want to wear anything out in the gearbox.

Little Kanute was up on the cabin top, next to Logan. He thought about re-rigging the bowline tomorrow so he could release the little boat from the stern. Then he could sleep in the cockpit tomorrow night. He had the bridle set up, and it seemed to be working. Could he trust it?

As he drifted off to sleep, Logan wondered what Cape Mudge had in store for them. "I'm so tired. No tricks tonight Points North, be a good girl for me, would you? I need some rest."

Logan woke with the first light of the morning sun. The eastern sky was turning pink with lightly scattered clouds. *What a beautiful country.* The sun had peeked around the clouds to give a little warmth for Logan and Points North. His boat cut through the water silently, smoothly, a beautiful young lady once she settled down, and not one problem last night.

*What day is it? Could it be June twelve? I have got to keep up the log.* Sitting on the bow, he tried to think what time they had passed Lawrence Point. Now, if he guessed right, they should be pulling up on Cape Mudge by six this evening. He thought they were still making an excellent five to six knots as Burnt had told him.

Going back aft, he opened the engine hatch to check the bilge, remembering he needed to block the shaft too. *Dad had us use two wedges to stop the shaft from moving, so the net wouldn't tangle up in the propeller.* He didn't want it to run the gear or ruin the gearbox. He found the blocks brought along for that purpose. Laying on his stomach, he watched the shaft rotate, studying it carefully.

*Now, how am I going to stop that shaft from spinning?* Right now, it was moving too fast to put in the blocks. The only time it would stop is when the water stopped, and he didn't want that, or the tow would be over. *Can I slow it with power from Putt, Putt?*

Logan thought he needed some breakfast first; confident a solution would come to him with some food in his belly.

The two lingcod from last night needed to be cared for. Firing up the stove, he warmed up the iron skillet and laid in four beautiful slabs of lingcod he had filleted on the counter. They fried up fast with the iron skillet right next to the fire.

As he ate, an idea came to him. After cleaning up the galley and stowing the extra cooked fish next to the hull to keep cool, Logan got down on his knees in front of the little motor. He gave her a spin with the hand crank, and she started right up. With the greatest of care, he started pulling back on the reverse gear lever.

Sure enough, that slowed the shaft and it finally stopped. Then the propeller shaft started going the other way. Once again, he eased the handle and the propeller shaft stopped.

Holding the lever in one hand, he slid two wedge blocks under the gearbox coupler close to the engine bed. Then he reached over and switched off the magneto, and the little motor stopped running. The shaft coupler rested against the two blocks, and the shaft was not turning anymore. It worked!

Logan finished his rounds, checking everything on the boat. Now it was time to look over the charts and tide tables. He liked the Coast Pilot best for US waters. The Canadian version of that book was called *Sailing Directions*.

Burnt had pushed him to spend the money to buy those two books. He said it could save his life someday.

Logan knew the tide information was useful for fishing because Dad had used them all the time.

Now the Coast Pilot was a well-designed book. It told you which chart to use, then told you about all the places along the way. It was apparent he had some reading to do and that took the better part of the day, as he sat in the stern of the boat.

Suddenly, the wind showed up, out of nowhere it seemed. The tug and tow were now in the northern part of the Straits of Georgia where the wind would come right through the middle.

*Is this the beginning breeze of what Burnt had been talking about?*

He could see the wind's speed over the water was increasing with little white caps all across the water. He could also feel the breeze overhead. It had doubled on his backside.

*Burnt was right again. Its going to blow.*

He had to wind that stupid pocket watch and keep it set. Not knowing the time could be a big mistake in this country. He couldn't see around or over the barge, so he didn't know exactly where they were.

The wind waves were now big enough to slap the stern of Points North one way or the other. She would shear easy and come back to straight ahead. To steady her up, Logan took to hand steering.

Within minutes, the waves were more prominent, and Logan was watching carefully now, not leaving anything to doubt.

*Yes, Burnt, I know. These could be ten footers with a steep backside after the swell tops.*

Now, Points North started surfing. On the swell's forward side, she would shoot ahead, making the tow line go slack. With all that slack, she would slow down and fall off the backside of the swell. Then the tow rope would tighten with a snap and give a big jerk on his little boat.

*Holy cow, I remember things like this on the fish boats. All you could do was be patient and steer the best you could. You would pull through, but it was hard work and took a long time.*

*Do not let go of that barge!* Logan thought. *Hang in there, and soon, the tide will change, and the water will calm down.*

"We'll be fine," Logan said, knowing it would be a long fight.

Two hours passed. Finally, the wind and water started to lay down, and Logan could relax his death grip on the tiller. Soon, they passed a huge cliff with a lighthouse that stuck out from the surrounding land. He was hoping that was Cape Mudge.

"Thank you, God, for watching out for me and my little boat. To think she seemed so big when I rowed her around the pulp mill."

As it was getting dark, Logan could see the lights of a big town. Was that Campbell River? What did the chart say? By now, the waters were calm enough that Logan didn't need to steer any longer. "Thank you, God, once again!"

Burnt had warned him about Seymour Narrows, and he knew that was next. They should be through it before it was completely dark.

Logan quickly made a simple dinner, watching how Points North steered as they ran with the current. The banks alongside him were much closer now, with high steep sides covered with beautiful fir trees—no Madrona trees like at home on the cliffs and shoreline.

The Narrows made a distinct right turn a little past the rock in the middle of the passage, the current gaining speed. They had made it into Discovery Passage and continued their way up toward Johnston Straits.

*Burnt said we should make it most of the way through Discovery Passage in one tide.* The tug would buck the last of it, but it is fast running in Johnston Straits.

Logan wanted to sleep in the stern tonight. There was more room back there.

He tried to count how many days had passed since he left home. He was on his seventh, no eighth, or was it the ninth day? He wasn't sure.

He did know that Mom would be looking for a phone call. *I'll call on my first stop in Alaska. Not much she can do then but say, "Ok."*

The stars were bright, with no shore lights to dilute the background. Logan could see the Big Dipper, and straight above it was the North Star. Dad always pointed them out to him when they were fishing.

Curled up in his sleeping bag in the stern, Logan rested his head on the guard rail next to the tiller. There, he could feel if the boat sheered on him.

Sleeping that night was fitful, as he woke several times when Points North took a light sheer. She corrected herself before Logan could come to his senses. *That harness is working out correctly.*

Soon, daylight was breaking, with the sky dark pink all over. *I know, pink skies in the morning sailors take warning. Thanks, Dad.*

Breakfast was in order. He fired up the cookstove, with mush being on the top of the menu this morning.

Logan stuck his head out of the cabin hatch and could see the barge had slowed to a crawl. Shutting off the stove, he stepped out on the well-deck and looked forward to the barge.

Two men were standing on the stern of the barge. *Oh, man! They're pulling in the emergency towline, and I'm at the end of it. What now? Am I in trouble?*

The men were laughing and smiling as they pulled up Logan and his boat. They reminded him of Burnt at home.

They stopped pulling when Points North was about twenty feet from the stern of the barge.

Logan was still standing in the well deck of Points North and said with a big smile, "Good morning."

The man that looked most like Burnt said with a booming voice, "Good morning to you, our young guest. There's a gale blowing out in Queen Charlotte Sound. Our captain thinks you might not live to talk about it if you hang on to us like you are. He would like you to let go and come alongside the tug for a visit. It's a bad place when it storms here."

Logan had been holding his breath, letting it out now with a sigh of relief. "Okay, thanks. I've got to unblock my shaft. Then I'll run up to see him."

After knocking the blocks from under the shaft and starting Little Putt-Putt, Logan went forward and dropped the barge emergency buoy back into the water. He increased speed, and Points North chugged her way up the barge's side to the tug. The tug had shortened the barge towline, and the barge was secure against the port side of the tug.

The crew was crawling all over the freight on the barge, checking the tie-downs, making sure everything was secure.

As he pulled alongside the tug, Logan tied off to one of the big rubber tires hanging on the side of the tug.

Looking up, Logan saw the Captain watching him from the walkway on the side of the tug wheelhouse. *This man looks like a real Captain.*

The captain smiled and said, "Good morning, friend."

Logan came back with his most respectful, "Good morning, sir," and a big smile. He still didn't know if he was in trouble for hitching a tow.

"You know she's blowing a gale out there? It could work itself into a storm."

"Yes, sir, that's what the man on the stern of the barge told me."

"I don't think you'll make it out there in your little tin tub. Now you can go west from here for twenty miles or so, and you'll find Alert Bay. There you'll be safe. Right now, you're in Blakeney Pass, just so you know.

"You'll find other tows coming through when the weather is better, and you do need to keep track of the weather. I wasn't sure if you were going to be there after Mudge last night."

"Thank you for the information, sir, and for the tow." Logan turned to untie Points North.

"Hold on there, young feller. The cook is coming out with some grub to pass over to you."

Right then, the cook stuck his head over the rail and, reaching down, handed Logan a big bag of food that smelled of freshly baked biscuits.

The cook said, "Here you go, sausage, scrambled eggs, and fresh biscuits. I threw in a few canned goods also."

"Thank you so very much. How did you know I could use this?"

"It was a good guess on Skipper's part." Looking up, Logan saw the Captain still leaned against the rail, watching him.

"Thanks again for all your help and grub." Logan gave him a respectful salute.

"You be careful. This country can kill you quicker than you think. You should be in Alert Bay sometime this afternoon. Now you travel safe and take care."

Logan waved to the Captain and the cook, untied Points North, and turned west using Big Kanute's old magnetic compass to steer by.

The sun was still peeking through the heavy clouds over his shoulder to the east and that light breeze coming on his backside. *That will help me make Alert Bay sooner.* With little Putt-Putt in gear and heading west, Logan put up all the canvas for the wind, now his friend, to fill.

Next, he wanted to see what is in the grub sack the cook passed over.

The Captain was right. It was somewhere past noon when he putted into Alert Bay.

# CHAPTER 13

Logan pulled into the dock with a large Shell Oil sign above it. The small native town with one main road winding along the rocky shore, sat exposed to the wind, its totem poles standing tall in defiance of the weather. Sturdy docks held many fishing boats and bald eagles harassed by crows picked through fish-cleaning leftovers.

The oil dock looked to be safe moorage for the upcoming storm. Tying up Points North on the outside of three side-tied fishing boats, Logan crawled his way across the boats to the dock.

A man sat on the fish hatch on the inside boat, a cigarette in his hand, sporting a well-trimmed beard. Logan nodded to him as he stepped across his boat and onto the dock.

Turning to the man, Logan asked, "Is there a Customs Office here?"

The man nodded toward the street. "It's right next door to the RCMP station."

"Is that where I check-in? I just arrived. It's my first-time landing in Canada."

"Yes, lad. You'll be needin' to check in with those folks. It's on the main street up a 'ways. You can't miss it. Good luck to you now."

"Thank you for your help. I'll get over there as soon as I figure out where it is."

The man laughed. "You go down the dock to the road, then take a right and follow it a ways. It'll be on your left as you go up Waterfront Street. You'll see a sign with big letters, RCMP, that means Royal Canadian Mounted Police. The Customs House is the big house next door."

"Yes, sir. Thank you again for all your help."

The man was right. It was up to the street, down a 'ways and on the left. Logan needed to go in and face the music, as they say. He wasn't looking forward to this at all.

In the Customs Office, a lady was sitting at the counter with short neater-than-a-pin brunette hair and a smile.

That smile gave Logan hope this was going to work out.

She sat higher than Logan, so he had to tip his head back to look up to her.

Taking off his ball cap and politely holding it with both hands, he asked, "Is this where I check in with Customs, ma'am?"

Once again, she smiled. *Just like my mom.* "Yes, you can check in with me, young man." She turned in her chair and opened a drawer in the filing cabinet. Reaching in, she pulled out a form of some kind. She smiled again and started asking questions.

Logan explained how he caught a tow with a tugboat for Alaska, and the weather was coming up. He hadn't planned on stopping in Canada and would get going once the weather got better.

The lady asked his name, address, and the name of his boat. She then asked for two pieces of identification and the boat registration.

*Wow, this is hard.* Logan did have his identification. Back home, he had taken his birth certificate out of his mom's files. And he had his student body card, but he had forgotten Points North's Coast Guard registration back on the boat.

As he finished explaining all that to the nice lady behind the counter, she replied with a smile, "You will need to go back to your boat and get that. We need to know that you didn't steal the boat and bring it into Canada."

"Yes, ma'am. I can do that for you. It's getting late in the afternoon. Do you close at five?"

"Yes. You have cleared customs for coming into Canada, but your boat hasn't. That will let you go to town. We do need you to come back before 5 o'clock and clear your boat with the Coast Guard registration."

"Thank you, ma'am. I'll be here before 5 o'clock. Then we can get it all taken care of."

As Logan walked toward the door, he looked back over his shoulder. The Customs Officer slipped out of her chair and walked over to the man sitting at a desk behind her.

Logan walked out the door and glanced through the window as he headed down the steps. The man reached for the telephone.

Logan headed back to Points North at a brisk walk, a feeling gnawing at him that the man at the desk was calling the law. As he crossed the street, the nice lady came out of the Customs House. Standing on the front porch, she called to Logan, "Young man, come back over here, would you please."

Logan turned, waved, and started walking back to her. He asked from halfway across the street, "Yes, ma'am. What can I do for you?"

"Would you come back in, please? We want to call your mother and confirm that she knows you're in Canada."

Logan had already thought about an answer if that question came up. "Sure, I'd be glad to, but she's at work right now. I need her work phone number, that's on the boat also." He kept a straight face, stalling for time, as he stopped in front of her. She smiled again. "That's fine. You can bring it with the registration for your boat."

"Yes, ma'am. I'd better get going then." Logan turned to leave.

"Yes, you do that. Hurry back now."

Logan's mind was racing as he walked quickly down the street. *You're into it for sure now, Logan. You dummy, these people flat-out don't believe you, and they're serious about this stuff. I'm not worried about Mom. I can work with her. I don't want them to put me on an airplane and leave Points North here with all my gear on her. No way in hell, I won't do that.*

*If I have to go on the run, then that's what I'll do.*

Logan convinced himself that was the right thing to do. As he turned the corner, he glanced over to the government dock and saw a truck under the hoist crane with gear being unloaded to the boat below. He stopped and watched a big man, as big as Coach, standing by the edge of the dock with the winch control in his hand, giving orders to the man on the truck, then to the man on the boat.

Logan noticed a couple of new chainsaws and some 5-gallon pails of oil for big diesel machinery. "I bet they're picking up supplies for a logging camp."

Logan decided to take a chance, figuring nothing ventured, nothing gained and walked right up to the man giving orders.

The man stood a full head taller than Logan and there was something familiar about him. He reminded Logan of the men he worked around in the fishing fleet.

"Excuse me, sir," Logan said in a firm voice. The burly man had a big smile as he turned to Logan.

He said, "Yaw, vut is it you need, young man?"

"I couldn't help but notice your loading a lot of logging gear with the chainsaws, chokers, oil, and everything."

"Yaw, dat is what we need to keep da camp running."

"You work in a logging camp?"

"Yaw, I own it."

Logan could feel the excitement rising in him. "I have my chainsaw with me. You wouldn't need a good hand, would you? I fall and cut cordwood with my friend at home."

"And where would your home be, young man?"

"Across the border in a small fishing town. I fished with my father until he went up to the Aleutians. He was fishing king crab and never came back."

The man lowered the winch controls, and the men on the boat stopped to listen to the conversation. "I am sad to hear dat. You said you cut cordwood at home?"

"Yes, in the winter, I did it with my dad a lot. Then when we moved to town, I worked with my friend."

The big man asked, "Have you heard of Scott Cove?"

"No, sir. I hitched a tow behind a barge up to Blackney Pass. The weather was coming up, so I had to let go and come into Alert Bay. My boat, Points North, and I are headed up to Alaska."

"Alright then, you should be able to make it to Scott Cove. I can pay you forty dollars a cord cut, split, and stacked. Do you think you can do dat?"

"Yes, sir. I'll go get my chart, so you can show me where it is."

"Yaw, first, what is your name, young man?"

"Logan, sir. Logan Johansen. Grandpa came from a town south of Oslo, Norway, by the name of Royken."

"Yaw dis is good. Ok, Logan, you get your chart. Hurry now. I got to get back before da weather comes up on me."

"Thank you, sir. By the way, what's your name, sir?"

"Oley Stimpson. I come from the old country also. Nice to meet you, Logan."

They shook hands. Logan almost burst with excitement as he grinned ear to ear. He hoped this was the start of a long friendship.

He ran to Points North and grabbed the Broughton Islands chart, hoping it was the right one. He thought it might be the wrong scale and the detail may not be good enough. *I guess it will have to do.*

As he ran back to the government dock, Logan could see the men had finished loading the boat. The big man was watching Logan run as fast as he could to get back to him. Logan didn't want to hold him up any longer.

Out of breath, he handed the big man the chart. Oley unfolded the paper chart and took a pencil out of his pocket. "You be careful now," he said. "There's a rock pile right there as you come in," pointing to the chart.

Drawing a circle around a cove, he continued, "Dat is my camp right there," pointing with the pencil. "Ven you get there, you find me, alright? I got to run now, so you take care. We see you soon."

"Thank you ever so much, sir. You can count on me. I'll be there as soon I can."

"You travel safe. Dat is some tough water out there now."

"Yes, sir, thanks again." As he headed back to Points North, Logan thought he had struck it rich. Forty bucks a cord when at home, he only made ten bucks as second fiddle.

Then he remembered the Customs people. "Oh, shoot!" He had to hustle. They wanted Mom's work phone number. *Guess I'll be late. Too bad,* he thought.

Back at Points North, Logan wrote his mom's work phone number on a piece of paper and gathered up the boat registration. He figured that would give him some extra time.

Logan headed back for the Customs office, not running as he had for Oley. He wished he had his pocket watch.

By the time Logan got back to the Customs office, he figured the day shift was over. *Oh well. I'll be leaving for Scott Cove tonight once it was dark.*

"Hello." It was a new person behind the desk, and this one had wedged herself into the chair. Oh boy, she looked like you didn't ever want to give her any lip. *It must be the night shift.* "Ma'am, my name is Logan Johansen, and I brought my mother's work phone number. Also, my boat registration for you."

"Oh yes, I have your forms here." She took the boat registration and reviewed it. "Alright, Mr. Johansen, you have cleared customs. Here is your number for clearing. You are to keep that number with you and your boat. Everyone has gone home for the night. You need to come back in the morning so that they can call your mother."

Logan's heart sank into his socks. "Yes, ma'am, right, first thing in the morning. You have a good evening now."

"You too. Remember, the day shift wants to see you in the morning bright and early to make the call, so don't go anywhere."

"Yes, ma'am, first thing."

Logan walked to the door, calculating he had fourteen hours before they started looking for him. *I think I'll keep moving toward Scott Cove,*

# CHAPTER 14

The westerly evening breeze helped push Points North along. Logan had all the sails up to be as quiet as possible as he passed Alert Bay.

*It will be a long night, like on the gillnet boats.* He remembered fishing all night, and his dad teaching him night navigation. Logan knew he was up to the task.

There were no navigation lights in sight. Big Kanute's old box compass guided his way.

Time dragged on as he sailed east into the pitch-black night. Finally, he could see a light off his starboard bow.

*That's Lewis Point.* Keeping it broad on his starboard bow, the scattering of clouds with a half-moon would peek out at him occasionally. Soon, he was out in the channel.

The ebb on Points North's bow slowed her speed. Soon Logan could make out the faint outline of islands on his port side. Checking his charts, he figured he was cutting across Pearse Pass as he went by Gordon Bluff.

He was favoring Lewis Point on his starboard side. *Now let's see, it got dark around ten and light should be breaking by five AM.*

*I see the south end of the Pearse Islands. We'll sail straight for that once daylight breaks, then start Putt-Putt.*

Thirty minutes later, the motor was running, and the tide was changing.

As he rounded the islands, he spotted a small channel in the middle, then more channels in between the many islands. *I can pull in for some sleep with the tide starting to run.* He noticed the sky closing in with low hanging clouds and thought it looked more like fog, and it was blowing in from the Queen Charlottes.

*It might be the storm the tugboat captain was warning me about.* As the fog bank rolled in, the visibility dropped immediately as Points North pulled into the first channel. *This is wee small.* It was more like a ditch with sharp rock cliffs on both sides. *Perfect. I'll explore the others later.*

Suddenly Logan heard an unwanted sound behind him, a rumble of diesel engines. Turning around in his seat in the stern, he strained to see.

The faint outline of a RCMP patrol boat filtered through the fog. Logan slowed Putt-Putt to listen closer. Once again, his gut was telling him they were looking for him and the lifeboat.

*How did they know I took off so soon? I don't think they've seen me yet.*

He quickly dropped the sails and reached for the throttle to speed up Points North.

Logan steered to the middle of the small channel as the fog wrapped around his little boat. With less than fifty feet visibility now, all he could see was the bullwhip kelp patch on his port beam. He slowed the engine to a crawl and shoved Points North's bow into the patch of kelp. Logan laid her flat against the sheer rock wall, between a couple of trees growing precariously out of cracks in the rock. He scrambled to get a line up from both the bow and stern to the branches sticking out.

Once Points North was holding good, Logan shut down Putt-Putt. Looking back, he could hear the RCMP still coming, but he couldn't see them with the fog as thick as pea soup. From the stern looking forward, Logan could hardly see the bow of his own boat.

He remembered fog being this thick from fishing with his dad. Occasionally, when running from the game warden, they would drive their boat up onto the beach so they wouldn't show up on the game warden's radar. He would see the outline of the beach, but there would be a bump like a big log on his screen.

No one said Dad was an angel, but he still had to care for his family. He would tell Logan, "We don't want to break the law. We only want to bend it a little."

The fog was still coming in, dense and heavy. Logan knew this was his one chance to lose the RCMP.

According to the chart, the channel went all the way through between the two islands and Logan could see there would be plenty of water at high tide. The RCMP boat could make it through there with no problem, without the fog, of course.

Logan could hear the other motor slow, then stop. There was shouting in the stone-cold silence wrapped around him. It sounded like they were right next to him in the stern of Points North.

Someone asked if it would be safe to follow the small boat ahead of the RCMP boat. Logan heard them discuss not going through the channel there, and if they didn't, they would have to go out and around the island. Then they could catch him on the other side as he came out.

*That is, if I come out on the other side.* He was amazed their voices traveled so well.

The police decided it was too shallow to go any further with the fog and the strong current.

One voice called out, "How about I take the skiff?"

"Then we would have two boats lost in there. No, not today."

There was a short pause. "It's a maze of channels with a heck of a lot of currents to push you around. No, we'll catch him, but it will take more time. Let's run around to the other side. We'll catch him when he comes out."

The big diesel engines rumbled, and Logan could tell they were backing hard. Someone yelled again, "It's so blasted thick in there, no one could make it in or out, not in this fog anyway."

Logan could hear the boat turning around, then the rumbling faded off into the fog.

"Well, nothing to do now but see if breakfast is waiting down there," Logan announced to Points North.

Using a small jig, Logan had six nice fat rock-cod on deck in a matter of minutes. That was the great thing about parking in a kelp patch, food was always waiting under your feet.

Cutting their throat latch, he let the fish bleed out. Logan decided cooking fish wasn't a good idea. He didn't want the smell of frying fish carrying through the channel.

*Guess there'll be fish for lunch instead.* Logan settled for oatmeal then laid down for a well-deserved nap. Soon he was deep asleep and slept hard for an hour. He woke up with a jerk.

He heard the RCMP boat again. Out on deck, he could hear them going away from him once more.

*Guess it's time to move. No, I'll wait until the fog lifts to about fifty feet. We'll take the small cross-channel if it's high tide.*

According to the chart, there was a small square bay on the northside of the island. That looked big enough for Points North to lay in with a stern tie.

Logan started to get anxious, but the fog was still there, at best twenty-five feet of visibility. He thought this would be the best place to wait for the fog to lift.

About noon, the fog finally lifted a bit more. Logan worked his way down the tiny channel until he could make out the small bay ahead of him. There was not enough swinging room to anchor in the middle, but he could tie a stern line to the beach and put the anchor stretched out in front of him.

*Good thing I threw in that old corkline Dad had for the salmon nets.* Logan let the anchor out in the middle of the bay and it fetched up hard right away. He put Little Kanute in the water, rowed the stern line to a tree on shore, slipped it around the tree, and rowed back to Points North, bringing the rope back to the stern again. That way, he could let it go without having to go to the beach.

Logan was ready for a change in the menu. He salted the rock cod and put them away, then baited an old rusty halibut hook with some of the morning's cod, lowered it to the bottom on a handline, and tied it off to the tiller. Fishermen call that a 'meat line' while anchored up. He busied himself with housekeeping chores, and with that done, he stopped by the to check how the handline was doing.

As he pulled on the line, it seemed to be hung up on the bottom. *That could be an old log. It's coming, but pulling hard.*

Suddenly, the line started running out fast, burning his bare hands. "Whoa! What have we got here?"

The fight was on. He pulled in ten feet of fishing line, hand over hand.

It took off again, pulling the line straight down. All Logan could do was to slow it down, trying to avoid cutting his hands. Now it was still, as if on the bottom, resting.

Then suddenly, off it would go one way, then another, then right back to the bottom. That routine continued for thirty minutes.

Finally, Logan could pull enough line in to bring it into sight. *That's a nice halibut! I'll bet it's sixty pounds or better. I can eat on him for a week.*

The halibut ran three more times before Logan could get him in close to the boat. Holding the line in one hand, he grabbed Grandpa's old gaff hook and drove it into the fish's head. That woke him up, and he thrashed about in the water slamming into the side of Points North.

Carefully, Logan pulled the line up and rolled the halibut over the gunnel into the well deck. He beamed with pride that he could catch a fish so beautiful.

The halibut was about four feet long and over two feet wide. The olive-colored top side of the fish had two eyes, and the bottom side was creamy white. It was still pounding the deck with its tail. Logan turned the giant fish over, so its white underside was up. It calmed down and died quietly after Logan bled it out. *This fish makes the whole trip worth it.*

Logan started filleting, wrapping each piece in plastic wrap then layering the meat down by the keel to keep it fresh. He was sure there was enough meat to eat for two weeks or more.

He thought if the RCMP boat were to catch him he could share it with them. No, bad idea. He didn't have a fishing license. *Were halibut even in season?*

Logan figured he'd better get serious about the RCMP boat. *By now, two things have happened. They're mad that I gave them the slip, and the customs people back in town know I'm missing. God, I hope they don't call Mom! She would be worried.*

*Should I go ahead and catch another tow north and pass up the cordwood job? No, don't do that. There's too much money to be made. Hopefully it will turn into a job for the summer. Points North, we're going to Scott Cove.*

With the halibut mess cleaned up, Logan spread the chart on the table, tracing possible routes with his finger. Going the short way, he might stumble into the law. *That won't work. The long way will be slower, but the odds are better not to get caught.*

The wind whistled through the boat rigging and Logan could hear it clearly from inside the cabin. He stuck his head out the hatch. *It's coming out of the West, and the fog is not as thick.* He thought he should run with the fair tide.

The wind whistled again, gusting stronger now. *It must be blowing thirty-five knots or more. Time to go. No, wait. The wind and cover of darkness would be the best time to go, so before daylight. That'll push me past Hansen Island. Then we can duck into Blackney Pass.*

Logan decided he had to make his move at the change of the tide. *Besides, the RCMP won't figure on me making a run for it with this weather. They'll be at anchor in some bay, safe and sound. This will work. Play it cool, Logan. Be smart like Coach taught you.*

# CHAPTER 15

Logan left his secure anchorage spot just as the eastern sky glowed pink. The wind had calmed to a nice fifteen knots dead on his stern.

The trip from Kuldekduma Island to Scott Cove started well with Logan pulling into small coves when the tide ran against him. He noticed it was flat out dark in that part of the world with no beach lights to help navigate in the night. What little moon there was hid behind full cloud coverage.

He couldn't believe Gilford Island was so huge. Logan calculated it would take him six days to come around the back way.

The only problem he had was when he started across Knight inlet to Tribune Channel. All the sails were up, and the engine at its top speed. Points North couldn't make much headway against the ebb current.

As darkness approached, Logan knew it was too late to keep going. They had to layup for the night.

He eased the little boat into a kelp patch and shut down, suddenly very tired. Logan fought off sleep as long as he could, trying to figure out where he had gone wrong. He finally succumbed to a fitful sleep, anxious for daylight so he could push on.

Fighting his way up Tribune Channel cost Logan an entire day. Sometimes he wondered if he would ever make it to Scott Cove.

On the sixth day, as he approached his final turn, Logan smiled, knowing he and Points North had made it in one piece and hadn't been caught and hauled off by the RCMP.

As he approached the bay, two prominent rocks stood awash on the port side, barely sticking up out of the water, just like Oley had told him.

Logan steered well clear of the rocks and came into the camp quietly. The bay was surrounded by rocky shores and dense trees. The logging camp was in a large clearing, with easy water access, with a large log home off to the left, a bunkhouse close to a shop and further around the bay, a log dump on the other side of a small point of land.

A boat ramp extended from the clearing and a long building that looked like an office to the right. The crew boat he had seen in Alert Bay six days ago sat tied to the dock. A float house and another dock to the left completed the camp.

It was late afternoon now as he tied Points North in front of the crew boat. The whole place was quiet, with no one in sight. Logan walked up to the building, knocked on the door with the Office sign, and went in. He saw a nice lady sitting at the desk with a name sign that said, *Allison Benson.*

"Hi, Miss Benson. My name is Logan Johansen. I talked to Mr. Stimson last week in Alert Bay."

"Oh yes, he told me about you. Did you take the long way around?" She gave a big heartwarming smile.

"Well, yes, ma'am, it was slow but sure to make it here."

"And no RCMP?" she asked with a smile.

"No ma'am, I didn't see any on the way I took."

"That's good. The RCMP stopped by last week looking for someone that fits your description."

"Well darn, that's too bad I missed them."

She chuckled and gave him another big warm smile.

"Are you here to go to work?"

"Yes, ma'am, I am."

"Good. You can put your boat across the dock down by the float house. The house belongs to my husband, Burney, and me. You can be our neighbor, okay?"

"Yes, ma'am. That sounds great."

"Oley is up at one of the sides. He'll talk to you when he gets into camp this evening, I'm sure."

"Thank you again, ma'am. I'll move my boat and wait for Mr. Stimson."

Logan turned to leave and paused, turning back. "Say, ma'am, would you like some halibut? I caught it this morning."

"No, my husband caught me one the other day, but if you go over to the cookhouse, I'm sure Ida would appreciate some."

"Okay. I'll move my boat and take that fresh halibut right over."

Firing up the little motor one more time, Points North putted out and around the float house then glided into the slip across the dock from the float house.

Once she was all secured, Logan dug out the forty-pound halibut catch. He was hoping the cook would like it.

The back of the cookhouse had a row of galvanized garbage cans with various methods of bear prevention. Some had chains through the lid handle, and others had snap locks and concrete blocks on top of them. In the middle of the building was a sturdy wood-framed screen door and a closed wooden door behind it.

Logan opened the screen door and knocked twice, as hard as he could.

Before he could knock again, the door swung wide open, and a large lady with a sweet, friendly smile filled the doorway. *Now she is not fat, mind you. Big boned, my aunt would say.*

The lady had a wide smile and a whole stack of braided blond hair piled on top of her head. She wore a clean white dress, covered by a white baker's apron. The apron hung under her chin and wrapped around her middle with a tie string. She looked at Logan, then the halibut. "Is dat fish for me, young man?"

"Yes, ma'am, I caught it fresh this morning."

"Well, you come right on in. You put it on the cutting board by the sink."

"Would you like me to fillet it for you, ma'am? I always did it for my mom back home."

She smiled and nodded, "Yaw, thank you."

He got right to it and started laying the fish on the cutting board.

She said, "Yes, that would be nice. My name is Ida. Who do you belong to, young man?"

"My name is Logan Johansen. I belong to my boat. Her name is Points North. I met Mr. Stimson at Alert Bay. He offered me a job cutting cordwood." He paused while putting the halibut up on a cutting board.

"I haven't talked to him since I got here, though. He's up on one of the sides, according to Mrs. Benson. She is the one that thought you might like some fish."

"Oh yes, Logan, I love to have fresh fish for the kitchen, and so do the loggers we feed here."

"Got a knife? And what size would you like them cut?" Logan asked, rolling up his shirt sleeves.

"About four or five-inch squares. That's a nice size. Ve can pan fry dem and hand out to the hungry loggers. I'm fixing dinner and could use some help when you've finished with dat fish."

"Sure, I'd be happy to, Miss Ida. Tell me what you want. I'll need to wash up first."

"Please call me Ida. That would be fine with me."

After Logan washed up, Ida gave him a white paper hat, and that was it. They were fast friends.

Logan finished up the fish, set the tables, and brought wood in for the stove.

Ida had him start the salad, as it was close to dinnertime. Mr. Stimson walked into the kitchen and smiled at Logan. He was a big man and looked a lot like Ida.

"Looks like you finally made it. Long trip? Logan, isn't it?" Logan kept cutting up the lettuce.

"Yes, sir, I took a long way around to be safe and sound." Logan gave Oley a big grin.

"Vel, I am glad you made it. It looks like you met my sister. How are you two hitting it off?"

Ida broke in, "Ve are yust fine, brother."

"She is a little shorthanded, Logan. Next week, her help should be here. Would you mind helping out until then?"

"Not at all, sir. I would be happy to. Do you think I could cut cordwood when Ida doesn't need me?"

"Yaw, dat would be yust fine, after breakfast tomorrow ve vill get you set up for dat also. Ida vill be your boss until help arrives, then you can do cordwood full-time."

Ida said, with the roll of her tongue, "This nice young man brought me a forty-pound halibut this afternoon. Vould you like some rolled in crushed crackers and fried up for dinner?"

"Yaw dat sounds good, but do you have time?"

"Yaw, I know yust how you like it. Logan here can fry it up for me, you'll see."

"Dis is good." Oley said, "I need to check-in at the office. I yust wanted to see how your new hand was doing."

It was a busy night. Logan fried up nearly half of the halibut for the crew when they came in. He cleared the tables and did the dishes. Ida was busy getting things ready for breakfast. They finished up around seven that first night. Ida said, "You be here by 4 AM tomorrow morning."

"Ida, I don't have an alarm clock."

"Oh no. Never mind, I have an extra I can loan you. Come with me."

Following her over to the house, Logan waited outside on the front porch. She brought him out an old Big Ben clock with big brass bells on top. Thanking her, he said goodnight. Logan was sure his bunk had never felt so good.

The clock started ringing, 3:30 AM, and he was off to the races.

He made it to the kitchen with ten minutes to spare. Ida was already hard at work and had Logan set up for breakfast, then set out all the food for the crew to build their lunches.

Logan couldn't believe how much food these men could eat. He thought they ate a lot on the fish boats. The fishermen never had a thing on these lumberjacks.

Ida was shoveling out scrambled eggs as fast as she could cook them. Logan was making toast and trying to keep up. He noticed the crew were easy-going, wearing the same dirty duds they had when they came in for dinner. Except now, the clothes were dry, and the men had taken showers.

*This is a tough life they live for sure. The money must be worth it.* He was hoping to make some of that money for himself.

As he finished up the morning dishes, Ida told him her secret. She took a long nap in the middle of the day. Then dinner was a snap for her.

Logan liked talking to Ida. "I know you said my relief would be here in a week. Then I can cut cordwood full-time."

"Oh yaw, it'll be my niece, Oley's daughter. She lost her mother, cancer, you know. Now she lives in Vancouver with her mother's sister."

"Does she like coming to camp?"

"Vell, she was raised here by her mother and father, sometimes me, here in camp. We all love her very much, and she is such a sweet girl. Now I tink she wants to stay in the big city, playing with her friends."

"How old is she?"

"Annie is 15 years, like you, Logan. You'll like her. She's a beautiful girl and smart, very smart."

"Ida, I notice everyone sits in the same chair and table. Where do I sit? On the fish boats, we never sat in anyone else's seat. If you did, you were in trouble."

"You're right. You can sit at this table and use that chair where you are right now. Dat's your chair now, from here on out."

Oley walked in, smiling as usual. "Logan, come vith me. Ida, she vill tell you all kinds of stories. You never know what to believe, even if she is my only sister."

Ida smiled, "Dat's my big brother. I know you'd have guessed it by now."

"What time do you need me back, Ida?"

"Make it at four o'clock. If you're not busy, come in earlier. There's always plenty to do around here."

"Come on, Logan, I vill give you the rundown." As they headed out the door, Oley asked, "Can you drive?"

"Yes, sir, but I don't have a driver's license."

"No problem. We're on private property."

Outside, an old flatbed World War II vintage Dodge truck waited for them. It was to be Logan's wood and garbage hauler.

Twice a week, he was to pick up all the garbage cans, burn the paper and cardboard at camp in the back of the shop, then take what's left to the dump.

Logan drove as Oley explained where everything was in the camp.

Pulling up to a massive log loader, Oley said, "Come on, Logan, I want you to meet Burney. He's your neighbor in the float house. You'll like him."

They got out of the Dodge and watched Burney glide the big rubber-tired log loader next to them. He stopped and climbed down the ladder from the cab, smiled and held out his hand to Logan. "Welcome to Scott Cove. You already met my wife, Allison. She told me you were our new woodcutter."

"Yes, I am."

"Good. See over there? I'll lay your wood out for you, and you'll do all your cutting, splitting, and loading there. Any questions?"

"No, keep it coming, I get paid by the cord."

Burney laughed. "We'll do fine. Any questions, ask me, okay?"

"You can count on that, I'll ask."

Oley smiled, "Come with me, Logan. I'll show you the rest of the stops."

They went to the repair shop, then all the places he was to pick up the garbage and drop off the cordwood.

Oley explained that this was an important job because they still heated with stove wood. He thought someday he would change over to oil, but he liked the wood heat for now.

The last stop was the office. Inside, Oley said to Allison, "Logan, here, will be our woodcutter." He paused and laughed. "Along with garbage, errands, and whatever else we need him to do."

Turning to Logan, he continued. "Now Logan, if Allison needs anything, you help her out. Next week, I'll take you up to the sides, then if you need to run messages or parts up to them, you'll know how to get there. And be sure you're on time for Ida. She is a hard one to live with." He winked at Allison, who knew he was kidding. With that, Oley gave him a nod and a big grin. The old Dodge was to be Logan's and he was on his own now.

Logan felt like he belonged. He liked the responsibility of working in the kitchen and in the wood yard and whatever else they asked him to do. He never wanted to disappoint Ida. She was the sweetest person. He did want to talk to her about Oley's daughter. She sounded like a nice person, and the best part was she loved to fish. *Now, this is my kind of a girl. We'll see.*

Logan needed his chainsaw, ax, the splitting maul, and splitting wedges. Then he had to get gas and oil at the shop for the old Titan saw.

The mechanics were friendly and explained where to get the gas for the saw and the old Dodge power wagon.

Once he had everything gassed and oiled up, Logan jumped in the old Dodge like he knew what he was doing.

Back at the log dump, Burney had a half-dozen damaged logs laid out for him. They were straight grain and easy to split since they were already half split-up from the damage.

"Can't sell them to the mill, so it's free heating wood for the camp, except for your wages, of course," Burney had told him.

After a few days Logan settled into a routine. *Wish the rain would slow for a day. Since I got here, it hasn't stopped raining. Now it's a low fog, drizzling, and everything is soaking wet.* Even being wet, he was happy making money for the summer. Good summer jobs like this were hard to come by. He figured if he could cut a hundred cord of wood, that would come to four thousand dollars cash in his pocket this summer. Then, he might be able to buy a small cross-sound Alaska troller for next summer.

Logan's process for cutting cordwood was efficient. He marked off the first log for stove-sized blocks. The wood was clean, and the jag-tooth chain made quick work of cutting the logs into blocks. The old Titan chainsaw fired up on the first pull.

He stood up each block while he was cutting off the next block. That took one move out of the process. Now they were ready for splitting with a sharp splitting maul.

The straight grain was beautiful, and the blocks split like butter. Logan decided a regular ax would be quicker. For sure, he needed to keep everything razor sharp.

He stacked the wood on the old Dodge flatbed into a pile, four-foot-wide by four-foot-high by eight foot long. That would be one cord. By the time the truck was full, he had four cords in the flatbed ready to go.

Burney kept track as he took the loads out. After a while, he and Logan became friends, and Burney told Logan to keep track of his wood. He said he was busy enough, and he trusted Logan.

Logan liked working alone. He never told anyone, but he especially liked the fact they trusted him. Their trust was essential for him. Being left alone did have its pitfalls. He had to keep track of the time so he wouldn't be late for Ida. It was so comfortable working on the cordwood he would forget what time it was. The pocket watch Grandpa had given him was wound every night. He knew he had to have it to make the job work.

Logan was looking forward to Ida's niece arriving. His job would be a lot easier then, only take care of the wood, haul garbage, and run errands when needed. He won't need to help in the kitchen anymore.

Listening to Ida talk about her niece, Logan thought she must be a beautiful girl. He would find himself daydreaming about her arrival while hanging on the backside of the noisy, smelly chainsaw. He hoped they could become fishing partners. It was much better to catch a perfect fish with a good friend.

On Sunday, the crew took the day off and laid around like a bunch of lazy cats. Ida would prepare a light breakfast and, in the afternoon, a long, late lunch. All the other days, Logan was off from 8 AM to 4 PM, then finish up dinner and do it all over again.

Having been there for a week now, Burney and Logan trusted one another. Burney liked hearing the story of Logan's trip to Scott Cove, especially the part about outrunning the RCMP boat. It made him howl with laughter, and of course, he had to tell the rest of the crew when he had a chance.

That story gave Logan some favor with the crew. They were a rough bunch but respectful. If they needed something done or needed help, Logan was always there giving a hand.

One day Burney asked, "Logan, did you know the RCMP boat was here looking for a boat like yours? Also, someone that fits your description?"

"Yeah, I know. Allison told me the first day I got here."

"Here's an idea. How about you pull the mast, then let me pick your boat up at the ramp with the log bull. She would saddle fine in the forks, and I can set her down behind the bachelors' bunkhouse. You could still sleep in Points North there and use the showers in the bunkhouse."

"That's a great idea. The RCMP wouldn't see my girl if they came back snooping around."

"Yep, and I don't think Oley would mind, but I'll check with him in the morning over breakfast. He already knows about the RCMP boat. Don't you worry none, I know he likes you.

"Logan, it took a lot on your part to get here. You're a good hand, so you stick around now. Keep doing what you're doing, and the summer will be over before you know it."

"I will. I like it here, and everyone is nice to me. Some of the loggers grumble at times, but that's fine. I don't have anything to do with them. I like my job here, and I want to make it through the summer, then I'll have to go home."

"I understand. You need to go home to school."

Burney talked to Oley about putting Points North behind the bachelor bunkhouse the next morning and Oley agreed it was a good idea. Logan could string out some power for light while he was at it.

"Oley," Burney said, "I like Logan. He's doing a good job, and he works smart. No wasted moves for that young man."

"Yaw, I've vatched him too. He is a hard worker, and Ida wants to keep him if we're not careful."

After breakfast, Oley had Logan move Points North to the ramp and Burney hauled her out with the log bull. Within the hour, Logan was blocking up Points North behind the bachelor's bunkhouse. She was safe there. Now Logan had his boat bunk and a place to take a shower.

Ida was as kind as ever, filling him in on all the rules and courtesies. She was firm in that he was to use that chair at every meal. It was his chair as long as he was in the camp.

"But Ida, I know this is the boss's table. You're all family, and I'm a piece of driftwood that came in on a windy day and got lucky enough to work here."

"No, Logan, you're not driftwood here. We like you and want you to stay. You're younger than the crew and don't need all their stories. That's a lot of talk and nonsense.

"You sit in that chair. It's yours, if someone asked you why you are sitting there, you tell that person to talk to me."

Ida chose not to tell Logan that her niece Annie would sit in the chair next to him.

Ida was a thoughtful, wonderful aunt and felt that Annie needed someone her age in camp, even if it was a boy and a polite one at that. *Who knows, they might become good friends.*

"Yes, ma'am. When your niece gets here, would you like me to wash your dishes still?"

"No, you don't have to."

"What I was thinking, Ida, is that I'm a contract worker. So, could I pay for my meals by doing your dishes? Then on Sundays, catching us fresh fish to feed the crew? I want to pay for my keep."

"Don't you worry about your keep. You more than pay your way around here. We like you, Logan, and I know my niece will like you when she gets here."

"Thanks for that, Ida. I want you to know I won't let you down."

Now the routine was like clockwork. Oley, Ida, Burney, and Allison became good friends with Logan. They understood he was younger than the logging crew. If he wanted to visit with any of them, they were there for him.

Logan liked his time alone, so he kept mostly to himself.

It was time to call his mom. For now, he figured a letter would keep things straight. He had his mind made up that he wouldn't let go of this excellent summer job whatever happened. This job would take care of him for the next school year and the following summer.

Besides, he was looking forward to meeting Oley's daughter Annie.

# CHAPTER 16

The seaplane landed and taxied to the dock. Logan watched as two new crew and a young girl got off the plane. *It must be Ida's niece or the boss's daughter, all the same.* He turned back to his cordwood pile. *This might be interesting. It would be best to lay low and keep my big mouth shut for now. Besides, from where I'm standing, that girl is beautiful. Oh well, never had much luck with girls, not even a kiss on a hayride. I guess I'm saving myself for the right one. It would be nice to find someone special. We could spend time together. Go fishing, hold hands, an occasional kiss. Yeah, all the basic stuff.* Logan continued to cut wood and carry on a conversation with himself. *Maybe when I'm 40 years old, and all this cordwood work is over, then there would be time for that stuff.*

When Logan showed up at the kitchen at four that evening, Ida had him setting tables and building the food line, then scrubbing all the pots and pans. By the time his chores were done, the men had come in, got their food, and started eating. Logan finally had time to grab a plate of food for himself and head to his chair at the table.

Ida's niece was sitting next to his seat, talking to Ida and her dad. Oley was sitting in his chair across the table from her. Logan could see she was noticeably confident with herself. That didn't interest him. He was glad to sit for a minute and eat his dinner.

He started eating, listening to her chirp away about her Aunt in Vancouver and the Bobby.

The chirping stopped mid-sentence. She glanced at Logan. "And who is this sitting at the family table next to me?"

Logan looked up over to Ida and Oley. They smiled. He turned to look into beautiful green eyes. "Hi, I'm Logan, the firewood cutter. As far as the family table seating, you can check with your Aunt Ida.

She gave me the chair for meals, and I was to send anyone that asked me about it to her."

He smiled and couldn't resist looking into her deep green beautiful eyes. *God, they were so deep, the prettiest sea of green, with a wee twinkle to them.*

Everyone at the table could see the hesitation coming from Annie. With a slightly bewildered smile, she looked back into his smiling blue eyes and took a mental picture of the young man. He was clean, smelled of gasoline and wood, slender, tall, looked healthy, and needed a haircut.

"Well, hi to you. My name is Annie. I'm the boss's daughter. You must know of me?"

"Yes, your Aunt Ida said you were coming, and I'm happy to see you. Now I can go to the woodpile full-time. If there is anything I can help you with, please let me know."

"Well, yes, okay. And who are you?" Her mind stalled for a split second again, trying to evaluate him.

Oley said, "Logan here, is our new cordwood cutter, as he said, and he's been helping Ida out until you showed up."

Everyone could see Annie was still too busy checking Logan out. She hadn't heard a word her dad said.

Oley was having a hard time not laughing.

Annie turned to her dad once she figured out what was said. "Now, Dad, I don't think I need to be a galley slave. I've been thinking I could be of more help in the office with Allison. Don't you think?"

"No, Annie, I don't think so." He gave her his all-knowing smile, being the kind, loving father that he is.

"You remember the deal ve made. It was two summers in the cookhouse vith Aunt Ida. Then ve vould see if you vould vork out in da office. That is if you still want to go to University?"

"Yes, of course, you know I do. I don't think I need to be a galley slave. Dad, you know that. No offense, Aunt Ida. It looks like you have one sitting here at the family table right now."

*Okay, I've heard enough,* Logan thought. He could feel his anger rising but she was too pretty. "Excuse me, miss. I am not a galley slave, for your information. Your Aunt Ida does a hell of a job here from what I can see, and she's my friend. Now you might be thankful you have a summer job here. I sure am."

Logan took a breath to let what he had said sink in.

"Besides, you might lighten up a bit. I hear you like to catch fish, and that is one of my favorite things in this world."

He leaned toward her, giving her a big smile, about six inches from her pretty nose.

She returned Logan's smile, moving away a bit. "You're right. What kind of fish do you like to catch?"

"Anything with gills and a tail. How about you?"

"Salmon, some halibut, but that's a lot of work, you know."

"Yeah, I know, but it's still a lot of fun."

Oley broke into their conversation. "Good. Annie, you be here at 4 AM, right Ida?"

Ida smiled warmly. "Yaw, dat vill be yust fine, Logan, you too? You can show Annie your routine. If you still want us to trade dishwashing for meals that would help us out a lot."

Logan looked over to Oley.

Oley winked as he nodded.

"Yes, ma'am." Logan stood up and collected dishes for washing.

Up to his elbows in soap suds in the kitchen, Annie came up beside him. "So, how did you land up here, and how old are you?"

"I'm fifteen, and I came in on my boat, Points North. I met your dad at Alert Bay, and he offered me a job cutting cordwood for the camp. I brought my chainsaw."

"You're a little young to be a logger."

"You're right, I am. But I needed a summer job, and your dad was good enough to give me one. You know everyone here respects him very much."

"Yeah, I know, he's my dad. He wants me to earn my way if I want to go to University. I just don't want two years in the kitchen. My interests are in business and accounting."

"That's good. My mom is a bookkeeper, and she likes it."

"Well, I'm not quite talking bookkeeping."

Logan wanted to talk about something more interesting. "Say, when I get done with the dishes, would you like to fish a handline for halibut on the log boom? There's an evening bite out there waiting, you know."

"Well, I just got in. I'm not sure."

"Okay. I'll be going down to drop a couple of meat lines in. You're welcome to come if you like. There are some nice fat chickens down there. It could be a twenty to forty pounder, you never know. One of them might have your name on it. Also, it could be waiting for Ida's skillet."

"I'll check with Dad. That sounds like fun."

Annie caught up with Logan down at the log boom. They both were wearing their rain gear with it raining as it was.

Logan had a couple of work lifejackets and handed her one then put his on. She smiled and looked at him, "How did you know I would come down here for fishing?"

He returned her warm smile, "Did I mention Aunt Ida told me how much you loved fishing? I knew you couldn't resist the invitation. Besides, you wouldn't want to miss out on all the fun."

She smiled again and laughed. "You're right. So, where is my handline, and what are we using for bait?"

They fished until near dark, with a lot of whooping and yelling going on when Annie caught a nice fat halibut.

They made it up to the cleaning station dragging the fish together, and Aunt Ida was standing there to see how they did.

Annie was so excited, telling Ida how much fun it was to catch the fish on a handline while trying to keep her balance on the log boom without getting pulled into the water.

Logan smiled. He was happy to share in her excitement. *What a great girl.*

Logan cleaned the halibut, and Ida opened the kitchen cooler, so he could let it hang for the following evening meal.

He told Ida, "This girl loves to catch fish. She lit up when that halibut tried to pull her into the drink."

As he crawled into his bunk on Points North that night, the girl was all he had on his mind.

*This could turn into a great summer being friends with Annie. The green-eyed, golden hair, very trim girl. She sure had a lot of fire when it came time to catch those fish. Maybe we could have a great friendship, fishing together, Bobby or no Bobby.*

Annie and Aunt Ida had walked back to Oley's house, where they both lived. The evening mist rolled in as the drizzling rain stopped.

"Auntie, do you think Logan will be here all summer?"

"Yaw, I tink your father will have to tell him when it's time to go home. He seems to like it here, and all of us like Logan. You will, too, you'll see."

"You knew that when you gave him a chair at the family table, didn't you?"

"Vell Annie, he is younger than the loggers. He doesn't need to spend a lot of time with them. God knows they are good, respectful, hard-working men. But all the same, men."

Ida paused to reflect a moment, then continued to explain. "Logan is young like you. He and you both need time to grow. Please, yust have fun like you did tonight. He will make good company for you. I would like to see you both be good friends. When summer is over, you can go back to Vancouver and your Aunt Samantha."

As they entered the house and took off their coats, Annie thought about how much she loved her dad's sister.

When Mother died, Aunt Ida was always there for her. They could talk about anything.

"Auntie, what about Bobby? What will he think about our fishing and spending time together?"

"Vat about Bobby? You're not engaged, are you?"

"Well, no, we're friends. We've held hands a couple of times to see what it's like."

"Vell, so you're not even going steady?" Oley was sitting in the living room, listening to the girl-talk, and keeping quiet.

"No, not going steady. No promises. That was how we left it."

"Sounds to me like he still wants his freedom. Yaw, dat gives you yours, so have some fun. Annie, you know this logging camp can be a lot of fun if there is someone your age. Yust tink, you have someone you can spend time with and share the one thing you enjoy so much."

They looked at each other and said, "Fishing!" at the same time, and laughed.

Oley was happy to hear laughter in his house again. It had been too quiet, too long for his family.

"Auntie," Annie said, "You might be right there, after this evening."

Annie spied her dad. "Poppa, I had the most fun tonight. I caught a 40-pound halibut right off the log boom. That darn fish wanted to drag me in. Logan told me how to land it. He said he would back me up, and he did. He was there when the fish started to run, burning line through my hands.

"Once we got it up, he gaffed it for me, then pulled it up and knocked it out to keep from bruising the meat with it flopping around on the boom stick. That was so exciting! He is a nice boy. Poppa, I like him."

"Yaw, I tink he is a good young man. He works hard and has good manners. You know he has his pride too and doesn't want to be called galley slave."

They all laughed at that.

Annie still had more to say. "I know, I grumbled when I first got here. I want to apologize for that, and this is my home. You are my family, and I'm glad to be here. It does make me miss Mother more, though. She was such a great mom and a good friend."

"Yaw, ve all miss her very much. Now you need to call it a night. 4 AM comes early," Oley said.

"Dad, do you have any boats Logan and I could use for fishing this summer? The log boom was fun tonight, but we need to get out and troll for salmon when they come in. Logan was telling me what kind of lures he uses."

"Ve'll see, there might be something laying around. I know Logan's boat is out of the water, so you do need some ting. Goodnight now and velcome home, my lovely daughter."

Annie kissed his cheek goodnight. Turning, she gave her Auntie a big warm hug. "I'll see you in the wee hours, Boss."

"Yaw, velcome home Annie. Ve have missed you so much."

Annie smiled and headed straight to her bed. She felt drained and knew it would be a big day tomorrow.

Ida looked over to Oley. "Our little girl is becoming a young woman of her own, Brother. I'm so glad you found young Logan for the summer. It'll give Annie a friend. He is a good boy, and he'll be good for her."

Oley agreed. "I like him and how he stood up to her at the dinner table. Dis is good, and she didn't resent him for reminding her to be respectful to my sister. I liked that too."

Logan came through the kitchen door at 3:50 AM Ida was already starting to set up breakfast. He put on his apron, hat and said with a huge smile, "Good morning, Auntie."

She gave him a warm smile back, "Good morning, Logan. Could you fry up some halibut strips for breakfast, please? Also, vould you make sure there is enough for sandwiches?"

"Yes, ma'am, can do."

She shook her head and smiled again.

Right at the stroke of four, Annie came through the door, nodding and said, "Good morning." She stood next to her aunt. "Reporting for duty, Auntie."

"You can set the tables and start setting up the breakfast food line. Logan is frying up some fish for me."

The morning flew by as always, then clean up and some quiet time to eat their breakfast.

Logan ate with the ladies, and they all talked about jigging lingcod. Annie asked about little Kanute, "Is he big enough for the two of us?"

"Yes, but it needs to be flat calm."

She said she would check again on a boat for them to use. Logan finished the morning dishes, fixed his lunch, and headed for the door.

"Logan, wait, please," Annie called to him, catching him as he was putting his coat on. She stood in front of him, nervously wringing her apron in her hands.

"What time do you stop for lunch, and where will you be?"

"Guess I'll be by the log dump cutting and splitting wood."

"Good, I'll come to have lunch with you. I want to show you a couple of sportfishing magazines that Dad had. There are some new lures you might like to see."

"That sounds great. I'll see you then."

Once he was out the door, Ida smiled her wide, warm auntie-smile at Annie. "So, lunch is it for the young fishing people?"

Annie blushed. "Auntie, we are so busy here in the kitchen, Logan and I don't have a chance to talk."

"Oh, I see. Yaw, lunch would be a good time to talk fishing lures."

Ida knew better, and she could see Annie was curious. This young man from the US was much different from the Canadian boys in her school.

Annie was at the woodpile at straight-up noon. It was drizzling, so they both were wearing rain gear. Logan suggested they sit in the cab of the old Dodge truck to eat their lunch. Then they could at least take off their raincoats.

Today, he planned on taking a thirty-minute lunch break. They crawled into the old Dodge truck. After the doors slammed, Annie started chirping like a little songbird. Then she handed Logan the magazines and kept right on talking. He ate his lunch, listened, and looked at the magazines for the new lures. Then he heard some more. As twelve-thirty came around, he knew he had to go back to work.

*If I could get a word in… Ya know she could keep talking for the rest of the afternoon.*

Annie paused and knew it was time to go. As she opened the door, she turned and said with a smile, "See you at four in the kitchen. That was fun to sit and visit. Can we do lunch again tomorrow? There is so much to talk about."

"Yeah, I guess there is. I usually don't have a whole lot to say. Guess you bring it out of me." They both laughed knowing Annie had done all the talking. Logan smiled and looked into her beautiful deep green eyes again. *She can talk as much, and as long as she wants, I certainly didn't mind.*

Annie started up again. "I'm over to see Allison, see if I can help her with anything, and I'll ask if she could check on a boat for us. If no luck, could we use little Kanute? I walked by Points North and saw it on the top of the cabin."

"Yeah, it's only seven-foot, small, but it doesn't leak."

She pulled the hood of her raincoat over her pretty blond head, turned, and started walking toward the office. Logan went back to his woodpile, thinking this could be a perfect summer.

Annie found Allison working on the books. She has known Allison since she was a little girl.

Allison had been Mother's best friend, and they would laugh and talk all the time.

"Hi Allison, how have you been?"

"We're good. You have been missed very much around here."

"I know, I've missed you all as well."

"I heard you wanted to stay in Vancouver and not come to camp this summer."

"Well, that was earlier. Now that I'm here, I'm looking forward to spending the summer with everyone."

"Burney likes the new Yank. He's hard-working and very polite. I think the word would be respectful."

"Yes, I know. I caught a halibut on the log boom last night with him."

"I know, we heard all the yelling, sounds like it was a lot of fun."

"Oh, yes! So, we'll start fishing salmon when they come in. He's smart that way. He started fishing with his dad when he was eight years old. Did you know he lost his father in Alaska fishing?"

"No, I didn't. You two have a lot in common, so enjoy your friendship. I'm glad you have someone around your age. It makes the time more enjoyable that way."

# CHAPTER 17

The next evening, Logan quickly finished the dishes so he and Annie could jump in the old Dodge truck.

They stopped alongside Points North, loaded little Kanute onto the truck, and hauled it to the log dump ramp.

It was a little crowded, but with Annie in the bow, they would manage. She chatted away, telling him about her school and studies.

Logan sat in the stern and rowed by pushing rather than pulling the oars. That made it easier to steer as he was facing forward. The tide was at slack water, and they caught four nice lingcod in an hour out by the kelp patch next to the rock on the right. Logan remembered it when he entered the cove.

As they returned to camp, they found Aunt Ida in the kitchen. *Come to think of it, she's always there, even before Annie came to camp.* Logan thought she liked the excitement of being around all the activities.

The fish were soon filleted and put in the cooler. Annie asked, "Logan, would you like to come to the house and play a game of chess?"

"I'm not any good at chess. My sister tried to teach me, but I wasn't interested. I liked other things."

Annie pushed until Logan said yes. *Guess she has to find out.* They sat at the kitchen table for an hour, and Logan was getting frustrated.

"Your sister was right," Annie said. "You're not interested, are you?"

Logan stood up. "I'm sorry, I better call it a night."

Walking into the living room, Logan said goodnight to Ida and Oley.

Then turning to Annie, he thanked her for the great day and said how he looked forward to seeing her in the morning.

"Goodnight, Logan, and thank you," she said as he let himself out the door. Annie said goodnight to her dad and aunt and headed for her bedroom.

Ida looked at Oley, "Dis is good, having someone her age around. It does make it easier and more fun for her. Did you know she vent down to the log dump for lunch to sit and talk? She needs someone to talk to besides adults."

"Vell, I am happy for her. I don't vant to lose my daughter to the bright city lights of Vancouver or her Aunt Samantha."

"She is home here now, and we need to enjoy her while we have her. She is growing so fast."

Logan washed up dishes after breakfast the next morning as Aunt Ida and Annie finished putting the lunch fixings away. Oley stopped by and asked Logan how the woodcutting was going.

"I have twenty cord done. The wood is perfect for splitting."

"Dat's good. Didn't you tell me your dad had you service boat motors and grease tings? And you startup da diesel buses for the janitor at school, right?"

Logan smiled, wondering where the conversation was going. "Yes, I did. He had me do all the oil levels and make safety checks. I liked doing it. I learned a lot."

"Okay then, tomorrow morning, I need you to go make the safety checks on all the log equipment starting at five AM. I vant you to start and warm dem up." Logan eagerly nodded yes.

"In the evening, when things cool off, you vill check the oil levels, and make safety checks on all da log trucks, including all the trucks and front loaders in the camp. Harvey Nelson, da lead mechanic, he can get you started on dat this afternoon."

"Sure, thing, boss, be happy to." Logan struggled to hide his excitement. He relished the thought of more responsibility.

Ida, listening nearby, chimed in. "Today is camp garbage day. Is da Dodge empty of wood?"

"Yes, ma'am. I can start on that right after I finish the dishes."

"Good. Den you can take Annie vith you, she can help too." Ida and Annie exchanged smiles. Ida knew that would give them a couple of hours to visit.

Logan was looking forward to that job too, especially with a chance to spend time with Annie.

Now having been there a couple of weeks, he had a routine for the garbage. Logan picked up all the cans in the camp, burned all the cardboard and paper, then drove out of the logging camp three miles to the dump. Usually, three or more bears were rummaging through the garbage. Sometimes, he had to blow the horn to get them out of the way. This time, Annie and he had fun watching their antics. Once back at camp, Logan scrubbed the cans and put them all back. He had marked the garbage cans when he first started and now, he knew which cans went to the kitchen, then the bunkhouse, the shop, and finally the boss's house. He worked it so he could drop off Annie last.

Lunchtime came and they shared their lunch half-hour. Annie chirped away while he munched on his fish sandwich. *She's never short on words and I sure like listening to her voice.*

That afternoon when the logging crew had ended their day, Logan used the lube truck to fuel each piece of equipment and check the oil levels.

With his added chores, Logan usually came in late for dinner. Annie would make him a plate and sit with him while he ate. Logan could set by the hour listening to her talk and hardly ever did she get quiet.

Sometimes Oley would have him go up to the log sides to help the mechanics service the equipment.

When he got back, Annie would be waiting for him and they would catch the tide for cod fishing. The salmon haven't shown yet, but they were coming soon.

Oley went to town for supplies one day and picked up a used fourteen-foot aluminum boat with a nine-horse Evinrude. Now Annie and Logan had a real fishing boat. Oley didn't want them to use little Kanute anymore. "Kanute is too darned small, Logan. Dis is big water up here."

Time was going by too fast. It was time for the salmon run to show. The early Kings had come and gone and now the Coho had arrived.

Annie and Logan tied their fishing gear on Oley's kitchen table. They would talk, then laugh about who would catch what and how.

Oley and Ida stopped to listen to them on their way through to the living room. They laughed at the two young "fishing people" as Aunt Ida would call them.

Sunday had finally come, and the camp took a day of rest. They planned on fishing all day together with the new boat and motor. Ida said she would take care of the camp breakfast so her two young fishing people could go out. Annie fixed breakfast for them at four AM before they headed to the boat.

Both Annie and Logan wanted to troll, and Annie got the first silver right away. Then it was Logan's turn and a nice one too. Everything else was small compared to his. Logan claimed first place, much to Annie's disagreement.

The misty rain started. They donned their rain gear and put their life jackets on again. Oley wanted them to wear life jackets while on the boat. That took some getting used to for Logan. They had to do it, or they would be in trouble, and they didn't want to lose their skiff privileges. After all, Logan had painted "Miss Annie" on the bow. That confirmed they were fishing partners and they agreed it was theirs to share.

Once the bite was over, they came into camp to clean fish, rest up, then go out for the evening bite.

They headed out around the northern corner of the cove. It was a fair bite with plenty of fish for the camp. They finished up with fishing near dark and headed back to camp.

Before they got to the corner, the motor sputtered and died. *This is not good. The sun's going down fast.*

"Don't we have some of the most beautiful sunsets up here?" Annie purred.

Logan grumbled, "This could be dirty fuel."

Tipping up the outboard, Logan got Annie to sit in the stern while he rowed from the seat in the middle of the little boat.

As darkness surrounded them, Logan kept pulling on the oars. As they came around the corner, they could see the lights of the camp in the distance.

"I sure hope your dad isn't sore with me. I didn't bring any tools to pull off the carburetor and clean it."

"Don't worry, Love. It's not your fault. The gas is dirty." Annie put her hand on Logan's knee as she spoke. As they faced each other, both with full rain gear and work lifejackets, they realized what a sight they were and started laughing.

Logan noticed how good the warmth of her hand felt traveling through his rain gear to his knee. For that split second, it was like lightning surging through his rain-soaked body. And she had called him Love. Her touch and tenderness he knew he would never forget. It almost made him feel light-headed. Or was that butterflies in his stomach?

Logan hoped he could tell her his feelings someday. That is, after they have had time to grow closer.

"Thank you for that. I hope Oley sees it that way," he said as the oars dug into the black water, toward the camp lights.

Then they heard the engines of the crew boat breaking the silence of the night.

"Sounds like the cavalry is on its way," Logan mumbled, thinking he was in hot water for breaking down.

"Shoot, I was rather enjoying our quiet row home," Annie said. "In the darkness, it was fun. I like watching the camp lights from a distance. Logan, promise me we can do this again."

"What? Break down with dirty gas?"

"No, silly. I mean, let's go for a row again, sometime soon. I enjoyed myself."

Still rowing, Logan said, "Ok, we could row to the other side of the log boom. There's a nifty little cove over there and we could have a picnic."

"That would be fun. We can't fish every day. Besides, Auntie will be running out of room in her reefer, or the crew will be sick of fish, whichever comes first."

"Alright then, let's plan on it."

Soon Oley and Aunt Ida pulled up. Standing on the crew boat deck, Oley asked what happened.

Annie answered. "Dirty gas. It killed our little motor, but not before we landed half a dozen Coho."

"Okay, come into the boat. Ve have been vorrying about you two. Logan, throw me your bowline."

Annie spoke up, "I'd like to stay in the skiff with Logan while you tow us in." She gave a big smile and patted Logan on the back.

Oley smiled, "All right then, have it your vay."

Oley didn't tell them that Bobby, Annie's "friend," was standing on the dock, hopping mad. He had come to the camp with his father, a Canadian Ship's Pilot. Bobby's father was taking a log ship out that evening that had been loading logs for the last week in front of Scott Cove.

Logan knew about the ship because he was to help handle lines to untie the ship that evening. As far as Bobby, Logan was hoping he would be there. Then each could stake their claim. Logan wasn't sure which way Oley wanted things to turn out.

As they approached the dock, Oley let go of the towline, and Logan rowed the boat to its usual tie-up spot on the floating dock.

In the broad beam of the dock light, Bobby stood, waiting. He was about Logan's height, skinnier, with gold rim glasses, pressed trousers, tucked-in shirt, and tailored jacket. Logan thought the look was "Continental."

Annie and Logan were decked out in their modern-everyday-logger apparel, with well-used rain gear, hats, boots, and lifejackets.

Logan expertly tied the skiff and hopped out of the boat, saying "Excuse me" as he half-shoved the stranger out of the way to help Oley tie up the crew boat. His gut churned. He had no patience for people like him, especially around the girl he wanted to spend time with.

Logan knew he had to be careful. If something started, he would be right in the middle to finish it and Oley would have to fire him for fighting. He would lose his excellent summer job, but more importantly, Logan would lose the finest girl that ever wanted to spend time with him.

Logan remembered the fight in the high school parking lot. Annie was too perfect to lose because of some stupid childish fight. No, he wasn't going to repeat that mistake.

"Annie, where have you been?" Bobby whined in a nasal voice as he leaned into Annie. Logan thought he was making a fool of himself in front of everyone.

"I've been waiting all afternoon and evening here for you. Now my dad has to take the ship out, and I won't get to see you until school starts." He paused to take a deep breath to start another whining spell. Logan hated whining, and Bobby was good at it.

"Who is that you're with, all alone, broke down out there?"

As Logan finished tying up the crew boat, he walked over to the skiff and stopped in front of Bobby, staring in his face. Everyone could see they were both headed for a nose-to-nose standoff.

Bobby ignored Logan and the whining continued as he cranked it up a couple of clicks on Annie trying to show that he was in charge, and she should apologize to him. He had sidestepped Logan and avoided any eye contact with him.

The look on Logan's face showed he wanted to drill this piece of milk toast into next Tuesday. *That's enough. I'll stand up for her if no one else will.*

Logan stepped right between Bobby and Annie as Oley and Ida stepped off the boat onto the dock. They had seen and heard everything. Logan could see Bobby's dad at the head of the ramp.

Moving in close, about 6 inches from Bobby's nose, Logan said, "Friend or no friend, you have no right to talk to her that way."

"Oh yeah? She's mine, and I can talk to her any way I want to."

"No, you won't. Annie does not belong to you, and she is her own person. She doesn't have to take crap from a garbage mouth like you. No one, including you, will disrespect this woman if I'm here. I promise you I will make sure of that. Now, why don't you tuck your tail between your legs and apologize for being such a spoiled jerk."

Logan could see Bobby's anger mounting.

"You can't talk to me like that. Do you know who my dad is?"

"Don't care what or who your dad is. Yes, I'm talking that way to you. Now, if you would like to dance, I'd be happy to oblige you."

Annie slid between the boys. "Bobby, quit running your mouth. Logan, you have fish to clean."

Bobby squeaked out at half throttle, "Annie, you never did say why you were all alone with this guy in a boat after dark."

"I don't have to explain anything to you. Besides, Logan is my friend. Do you remember when we said goodbye? Let me help you remember. You said you wanted to play it 'loose.' We could see whoever we wanted. And right now, it is not you with your big mouth that I want to spend my time with."

Oley spoke up. "Logan, you go ahead and clean your fish now. Ida will open up the kitchen for you."

"Come with me, Logan," said Ida.

"Okay, boss, whatever you say." Logan looked straight at Bobby. "You, if you talk to her and make her cry, I will hunt you down and make you cry. I don't care who your father is. You got that?"

Oley tried to calm down the drama. "Alright, Logan, let's leave it at that."

Bobby's father was still standing up at the head of the ramp and said loudly, "Oley, I need to get out to the ship. The tug should be here soon."

Oley replied, "Come on, then, I'll run you out in the crew boat. Logan, you take care of your fish, then you come back down here. I vant you to deck for me tonight while ve let go of the ship."

Annie spoke up loud enough for everyone to hear, "Dad, I'll ride with you and Logan tonight."

She stepped over to the crew boat and climbed aboard, leaving Bobby standing on the dock alone, staring out in the darkness. She could tell he did not believe anyone could do that to him.

Annie went to the bow to take the line as Logan let go of the dock end for her. She smiled at Logan. "Don't worry about me. I can take care of myself, Mister Nice Guy." Secretly though, she beamed with the thought that Logan had backed Bobby off.

Aunt Ida was standing next to Logan and patted his shoulder. "She is right, Logan. She can take care of herself."

Auntie and Logan went up to the kitchen to take care of the fish and Logan immediately went back to the crew boat. When they returned, no Bobby.

Oley shut down the crew boat. "I'll be right back. I have to go up to the office for a minute."

Annie paused and said, "Thanks, Dad." She knew her dad was giving her a minute alone with Logan.

Logan sat down on the gunwales of the crew boat with his feet on the dock. Annie sat down next to him, reached over, took his hand, and held it.

"Logan, you know you don't have to protect me. It is very sweet of you to want to stand up for me. You're the only one, but for my dad, to speak up like that. I know you would have fought him right then and there."

"Annie, you are my friend, and you are a woman. My mother and father raised me to care for, respect, and protect a woman. I don't ever want to see anyone talking to you that way again. You're very special to me, and I want to keep it that way." He squeezed her hand and felt her response.

Oley came back to the boat. "Here comes the tug, let's go."

After the ship was gone, Logan held Annie's hand as he walked her home. They saw Oley watching them. Logan guessed he didn't mind, and neither did they.

# CHAPTER 18

That little show-down with Bobby was good for both of them. It gave Logan a chance to show Annie his feelings for her. As well, she was able to show him that she cared a lot for him.

A floatplane landed four days later.

Logan was working at the woodpile when a seaplane pulled up to the camp dock. He watched a skinny primped-up middle-aged woman climb out of the plane.

The pilot sat her bag on the dock, hopped back in the plane, and took off.

The lady stood on the dock in the drizzling rain, her arms wrapped around her skinny chest. Logan guessed she was waiting for someone to come to get her bags.

No one told Logan to get any bags today. He thought she might be a tax collector or something like that. Or maybe an undercover RCMP itching to drag him in?

Logan went back to splitting his wood, occasionally looking over to the dock. The lady was getting a soaking and a good one too. Hair, suit, and now that primped hair-do was limp and plastered against her head.

Finally, she picked up her bag and stomped up toward the kitchen.

*Wonder what all this is about? She could be on Bobby's side. Guess we'll see.*

Logan hustled to get his equipment checks completed that evening, then headed in for dinner.

Everyone was there, and Aunt Ida was finishing up serving. She went straight for her chair as Logan was getting a plate of food.

Annie was in her chair, and next to her was the lady from the dock. *That must be Aunt Samantha.* She was talking a mile a minute, in the same winey voice Bobby had, burning holes into Oley with her stare during every blistering word.

Oley was sitting in his chair, across the table from her. He was calmly nodding his head, a very bored look on his face.

Annie saw Logan walk in, smiled, and patted the chair next to her.

*Well, boys and girls, here we go.*

With a full plate, Logan walked over to his chair, sat down, and started eating. He didn't nod or smile to anyone, but he gave a small pat on Annie's knee under the table to say hi.

Logan glanced sideways at the lady, two chairs over from him, and couldn't help but think, *this woman was a real piece of work, like a gunnysack of deer horns rattling around.*

She had lit right into Oley, hard, like she was somebody. Why no one had met her at the docks, and her new "do" was soaked. "That cost a bundle too."

"No one knew you were coming." Oley spoke in a relaxed quiet voice, trying to calm her down. He took a deep breath, smiling, but not looking at her.

She demanded, "Oley, why would you hire some ruffian? And to have the nerve to threaten good stock from the social pages of Vancouver."

Oley replied, "I didn't tink I did hire someone like dat. It could be I hired someone that would stand up for my daughter's honor. That would be what I saw. If we are talking about the same ting, Samantha."

"You know I'm talking about Bobby. There was no reason for one of your logging hooligans to intimidate him."

Samantha took in a short gulp of air, and Oley spoke up. "He's a nice young man and comes from a good family. He has a lot to offer for Annie and her position in our circle." Oley couldn't contain a smile, pleased with his comment.

"Oley, I think you should fire this ruffian immediately."

"Now, Sam, you veren't there. How can you say to fire someone you never met? For sure, I don't tink you got all your facts straight here."

"Oley, you know my name is not Sam," she said, raising her voice and getting the attention of the eating crew.

"You are to address me as Samantha, thank you. With my sister Sarah passing and Annie living with me during school, that does give me some say as to who she is spending time with."

*No doubt about it*, Logan thought, *she is on a roll.* It was easy to see she was enjoying the power it gave her. This woman was feeling good about herself raking over Oley.

Oley took a deep breath, looked to Logan, then Samantha, and said, "If you vould like to know who she spends her time vith, I vould like to introduce you to Mr. Logan Johanson. Logan, meet Annie's Aunt Samantha."

She leaned forward, looking around Annie. Logan did the same and bent forward. He had a fork full of food midair, laying it back down on his plate. He spoke first, "Evening ma'am. It's a pleasure to meet you too. Annie has spoken of you often."

"Yes. Well, we spend a lot of time together in the school year. You don't sound Canadian."

"No, ma'am. I'm from a small fishing town south of the border. It could be only an hour from your place in Vancouver."

"US? How are you here? Oley, you are subject to a fine."

"Samantha, he's a contract worker on a visa. You don't know him, but he is a fine young man. Logan vorks hard, he's responsible, and everyone here likes him, including my daughter."

"I can see that he has a chair at the family table next to my niece."

Aunt Ida recoiled on that one. She hadn't said a word until now, and Logan could see she was ready to come on strong.

"Samantha, I gave him dat chair because he has earned it and is a welcome friend at our table, not like some others."

"We never did get along, Ida, but your judgment has always been a little skewed."

Logan figured that did it for Ida. He leaned forward and said, "The only thing I can see a little skewed at this table would be an over-inflated busybody with an ego sloshing around insulting good people."

Oley chimed in, "Okay, come on, Samantha. Let's go over to the house. This is going nowhere."

He stood up, staring at Samantha. She gulped for air like a goldfish out of water. With Oley towering over her, she slid her chair back, not giving anyone at the table a second look.

Oley was a huge and powerful man, as gentle as they come, but you didn't want to make him mad for sure. She was testing him, and she knew it.

Samantha stood up and cast a sour look at Annie. "Come along, Annie, we need to talk."

"No Auntie, I need to clean up in the kitchen. It's my job."

Samantha groaned, "Oh, no! They have you doing kitchen work with Ida?"

"Yes, Logan helps with the dishes, too, so we can go fishing in the evening."

Logan smiled his best warm, friendly smile as he looked over at Samantha. "We have a great time. There's an extra pole with your name on it. That is, if you would like to come with us for the evening bite? You'll need rain gear for the mist, ok?"

"I wouldn't consider it. I came here to straighten some things out, and you are one of them."

"Ok, yes, ma'am." Logan looked to Oley. "I'll have Annie back by dark. Is that okay with you, boss?"

"That would be fine." Oley smiled and nodded his head.

Samantha bellered like a wounded cow. "Annie, when you have completed your duties of cleanup, I want you to come to the house. We need to talk. That's why I am here. I don't have time to wait for you to come back from fishing."

"Yes, Auntie. I'll be along when we've finished with clean up."

Samantha strode out of the cookhouse, followed reluctantly by Oley.

The cleanup was quiet. Logan thought he could hear a pinecone drop at 100 feet. Not a word was spoke by Miss Annie.

With the dishes done, she hung up her apron, put on her coat, then slipped out the door. Logan peeked out the kitchen window and saw her heading straight for the house.

Logan collected all the garbage for the cans while Ida set up food to defrost for breakfast. She looked at Logan. "Logan, don't fret. Enjoy the time you and Annie have together. She has a lot on her plate right now. I know my little Tulla. She's smart and can tink on her own two feet."

"Ida, that aunt is overbearing. Should she have that much influence on Annie?"

"Vell, she lives with her aunt most of the year now. Annie wants to please everyone. Like you, my young man, unless someone says something you don't like about your friends." She gave him a warm smile.

"Yeah, you're right about that, Auntie. We had it drilled into us early to be loyal."

Ida smiled, liking it when Logan called her Auntie. "Oh Logan, I thought you did a good job needling Sam when you told her you lived less than an hour from her house. Remind me never to make you unhappy. You have a way of planting the right words to rattle a person."

"Thanks, Auntie. You never have to worry about that. You're my good friend. Think I'll go down to the shop and work on my chainsaw for tomorrow. Goodnight, Auntie."

Logan tore apart the chainsaw carburetor at the shop, blew it out, put it back together, then started to sharpen the chain. He heard the small shop door quietly open and close.

It was Annie. He could tell by the way she moved and walked over to the bench. Logan didn't turn around. He kept filing the chain, tooth by tooth, one at a time.

"Ida told me you were here. She thinks a lot of you, Logan."

"Ida and your dad are important people to me. I'm better off for knowing them, and that goes for you too, pretty lady."

Annie took a long quiet pause. "I think a lot of you also. Things are so confusing for me right now."

She stopped to look around the shop, trying to collect her thoughts. "Aunt Samantha has her thoughts and opinions about what I do and think."

Her lips turned up in a shy smile, but Logan couldn't see it. "Ida, she loves me and wants the best for me. Dad, of course, has his thoughts too."

Logan stopped sharpening the chain and turned to Annie. She looked into his bright blue eyes as he stood there, thinking back to the first time they had met at the dinner table.

He leaned his back up against the workbench. Annie was so close she could feel his warmth radiating as he gave her that confident easy-going smile of his. If she weren't so confused with Aunt Samantha, she would have collapsed into his big strong arms. *God, why won't he kiss me?*

Annie collected her thoughts and continued to say what was on her mind. "Now, where you are in all this, Mr. Logan? You ask for nothing, not even a kiss. I'm the one that holds hands. You seem to be the center of attention that Aunt Samantha has focused on. She wants me to wait around for Bobby, whatever that means, and I don't know. Are you following me on all this?"

Logan said gently, "Yes, I am, tell me more, please."

"Mother, before she passed away, wanted me to have a chance at a real life besides living in a logging camp. I'm not sure now. Before I came here this summer, it was clear to me what I wanted."

"And that would be . . .?"

"You know, a good life after University in Vancouver. Department stores, theater on the weekends. A condo overlooking the city with a job in business management."

"So, what happened?" Logan already knew the answer. He felt she had returned to what her parents raised her to be.

"You know what happened. You came along. We've had so much fun spending time together and always doing things." Annie paused. "The best part of our relationship is we can talk. You know that's what I like to do best. We can talk about anything. That, Mr. Logan, has been one of the kindest gifts I have ever had in my life."

Annie stopped again. They were still gazing at each other, enjoying the warmth and chemistry they shared as friends. There were awkward moments as a couple, but as friends, it was perfect.

"When Mom died, something died inside of me. We were very close. I loved my mother so much. She was always there for me like I've told you before. The other night, if Mom had been there on the dock, she would have been shoving you out of the way. I'm sure she would have been the one telling Bobby a thing or two."

Annie smiled, picturing the scene in her mind.

"I miss her so much. At first, I thought Aunt Samantha was like my mother. After spending a winter with her, there was no comparison, they are two completely different people."

Logan had enough time with Annie to know when to let her say what was on her mind. He knew not to interfere with any questions or stop her in any way. It was the best way, and he was okay with that.

"Now you're here and turned a switch on inside of me. I can't hold back. I blurt out whatever is on my mind."

She took a deep breath. "Do you understand what kind of freedom it is for me? There are times I just want to find you and talk to you. It is almost an urgency to be with you. Do you ever feel that way?"

Logan saw a tear on her cheek. He held out his arms and she came to him, tucking her face into his shoulder.

He gave a deep sigh, "Yes, tonight I wanted to talk like we are now. I don't want to lose our friendship, Annie, it's so precious to me. I've never felt this way before."

He paused to give Annie time to think over what he had said, then continued.

"I understand how you wouldn't want to spend your life here at the camp. I don't know what I want right now other than to be your best friend and make it through the summer. After that, we both need to go back to school."

Annie took two steps back looking into Logan's eyes again. "I was hoping you would say that. I feel much better now knowing we can keep things like they are."

She came over and gave him a long hug, then stepped back, now nose to nose.

Logan had more to say, "I could take your hand to hold, but I wasn't sure if you wanted me to. That goes for a kiss also. One of those is there if you want it."

She smiled, "Thanks for the offer. Later, okay?"

"Sure, later. Come on, I'll walk you back to the house. You need an escort. You know there are bears out in them timbered lands."

She gave a weak smile. They held hands, walking in the dark to the house. Both said goodnight at the same time. Annie slipped into the house just as she had come into the shop.

Once back in the shop, Logan stood resting his hand on the chainsaw sitting on the workbench. The air was thick with the smell of gasoline he had spilled working on it.

Logan's mind started working on him. He couldn't help but think what he would have said if she had stayed to talk more.

That would be an incredibly involved conversation. Logan felt he couldn't talk just to be talking. He knew he could do damage if caution were thrown to the wind. The girl had sensitive feelings that required extra care.

And Annie was right. Her aunt had her tentacles, like an octopus, in her life. She wasn't sure how she was going to handle the situation, but Logan knew Annie had the grit to back her aunt off, if need be.

For sure, she had to do it her way. And for now, he needed to lay low and stay out of it. *Let time do its magic, Logan.* It was evident that he had stirred the hornets' nest enough already.

For what it was worth, he knew there was no room in Annie's life for a person like Mr. Front Page of the Vancouver social pages. Well, for the rest of the summer anyway. Logan figured that Mr. Front Page wasn't Annie's style.

Logan also knew she could not deny her roots.

Someone once told him, "You are a product of your environment." *And your environment roots are here, Miss Annie. Right here in this logging camp, and you can't deny it. The truth will continue to come bubbling to the surface. The sooner you accept it, the sooner you will be at peace with yourself. Then you can move on, go to University, and work in the business field with the best of them. You haven't figured that out yet. You are the best, and I know the world will know it soon enough.*

Logan thought if he told her that, she would laugh and say, "You're saying that because you like me," making light of it.

But he knew better. He had met people like that, even at his age. When a certain kind of person walks into a room, people notice them, and they will love them or hate them. Now for the latter, it's jealousy. That comes from human nature.

*Annie, I wish I could share this with you. Ugly and straightforward jealousy is easy to understand. What you have is what they want. That's where your aunt comes in. She hasn't got what you have, and she can't have it. So, she tries to control you or use her power over you.*

*Right now, she has all the cards - money, location, and don't forget, the ego. I know I am a simple fisherman's son, but believe me, all this is true.*

*The ego makes people get up in the morning, and then during the day, it is like the rudder on Points North. A touch of ego or rudder can turn your bow a tad, and before you know it, you are on an entirely new course.*

*I was so lucky to have Big Kanute Johansen as my grandfather. I heard him loud and clear when he spoke to me. It has made me who I am today. I know in my heart you come from the same place. We are back to our roots again, knowing your father and your Auntie Ida as I do.*

*You are so straight and true, and someday, I hope you can share that with me.*

Logan talked to his chainsaw, "Now, if I only had the guts to sit down and tell her all that. Like those people walking into the room, she will hate me or love me if I do."

Logan almost scared himself with the terms of raw honesty he was feeling. For now, he'll tuck it away and pull it out on a bright and sunny day to share with his Annie. He wanted her to be his Annie.

# CHAPTER 19

Over the next morning's breakfast, Oley asked Logan, "Logan, you tink you can be a runner for a yarder?"

"Sure, I chased chokers behind my dad while he skinned the cat."

"Yaw good, you will be Burney's runner on Side 2 for two weeks, no more. Then I want you and Burney back at the log dump." Oley paused, watching the excitement in Logan's face.

"We need to start up that second side as soon as we can. We're shorthanded, and I need to hire more crew."

"Sounds great, Boss. Can I buy a pair of cork boots from the company store?"

"Yaw sure. Ida, could you help out Logan here?"

Once he got his new corks, Logan ran over to Points North to grab his rain gear. He was excited to go up and work on the landing, especially with Burney.

They had become good friends and Logan knew this would give him a chance to learn more about what they were doing on the side. The only time he had been up there was to run parts or work on one of the machines.

Within minutes, he was standing by the crummy as everyone came out to climb into the back. The crummy was a cross between a truck and a crew bus.

Logan had not said anything to Annie about working on one of the sides. He hadn't talked to her since the night before, out in the shop. He was hoping Oley had filled her in.

Before he climbed into the back of the crummy, Annie stepped out of the kitchen door and gave Logan a little wave. Ida must have told her.

The crew saw it too. Winding up the road to Side 2, the crew kidded Logan relentlessly until things finally quieted down halfway up to the new job site.

Logan knew Annie did not want him to be up working on one of the sides. She grew up in the camp and knew how dangerous the work was.

She had told him she wanted him around so that she could see him during the day. He said he was happy cutting cordwood, but he would do whatever Oley ask him to do. Logan didn't think he could turn Oley down. He had given him a job, and that bought Logan's loyalty with him.

On Side 2, Burney was the yarder engineer, so he and Logan were working partners.

Annie knew more than Logan. Allison gave her an early warning of what was going on.

Oley needed Burney up on a new side for two weeks to get it up and running.

Burney had said, "Fine, but I want Logan for my runner. We work well together, and Logan is one of the best hands in camp."

Oley wasn't so sure. He knew Annie would have her thoughts about him chasing chokers and running a chainsaw on the landing for a yarder.

Oley knew she understood this was dangerous work, and she might not like Logan working there.

"Dad, are you sure there's no one else that can be the runner on Side 2?"

"No, Annie, you know we need more crew. Also, you know that Burney asked for him. We need Logan on the side for two weeks, that's all."

The job was fun for Logan. With working there, he was always busy. It was the way Logan liked it. What a great place to learn new things.

As for the job of a runner, it was not that hard. He had to keep his eyes and ears open, always listening for Burney's whistle signals.

When a turn of logs came in, Logan would unhook the bell chokers then back out of the way so Burney could pull the chokers out from under the logs with the yarder. Burney would send the rigging back out into the woods for another turn of logs.

Grabbing the chainsaw, Logan would bump off all the limbs and knots, making sure there were no branches left on the logs.

Oley had given strict instructions, "No logs ver to leave der landing vith a limb on it."

Logan also had to pull the straw line for moving the tail hold block from the yarder. It was once again easy, pulling a handful of 3/8" wire across the landing. The choker setting crew had the hard job, pulling that darned wire up the face of the steep mountainsides.

He had some mechanical duties as well. Logan had to keep the yarder well-greased and oiled using the grease gun, some parts he had to grease twice a day or more, and climb around the big machine, checking oil levels and inspecting for mechanical problems.

Burney trusted Logan. He had started to teach him how to splice wire and rope down at the log dump. Up on the side, they were finishing up his training on the landing as time would allow. Logan was a quick learner and took to splicing like a natural. Burney told Oley this one day and Oley's only comment was, "Yaw, he is a good hand. I only vish ve had more like him."

* * *

A few days later the crummy, with the crew in the back, was returning to camp at the end of a long day. Cutter Malone was driving. Out of nowhere, the crummy made a fast-jerky sliding stop, tires locked, in the middle of the road. Cutter got out from behind the wheel in the cab, came around to the back, and threw open the doors. "Hey Logan, you might want to go pick some berries with the bears. The RCMP boat is at the dock by the log boom."

Logan piled out quickly and smiled. "Thanks, Cutter, I'll pick a handful for you."

Everyone knew the story about how Logan arrived at Scott Cove, outsmarting the RCMP boat. That was the best part of it all in camp scuttlebutt.

Logan started walking back up the road toward Side 2, disappearing around the bend.

Annie was outside the office, waiting for the crew crummy from Side 2 to come in as Cutter pulled up and parked. The loggers piled out, and to her disappointment, no Logan.

"Burney, where's Logan?" Annie demanded. Burney and Cutter both could see she wasn't happy at all.

"Wasn't he working with you today?" Annie continued, holding her apron, and wringing both hands in it.

Burney smiled. "Yes, he was with us, but he decided to pick some berries with the bears." Burney gave a big nod toward the RCMP boat.

"Burney tell me now, please. How far is he up the hill?"

"Where it breaks out, you can first see the log boom there." Burney was thinking it wasn't a good idea to tell her.

"Darn him. It's time to take care of this once and for all."

Annie ran over to her dad's truck, jumped in the driver's seat, started it up, and went tearing up the hill to find Logan.

Oley came out of the office when he heard his pickup start. He could see Annie was driving.

Burney was standing by the office door when Oley came out. "Now, where is she off to?"

Burney laughed. "I think she's gone to fetch my young runner."

"Burney, I am not sure it's a good idea for a half-shook-up 15-year-old girl to be driving my truck. Especially at breakneck speeds up a gravel logging road."

Burney smiled and shook his head. "She does have her emotions running a tad bit high, Boss."

As Annie came peeling around a corner, she saw Logan sitting on a stump, smiling. It was a beautiful day with the sun still high and bright and only a few scattered clouds drifting overhead.

She slammed on the brakes, putting the pickup into a slide, stopping sideways in the road. She threw open the driver's door and hopped out.

Logan could see the girl wasn't her usual happy self.

"Hi, there, pretty lady. You come out to pick some berries too? The only problem is we need buckets."

"Need buckets! Logan, you need to take care of this problem. And for God's sake, right now. You know you can't run from it. We have to deal with it, and right now."

Logan wasn't as worried about the RCMP as he was about Annie cooling off. And he, for sure, didn't want to talk to the RCMP.

"No, thanks. I think I'll sit here until I see their tail-lights in the distance."

"No, Logan, now. I won't let you run from them, not again." Annie was about two hands in front of his face.

"Dad has talked to them. And, he talked to your mother a couple of weeks ago. Everything is fine, and your mother got your letter when you first got here. Now would you please come with me? They only want to see if you are the person they're looking for."

*Talked to his mom a couple of weeks ago? Why didn't he say anything? How long has Annie known this? What was all that talk about trust?*

"No, thanks. Those people will lie to you to get what they want."

"That is not true." She reached out her hands and held his face in them. He could feel the warmth of her breath as she talked to him and his heart melted.

"Logan, I won't let them take you or your boat. Is that's what you're worried about? That they would keep your boat if they sent you home?" She paused, staring straight into his eyes.

Logan looked down to the ground. "I am right. Yes, I thought so," she said.

"You're partly right. If the RCMP takes Points North, it's all I have left from my dad and grandpa. Don't you see how much that means to me? Also, there is one other thing."

Annie barely heard him say there is one other thing as his voice trailed off.

"I know," she said as she pulled him to her and put her cheek next to his.

"I know," she said again. "I won't let them take Points North from you. Now let's go down there and work this out. I'm confident it will all work out for the best."

"All right?" she asked, looking for reassurance as she stepped back, a shy smile showing on the corners of her mouth.

"Well, ok. I outran the cops once. I can do it again."

"Come on. Get in the truck now, would you please? Half of the camp is waiting for you."

"Hey, don't you want to hear what the one other thing is?"

"Yes, I do. But we don't want the 'cops,' as you call them, to be mad from waiting too long, do we?"

"No, I guess not." They got into the truck, and Annie drove down the hill to "face the music" as Grandpa would say.

She was right. The crew had all gathered around the office door. Logan thought if the RCMP were to cuff him and start to haul him off, they not only would have to fight off Annie but half the crew to boot.

Annie was right again. They only wanted to check his ID and told him never to run from them again.

They admitted that Logan was one of the few that had ever successfully given them the slip.

Oley's paperwork was in order as he had been working on it the last month. Now Logan was legal to keep working with a temporary work visa for the summer.

The RCMP folks thanked them and were gone.

Logan thanked Annie and Oley like he had a hundred times before for all their support and caring.

Logan tried to have a quiet dinner, but the crew gave him a good ribbing. They were glad he wasn't hauled off to the poky for the night. Ha, ha, they laughed, meaning no harm. It was their way of saying they were glad he could stay.

After dishes, he went over to his chair and took a seat. He was hoping Annie would come to sit with him for a minute.

He got lucky. Not only Annie, but Auntie Ida had a seat too. Then the door swung open, and in walked Oley. He came over to the family table and sat in his chair.

Oley volunteered, "I saw the lights on and thought I should check in here. Is something going on?"

Auntie Ida cleared her throat, "I tink Logan here has something he vould like to share with us. How about it, Logan?"

Annie slid her hand over to Logan's leg, taking his hand in hers. She looked into his eyes, then said with a small smile, "I would like to hear that one other thing you were going to tell me up on the hill."

Ida spoke next, "Yes, we all would like to hear what you have on your mind."

Logan looked down at the calico tablecloth, practically staring a hole in it. Taking a deep breath, he started. "After thinking about what happened this evening, there are two things I would like to bring up. The first thing would be that I think Aunt Samantha in Vancouver ratted me out and called the law. Would I be right on that Boss?"

"Yaw, I have my suspicions. I knew ve were just a step ahead of Sam, but it all turned out yust fine."

"Thank you for that, sir," Logan said. "I know she will go to any means to clear me out of Annie's life." He turned to Annie, "And unless you are the one running me off, I'm not going anywhere. Our friendship is too good to walk away from. If you like, you can tell her that. Or better yet, I could tell her that the first opportunity that comes up."

"No, I don't think that would help very much," Annie laughed.

Oley smiled, imagining Logan unloading on Samantha.

"And what was the second thing you had on your mind?" Annie asked in her soft voice.

"I didn't want the RCMP to haul me off. I have found myself a place here. After losing Dad and Grandpa, I was pretty much rudderless. Then I got started on Points North, and the adventure began."

Logan paused to take a breath. He wasn't usually this open with his feelings.

"You all are like my family now. It would be hard to let them haul me off and leave you here with my boat." He squeezed Annie's hand and looked into her beautiful bright green eyes.

She smiled and nodded in agreement.

"That was my greatest fear," Annie added. "That's why I wanted to clear this matter up, so we would have the rest of the summer together." She gave him a shy smile. "Summer is short enough without all the distractions of you wanting to hit someone and or scolding my aunt from Vancouver. Oh yes, and outrunning the authorities again."

Logan smiled and nodded. "How about we walk over to the stream on the way to the house? We can check on how the salmon run is coming along."

The rest of the evening, like so many of the evenings before, went by too fast. Annie still didn't like Logan working on the logging side. She wanted him safe in camp and, most of all, close to her.

# CHAPTER 20

Burney and Logan made a good team, and they knew the work at the side was only temporary. They could get back to the log dump once the boss hired more crew.

On the landing, when the tail hold block needed to be moved, Logan would pull the straw line, a light wire line, through the woods, then hook it to the mainline to allow the tail hook block to be moved by the heavy equipment. That allowed them to pick up logs from a new area. The choker-setters had their own man to do the light wire. Logan liked assisting the crew, and they appreciated the help.

Today, the landing was buried in bone-chilling cold fog. Cutter Malone was down at the yarder getting an armful of straw line as Logan was cutting limbs off the last turn of logs.

Cutter wasn't the sharpest knife in the drawer, the boys would say. He was a nice guy and huge, like a big furry bear climbing up the side of a mountain. He had a coil of wire on his arm and over his shoulder.

Burney had brought in a turn of logs, and as usual, beeped on the horn to make sure Logan was clear. Cutter didn't hear the heads-up horn beep.

Burney lowered the turn of logs down onto the landing. The pile of logs usually relaxed and laid in a heap. Suddenly, one log caught on something and swung the butt a hard left, catching Cutter in the hardhat and knocking him to the ground, out cold.

Logan caught the movement of the log out the corner of his eye as it hit Cutter's hardhat and saw him go down.

He shouted to Burney to shut down and call for help. Cutter was not moving as Logan climbed over logs to get to him. He was breathing, but that was it. Logan ran toward the crummy to get the man-basket to put him in, the three inches of ooze and mud covering the landing slowing him down as it pulled at his boots. He grabbed a blanket and the first aid kit. It was a miserable place to be, lying out in the mud, unconscious. Other men ran over to help bundle him up as best they could.

Burney called out on the radio, "Man down on the landing, Side 2, hit in the head with a log. We need help up here and fast." In camp, the radios in the office, kitchen, and shop all came to life.

Annie heard the call in the kitchen, and a chill ran down her spine. Logan was working the landing at Side 2. Ida heard it at the same time. "Oh, my God."

Annie looked at Ida with fear in her eyes. "Oh no, it could be Logan. I'm going to get Dad."

Annie, her apron still wrapped around her, grabbed her raincoat off the coat rack as she headed out the door. At a full run, she struggled to put her coat on while getting to Oley's pickup truck parked in front of the office.

Annie jumped in the driver's seat. The keys were there. She drove straight over to the log loader Oley was operating at the log boom.

"Dad, someone is down up at Side 2. It just came across the radio a minute ago."

Oley shut down the loader, jumped down, and climbed into the pickup passenger seat.

As they sped off toward Side 2, Oley thought this might not be such a good idea. Wasn't he saying the same thing a couple of days ago? Here he is again, letting a 15-year-old girl drive his truck up a tight, twisting log truck haul road.

Oley started calling on the radio to find where all the log trucks were and announcing they were on their way up to Side 2 for the injured man.

Now, if he had missed one of the log trucks, he and Annie would be meeting them on a corner. There was no room for both a log truck and a pickup.

Arriving at the landing, they both jumped out and hurried toward the group standing around the injured man.

Cutter was in the stoke-sledder bundled up, with one man beside him on his knee.

Annie came running up. "Oh Logan, are you alright?"

Logan turned and smiled, "Sure, but Cutter here will have a huge goose egg in the next hour or so."

She stopped cold with Oley beside her. Logan smiled, looking back to Annie. "If you want to work up here, you need cork boots on, not an apron."

She looked down, saw her apron on and gave a disgusted groan. "Oh, Logan," she said as she turned and stomped off for the pickup. Everyone gave a light laugh to help relieve the tension.

Annie didn't think it was funny.

Logan followed her to the pickup. "Annie, I'm sorry. I was trying to make light of a serious moment over there."

She turned and fell into his arms with a whimper, then a sob of relief. "I thought that was you on the ground. This is such a dangerous place to work." Logan heard a muffled sob, with her face buried in his shoulder. He wrapped his arms around her a little tighter.

"I know," he said, as he patted her on the back and gave her one more squeeze.

Annie moaned, "I don't know what's wrong with me. I've never felt this way before. It's you, and you make me this way. Logan, you mean more to me every day."

"I know. It's the same for me. Can we talk about it tonight?"

"Yes, let's do that." She sniffed as she stepped away from him and slid back into the truck. Not thinking, she got behind the steering wheel.

Oley had the crew put Cutter in the back of his pickup. He looked at the driver's seat where Annie was sitting, waiting for him to get in.

"I guess the lady is driving, boys." Everyone gave a hearty laugh as Annie backed the truck around and started the long slow ride back to camp.

Most of the crew had known Annie from the time she was a baby. Now here she was, growing into a woman, driving her dad's pickup.

Returning to camp, Annie's driving was not so erratic. Cutter seemed to be comfortable riding in the back. Later that day, Annie told Logan that Cutter had been flown out to Port McNeill and the doctor said he could be back as soon as tomorrow.

At the dinner table, Annie said to Logan, "Dad said he talked to you a couple of weeks ago and asked you what you wanted to do when you come back to camp."

"Yes," Logan replied. "Cordwood was okay, but if I could, I would like to work on or around the water."

"It looks like you'll get your chance. Next week, the log bronc operator will be going out for time off and Dad told me he was going to let you give it a try."

Logan looked up to Oley, sitting across from them listening. He smiled and said, "It's yours if you vant it, dat is until Irvine comes back from time off. That vould be four weeks from now. Burney vill goes back to his log bull, so you vill be working together as usual."

"What about my cordwood?" asked Logan.

"There's plenty of time for that, yust keep doing vat you are doing for now."

Logan could see Annie was happy to keep him close to camp. Now they could finally get more time for fishing.

# CHAPTER 21

Burney and Logan still had four more days on Side 2. The two weeks working on the landing had gone by quickly.

Not for Annie, as she was anxious to get him back into camp to have their lunches and fishing time together.

Logan had told her, "What could go wrong in four days?"

Every day, Annie lectured him on being safe. She didn't want to make any mad dashes up the hill again, thinking he was injured.

Thanking her for her concern, Logan said he would be as safe as the job would let him.

That was the wrong answer. Then the chirping would begin about being safe all over again.

Ida and Oley smiled, watching the happy couple. They could see the genuine feelings they had for each other.

On the last day up on the landing, the crew worked a steep turn out of a rocky canyon. The boys had hooked up a hefty turn hoping that would be the last one there.

Burney was pouring the coals to the old yarder. She had a big, tired turbine Cummins diesel engine for power.

The engine struggled to get the load up to the landing. Burney coaxed the levers trying to get as much power as he could without straining her.

The poor old yarder vibrated with the strain, and suddenly, the turbo oil line snapped, spewing engine oil on the hot exhaust manifold.

Flames and smoke bellowed out from the engine covers. With no oil in the turbo, it overheated and melted down, followed by an explosion that sent a thousand pieces of metal outward with scary force.

The motor hood was blown off, and large chunks of hot, fast-moving motor parts flew everywhere. Two pieces hit the safety glass in Burney's operator cab, caving in the side window next to the burning motor.

A third chunk caught Burney upside his head, knocking him out. Flames shot out all around the engine and under the floor of the cab where he was sitting.

Logan was standing next to the yarder waiting for the turn of logs to come in when the explosion happened. He grabbed the nearest fire extinguisher and started to climb up the yarder to the engine and bottom of Burney's cab. Both areas were completely engulfed in flames and smoke.

Logan held on to the railing with one hand and operated the extinguisher with the other, spraying the fire-retardant toward the cabin and engine. He couldn't get close enough to have much effect on the flames.

Continuing to spray, he made slow headway on the flames under the cab as the fire licked the floor directly under Burney's feet.

Logan cautiously worked his way to the engine. The flames were finally beaten back, just as the extinguisher went empty.

The intense heat crept into the handrail as Gunner hung on, burning through the thick leather glove, the extinguisher still in his other hand, aimed at the fire. As the flames died down, Logan climbed up the ladder to the cab and tore the door open. The operator's cab had filled with heavy smoke and Logan found Burney slumped over the yarder controls in front of him, unconscious.

Reaching in, Logan blew the whistle for the danger signal. That told the crew he needed help right away. Logan pulled Burney onto his shoulder with one hand while hanging on to the ladder with the other.

Burney was a dead weight on Logan's shoulder as he worked his way to the ground, laying Burney down on the wet ground and kneeling beside him. Logan pulled his raincoat off and put it under the injured man's head. Blood was pouring out his temple from a deep cut caused by broken glass.

Logan took off his shirt, tore it into strips, and started wrapping Burnie's head to slow the bleeding. *I don't think he's going to make it.*

He needed to get the bleeding slowed down. Burney had already lost a lot of blood from the head wound.

By now, the crew had arrived and finished putting out the fire on the yarder.

Someone backed up the crummy, and as soon as Logan finished wrapping Burney's head, the crew loaded him, flat, on a side seat in the back.

Logan crawled in next to him, holding him on the seat while trying to slow the bleeding.

The crew sped down the hill for camp. Their only radio had burned up in the yarder, so no one in camp knew what had happened. As they met log trucks coming up, they relayed the emergency back to camp.

Everyone from camp was waiting for them as they arrived. "This was bad," Oley said, helping move Burney to the dock. They loaded Burney into the floatplane, and Allison climbed in beside him. The pilot already had the plane warmed up and called the hospital requesting an ambulance to meet them in town.

Annie insisted Logan come to the cookhouse where she and Ida could tend to his burns. They made him sit in his chair, carefully removed the glove, then cleaned and dressed his burned hand. Annie put ointment on parts of his face where the hair had been singed off.

When they had finished, Annie sat and held his right hand.

Ida was putting things away when Oley came in.

"Burney vill be okay, thanks to you, Logan. You most likely saved his life putting out dat fire, den getting him out of the cab." He paused, going over the sequence of events in his head.

"Slowing the bleeding with your shirt helped. Thank you for dat." Oley looked at Logan, then Annie, and asked, "Vill he live?"

"Oh, yes, he will live," Annie said. "Some singed eyebrows and a burnt left hand, but I'll make sure he lives."

"Good, I vouldn't vant to lose my new bronc driver."

Ida sat down at the table next to Logan, reached over, and patted his arm. "I always knew you were good for us, Logan. Could be a little bit more for Annie here."

Ida and Oley gave knowing smiles.

Oley took a deep breath, looking over to Logan and Annie. "I talked to the medical people that picked up Burney. I asked about you, and how long you would need to not use your left hand."

"Oh no, Boss, I'm good to go. I want to start my work on the log bronc as soon as I can, please. I can do the job, watch me. If I can't do it, pull me off then."

"No," Oley said, shaking his head. "I have a better idea. I know you've been talking about the waterfall up at Kwatsi Bay and doing some panning for gold there. Right now, you need to take a veek off to give your hand a chance to heal."

Annie started to rise in her chair in protest. "Dad, you're not going to let him go up there alone, are you? That would be crazy. He only has one good hand. Are you sure about this?"

"No, I didn't say vat or suggest it. Logan has a good seaworthy boat behind the bachelor's quarters. And I know a capable deckhand with two good hands. Besides, she knows how to cook now."

Annie couldn't believe what she was hearing. "You would do that? Let us go up to the falls for a week? Oh my, thank you Dad." Annie said. "Logan, can we take some shrimp pots up there and see if we can get a bucket or two?" The excitement showed in her voice as she smiled at her dad.

Logan was stunned, sitting in his chair, thinking about what was said.

"Whoa there, Miss Annie. I want to go back to work to earn money for next winter."

"Well, you heard the boss," she said. "You have a week off, so we can go exploring. It is what you always wanted to do, right? Besides, it would be fun to take Points North out sailing."

Logan gave a quick look to Auntie, who was smiling and nodding her head. "Auntie, you got anything to add to this idea?"

"Yes. You two be safe and bring me back lots of shrimp prawns, big fat ones, please."

# CHAPTER 22

O ley smiled. "Good, it's final then. Logan vill take a veek off, and Annie goes along to keep him out of trouble."

Oley gave a big loud laugh. "Now, I don't want any visits from the RCMP in the middle of the night. They would be telling me they're looking for Logan and his boat." He followed with another big belly laugh.

Oley regained his composure and continued, "I do have a couple of requests for you. One is to tow the aluminum fishing boat behind you. Yust in case, you never know if you might need it."

"Also, take my 12-gauge pump shotgun with a box of birdshot and a box of slugs. Like before, you never know when you might have to defend yourself. Annie here knows how to shoot it, and she can show you."

"Dad, Logan can shoot a shotgun, can't you?" She looked to him for agreement.

"Yes, I have a single shot on the boat now. A friend gave it to me before I left for the north country."

"Good, then you are all set. Ida, could you make sure they pack plenty of food for the trip?"

"Boss, could we put Points North into the water right after breakfast tomorrow?"

"Yaw sure, you betcha. Now Annie, you best pack up tonight. I have a feeling Logan here will want to get going first thing in the morning." He laughed again, knowing his daughter would be the first one up in the morning.

Logan looked over to Oley. "Before we go, the four of us should sit down and discuss where we are going and how long we'll be gone, in case you want to stop by for dinner."

"This is good. We vill do it over breakfast, so you two have time to make your plans tonight."

"Yes, sir, that's good thinking. I want to thank you both for trusting me with the safety of your daughter."

Annie was still holding his hand and gave him a big warm squeeze. She spoke up, "May I say something? We need to get going, so I can be back in the kitchen at 4 o'clock. Logan, could we check the galley on the boat? I have no idea what you have for cooking pans or if there is any food. Let's make a list, and then I can talk to Auntie about how to plan and fix meals. Would that be okay with you, Auntie?"

"Oh heavens, that vould be so much fun to help you with."

"Thank you, Auntie. I'm so excited. To think, a whole week off."

Logan asked, "Auntie, what about your kitchen help?"

"Don't you vorry any. I'm sure my big brother already has that figured out."

"Yaw, I do. You two go have a good time."

Annie was all done talking. She stood up and had her coat on with a pad of paper and pen in her hand. "Come on, Logan, we don't have any time to waste."

Logan was up and putting his jacket on.

"I need to get a shirt. My last one went to town with Burney."

Oley and Aunt Ida chuckled.

The two adventurers went out the door with Annie chatting up a storm.

Once the door closed, Ida looked over to her brother. "You vouldn't be putting two puppies in a pen to see vat happens, vould you?"

"No, sister. I know our Annie. She'll soon be 16, yust like Logan. I trust them both. You will agree with me, I'm sure. The only thing that'll happen is they will know each other better. It is good to be closer. It helps to let their feelings grow for each other."

"I agree, they are both good children. They both know the difference between right and wrong."

"Sister, it is the happiest I've seen our little Annie since her mother passed away. I don't think Logan would ever do anything to hurt her."

"What about her Aunt Samantha?"

"You have a point there. I should tell Sam how happy Annie is. Dat vould be a slap, don't you tink? No, on second thought, ve mustn't tell her anything. It's Annie's business. Sam vould get on her high horse and talk mean to Annie. She deserves a break too."

"Yaw, she can do dat. You do realize our little Annie is smitten with young Logan?"

"Yes, sister. But we have our girl back, and she is so much like her mother. I vould like to keep it dat vay."

"So, who have you got coming in to help me in the kitchen? Ve vill needs two helpers to replace our Annie. She is such a good worker."

Logan and Annie climbed over the gunnel of Points North and into the tarp-covered well deck.

Logan slid the upper hatch forward then opened the two small hatch doors. "Wait for a second, I'll get my only bulb on for you."

"Well, thank you, kind sir," Annie replied with a smile.

He entered the forward cabin. Annie stepped in behind him and leaned over him as he turned on his single-bulb trouble light.

"Welcome home. The galley is on your left, equipped with one very used white gas stove. As you can see, it's the modern single-burner version, trendy, of course, for the Northwest Explorers Club.

"Now looking to the right is your portable sink, known as a wash pan, and it is fashionable battered white and also heavily used. Then, under that, is the sought-after used pots and pans locker, for the lady's convenience."

Annie started laughing.

"Annie, I'm ashamed for you to have to use this galley," Logan said, his heart sinking to his knees.

"Why? It's so cute. I love it and look at the seat across from it. On rainy days, we can sit together and eat our meals. That would be after I fix them for us, of course. Logan, this is just how I imagined it could be for us."

He shook his head in disbelief. "Really? I'm glad because that's all I have. You make a list, and I'll find a shirt. I need to check out Putt-Putt to make sure she's ready to go. She needs to be running when your dad puts us in the water."

Annie had already turned away from him. She was opening lockers and writing things down, all the time mumbling to herself.

"Do we need white gas for the stove?" she asked over her shoulder.

"No. We have 4 gallons from home."

"Okay."

Logan pulled out a shirt and, with Annie's help, got it on past the bulky bandages.

As they finished checking out supplies and the engine, Annie looked at Logan's alarm clock.

The time had escaped them. "Big Ben there, says it is 3:45. I need to go now and get back to the kitchen."

"Okay, I want to get a can of gas to fill our fuel tank. I'll catch up with you for dinner."

"You think we can get everything done tonight?"

"Sure. I'll work on your list during dinner. After dinner, we can stow our supplies on Points North, then we'll get your gear and guns."

Logan paused, mentally going over his to-do list. "In the morning, I'll make sure the skiff is ready to go."

Annie exclaimed, "I'm so excited. Thank you for the coming week. We'll have lots of fun. I know you're happy having Points North running again." She patted Logan on the shoulder. "Don't be late for dinner. Bring a chart with you so we can show Dad and Aunt Ida where we're going. Tonight will be a better time to show them. I think tomorrow morning might be too busy."

By dinner time, Logan had the gas tanks filled on Points North and the dinghy, and a spare can of gas stowed for the week's trip. He had also dug out all their fishing gear.

Annie and Ida were cleaning up in the kitchen when he finally came in. Annie pointed and smiled. She had a covered plate of food sitting in front of his chair at the table.

Oley was still sitting in his chair. Logan walked over and laid the chart down in front of him.

As Logan sat down, Oley already had the chart spread out across the table and asked, "Show me where Cutter said the waterfall pool is, would you?"

"Right here. The marks are Cutter's. He said there was some color in his gold pan. He loaned me his pan, and I borrowed a shovel from the shop."

"Vell, dat looks good. Yaw, I do tink it was years back, maybe before the turn-of-the-century, the loggers would go in and hi-grade the virgin timber there."

The ladies came over and sat down, looking at the chart with the men. Within the hour, they had their trip all laid out. At most, they would be only thirty miles from camp.

Oley said, "You remember, it's salmon season and time for bears. They need da fat to make up for their loss last vinter. Dat means they vill be on the move. Keep the eyes in the back of your head open. The mountain lions are around up there also. Vith you being on the mainland, be careful, they vill stalk you."

"Thanks, Oley, we'll be careful."

Annie finished up with her chores and wanted to get home to pack her gear.

The family walked up to the house together. Oley handed Logan two boxes of shells and the old 12-gauge pump shotgun.

Soon, Annie had everything packed in a bag and was ready to go to the boat, excited to get everything put away and organized.

By ten o'clock, Logan and Annie had returned to the front door of the house. She said, "Come in and let me check the dressing on your hand."

"No, it is okay. You go to bed. We can do it tomorrow." He squeezed her hand and said goodnight.

The sky was clear as Logan walked up to the kitchen the next morning. Annie was already inside, helping Ida with the set up for breakfast and showing the new helper the ropes.

She insisted Logan sit down so she could redress his burned hand and put ointment on his face.

"You know, we need to be careful with this. It could get infected if we don't watch out."

"Yes, ma'am," he said, smiling. He didn't mind following orders from his good friend.

Oley stepped into the kitchen. "It is time to put Logan's boat in da vater and get these two young people on their holiday."

Thirty minutes later, Oley had Points North in the log forks and hauled to the water's edge. He stopped before setting it in the water and signaled for the kids to get on board. Oley slowly moved the log bull forward and gently lowered Points North and her crew into the water.

Oley didn't completely float the boat yet, as he waited for Logan's all-clear signal over the noise of the bull's roaring engine.

Logan checked the bilges and they were good and dry. Putt-Putt started up on the third crank and he signaled Oley that they were ready.

Oley finished setting the boat the rest of the way in the water, and Logan and Amy shoved her off the log forks by hand. Logan waved to Oley as he reached down and clutched the motor astern.

Smiling to Annie, Logan said, "It feels good to be back on my boat. It makes me think of all the work and time it took to put her together."

Annie said, "I'm so happy we have her and have a chance to share this time."

"Annie, I'm so happy to share my girl with you."

Across the way, they passed Burney's houseboat. They could see it was still empty with Burney recuperating in the hospital in town.

Annie looked over to Logan. "It's terrible what happened to Burney. I don't ever want that happening to you."

"No, I won't let it happen. Besides, I still want to fish in Alaska. For some reason, I've always had the best of luck. You know why?"

"No, why?"

"I have an angel on my shoulder. Stick around, and you'll see."

"Oh, brother, listen to you now."

Logan steered Points North to the dock by Burney's houseboat. They put up the mast and readied the sails, then Logan pulled the skiff over and tied it off to Points North. The sun was high and warm in the sky by now, with hardly a puffy white cloud overhead.

Ida and Oley came down to see them off with a wave and two delighted smiles. Putt-Putt was running, and lines were taken in. Points North's bow pointed for Hornet passage to round Evangeline Point.

Logan and Annie sat in the stern with the tiller between them. Looking out across the bow, Logan could see the Burn Wood group of islands.

"Here, you steer," Logan said. "I'll put up the sails to catch this light breeze we have."

Annie took the tiller. "What do I steer for?"

"See Walker's Island and King Point there?" he said, pointing dead ahead.

"Yes."

"All you have to do is steer between them. We'll be in Tribune Channel once we pass Smith Rock."

Annie nodded a confident yes, concentrating on her task.

Logan could see this was important to her. It was probably the first time in her life someone wasn't standing over her shoulder.

Now he was letting her make her own mistakes. They were friends, doing this together.

Logan was beside her on their adventure, not leading or telling.

*It will be such fun for both of us,* Annie thought.

Logan put up the mainsail, then the jib sail. The light breeze filled the sails as soon as they went up. Logan reached down and shut off the little engine. The silence was deafening.

Annie couldn't believe how well the boat handled, with only the wind ghosting them along.

"Am I steering all right?"

"You're doing fine. Keep the sails full now."

"How do I do that?"

"You'll know it when you see it. The sails will talk to you, Grandpa would say. They'll start flapping, and the boom will swing out of control."

"Ok, I'll try."

"I'll do some troll fishing while you're sailing the boat. I might catch us some dinner."

"What if you catch a fish? What should I do?"

"You can drop the sails by letting go of these two lines," he said, pointing to the lines running back from the mast. "Then get the gaffe hook for me . . . please."

He smiled to himself, knowing that if he caught a fish, Annie would grab her fishing pole and tell him to run the boat.

Sure enough, he soon caught a nice bright Coho.

"That looks like too much fun," Annie said, letting go of the tiller. She couldn't help herself, grabbing her fishing pole and telling Logan he could sail the boat.

She caught two nice Coho salmon. They had to stop fishing because that was all the room they had in the fish box. Annie put the fishing gear away while Logan started up the little engine now that the breeze was gone.

They were well past Smith Rock. Annie had a death grip on the tiller again. She wasn't letting go of her steering opportunity out into the channel.

Logan was okay with that. It gave him time for the boat and navigation.

Pulling out the chart they had poured over the night before, Logan asked, "Can you see way out in front of us on the port bow?"

"Yes, it looks like a notch in the mountainside. Those are all granite, wouldn't you say?"

"Yes, that sounds right."

He pointed to a small cove on the chart. "That's Watson Cove. I want to pull in at the head of the cove. We could look around and do some panning for gold. How does that sound?"

Annie beamed, "That would be great. I want to stay there (pointing at the chart) for a day, and then we can go to Kawatsi Bay." She nodded, staying focused on her steering chores.

Logan had fish to clean. The sun was straight overhead, and without a cloud in the sky and no wind, it was hot. They both were happy the trip had started, and now it was time to make their first stop.

Logan pulled the skiff up close to the stern, tying it off with a short bowline. It would make Points North easier to maneuver in the small cove. "Do you want to take her in?"

"Oh, yes, show me what to do."

"Alright. I'll stand on the bow and watch for rocks. These are my signals that will tell you what I need you to do." He was pointing to the left, then right, motioning a come ahead, then closing his fist to signal out of gear. "Once we're in there, we'll find a safe place to anchor."

He went forward, reading the chain and anchor line, while Annie lined up on the cove entrance.

Annie's brow furrowed with concentration as she watched ever so closely to make sure she didn't get set to one side or the other with the current.

Logan cautioned there was a rock to the starboard side.

Annie asked, "That's on the right side, right?"

"Yes, on the right," he smiled. Annie was doing a great job.

Annie grew up fishing in boats with her dad. This girl could take care of herself with no problem.

He signaled to go left then to take the engine out of gear. They drifted for a short distance. Logan sounded the depth with his lead line, making sure there was plenty of water under their keel when the tide went out.

Annie put the little engine in reverse to stop their drift. He threw the anchor over the bow then put out enough anchor line for scope.

Annie gave Putt-Putt a little throttle to back more. They waited for the anchor to fetch up.

He signaled out of gear one more time. He felt the anchor take hold, and Points North settled down for the rest of the day. There was no strain on the anchor line on the bow.

He told Annie to turn off the engine as he sat down in the stern across from her.

Annie smiled. "Thank you for letting me bring her in. Dad would only let me run the outboard boat with him in it. This is not the same."

"You're right. This is a lot different."

"I know if I were to do something dumb or make a wrong choice, there could be a lot of damage to our boat. Thank you for trusting me."

"You're more than welcome, nice lady. It is our adventure for the summer, and we need to enjoy it."

"Would you like some fresh salmon and rice for lunch, sir?"

"Oh, yes," Logan smiled. "I couldn't think of anything better. If there's time, I'll set up for a stern tie to that boom-stick log pointing out from the shore," he said, pointing toward the beach.

"That's a great idea," Annie smiled. "Then, we could walk on the log to shore anytime we want to."

"Maybe, but I prefer to be free and clear with only an anchor line and just use the stern line tethering us to keep the boat from swinging."

"You know best, Captain. Could you show me how the cookstove works, please? I'll leave you to the stern tie."

The small cove had a sheer granite wall to the north. Up at the head of the cove was a creek bordered by tall, beautiful green timber. Looking south was a well-treed peninsula. *What a great place for the night*, Logan thought. *You could hear a pinecone drop from the trees, it was so quiet.*

He heard Annie's fish frying in the pan followed by a pleasant smell rolling out onto the deck. That completely derailed any daydreaming. "Can I help?"

"No. Sit and visit while I finish cooking the fish. We have cold rice to go with the fish that Auntie sent with us."

The day was still quite warm, with not a breath of breeze. They talked like they had done all summer. Soon the dishes were cleaned and put away and fresh fish and the rest of the fried ones went on ice in the cooler below the well deck.

Logan slipped the skiff aft alongside the log on the beach, then tied the skiff stern to the boom log. By pulling on the line connected on Points North, the two boats swung and came together.

Annie said, "Let's leave it tied as you have it. We won't have to tie and untie the skiff. It would make it easier for us to go to the beach."

Logan wasn't sure about that.

Once on the beach, Annie said in a quiet voice. "You know, I've been here before. Mom, Dad, and I came here for a picnic one summer Sunday. I remember the waterfall we passed on the way here. Do you know the name of it?"

"No, there isn't any name on the chart. Let's check the Sailing Directions when we get back tonight."

"For our picnic, we hiked into the woods to a huge old tree. The more I think about it, the more I remember. Dad told us it was over a thousand years old. We had the best time. Let's go up there. Mother would like that if she were here."

They walked up into the forest to the great tree. Logan suggested one word, "Majestic Old-Timer." That was what they decided to name it.

Annie laughed at him. "That would be three words, and you talk like it is a living thing."

"Well, it is, to me, anyway. It is well and alive, and that's why we, as human beings, need to protect it. What a wonderful piece of work Mother Nature did here. I hope it can live for another thousand years so others can enjoy it like we're doing today."

"I like that. Mother would also have said that if she were here with us today."

"She is Annie. In spirit, she is with us."

Annie went quiet, which was a surprise to Logan. She hardly ever stopped chattering away.

"You okay, Miss Annie?" He asked as they approached the tree.

She stopped walking in front of him, turning to face him. Her eyes were all misty and with a shaky voice she said, "This is so beautiful, now I see why Mother loved it so much. It was a big part of her appreciation for the Broughton's. She loved us, her family, the house at Scott Cove, and the beauty of this land."

Annie gave a heavy sigh. Logan stood quietly, giving Annie space with her thoughts.

"She had everything she ever wanted in her life, and then it slipped away from her. Cancer gave her no time to see how the story of her life would end. Dad wanted her to stay in Vancouver at Aunt Samantha's for treatments. Mother wouldn't hear of it, and she demanded to go home to Scott Cove." Logan could feel the pain she was sharing.

"Aunt Ida and Allison helped take care of her. Dad and I were there and did what we could. It gave her time in her house with her family around her. She was comfortable in those last few short weeks of her life."

Logan remained quiet, listening. "I see now how Mother planted her roots, not giving in to the city lights . . . like I am by living with Aunt Samantha."

Annie looked at Logan, "That silly little word of yours, 'roots,' keeps popping up."

He smiled at her. "Not so sure about that."

"And why not?" She asked, her face suddenly nervous.

"You and I both know we need to finish our education. That's our job for now. Then we can return to our roots if there is the calling. I try never to forget where my roots are."

"Yes, you could be right. Can I have a hug, please?"

They stood to hug one another beside the great tree.

Shadows were getting long in the deep forest. They worked their way back to the boat. Once again, Logan made sure everything was secure for the night. At Annie's request, the boat's stern was left tied securely to the boom log.

Annie was quiet through dinner.

Having the dishes put away, she insisted on redressing his burns before it got completely dark.

The day's light was slipping away fast, and it was time to call it a day.

Logan thanked her. "You go ahead and get ready for bed. Give me a call when you're tucked in, and I can come in."

Annie was in her sleeping bag in no time and gave Logan the ok to come down. He slid into his sleeping bag in the dark.

"Goodnight, Logan. Thank you for today. I'll never forget it."

"Thank you for trusting me with your thoughts about your Mom. Goodnight, Annie."

"You're the only one I could talk to about her like that. It hurts so much, missing her as I do. You've become my best friend, you know."

"My pleasure, nice lady."

He heard her wrestling around in her sleeping bag in the darkness.

Annie mumbled, half asleep already, "Give me your hand. I want to hold it while we fall asleep."

He pulled his hand out and found hers, falling asleep in the total darkness of Points North's tiny cabin, the water gently lapping against her tin hull.

# CHAPTER 23

Annie sat bolt straight up in her sleeping bag, giving Logan a jerk with her hand. "Did you hear that?" she whispered.

Half asleep, Logan forced himself to come fully awake. "I think that's the skiff bumping us with the tide going out. It would slack the on-shore tie-line."

Then there was the noise. "Thump," pause, "thump," "thump."

Then stone-cold silence.

Logan slid out of his sleeping bag and leaned over in front of the stove, straining to hear any sound at all. The thumping of his heart and Annie's quickened breathing was all he could hear. Logan pulled the 12-gauge shotgun out from next to his side of the bunk.

Then out of nowhere, another rapid thump-thump and a loud scratching noise on the cabin doors.

"Mountain lion," he whispered to Annie.

"Do you think it could be a bear?" She asked.

"No, too quiet, it's too light on its feet," he said, determination in his voice.

Logan laid the shotgun on its side in his hand and started shoving shells into it.

He wasn't sure what load he was loading as there was zero light to see. With a quick motion of his hand, he racked a shell into the chamber, safety on but ready to fire.

"I am going to yell at it and see if it'll go away. Could you hold a flashlight on the door? Don't turn it on until the door opens and hold it over my shoulder so you don't blind me with the beam, please."

"Okay, you want me to yell at it too?"

"No, that might confuse us, with a whole bunch of yelling going on. It's trying to get to our fish under the well deck. You ready?" Logan asked.

"Yes."

Logan was sitting on the cabin floor with his back to the head of the bunk. Annie was still in her sleeping bag, leaned up on her elbows, flashlight at the ready over the top of Logan's head.

He started in a low, calm voice. "Okay, cat, we know you're there. It's time for you to leave now."

It was eerily quiet. Logan took a deep breath and switched off the safety. He yelled now, as loud as he could, "You hear me cat? Get off the boat now!"

They waited in the profound silence of the little cabin.

"If he decides to rattle the door, I'm going to let him have it, okay?" Annie didn't answer, just patted his shoulder.

The clawing started at the split doors, the cat deciding it wanted into the cabin. Logan knew they weren't mountain lion proof, and the cat could pull them open.

With the doors being all that was between them and the intruder, he aimed in the darkness. "Hit the light now," he said. With the beam of light dead center on the door, the gun went off. In the small cabin the noise was deafening.

The noise was louder than anything Annie had ever heard before. She kept a steady hand on the flashlight even with the thundering blast. The shattered door, with wood splintered from birdshot, now had a hole through the center.

As soon as he fired, Logan pumped another shell into the shotgun. They could see the mountain lion recoil back, appearing to think about what had happened as blood covered its chest.

The darn thing wasn't dead, and Logan knew it wouldn't be for a long time. He wished he had loaded a slug instead of birdshot. Maybe the next shot would be a slug.

The cat stood in the stern well deck, staring into the flashlight beam. Its lips curled up, showing its teeth and a low growl started in its throat, then turned to screeching a blood-curdling howl. The gun was ready to fire again, in position, tight against Logan's shoulder.

Logan paused, not firing, hoping the cat would leave. *Looks like that's not going to happen.*

The cat crouched, and Logan knew it was coming in for the attack.

The gun barrel pointed at its wide-open howling mouth. Logan was waiting for the cat to close the distance between them.

The cat gathered up its remaining strength, mouth still wide open, making that god-awful sound. It leaped toward the end of the shotgun. Logan was sure the cat was going to bite the end of the barrel.

As the cat got within twelve inches of the barrel, Logan pulled the trigger for the second time, followed by a resounding boom and fire out of the end of the barrel.

This time, the shot went into the mouth of the big cat, then out the back of its head, the force throwing it into the stern of Points North.

The cat landed sprawled across the stern steering seat. Logan stood up and approached the animal cautiously, continuing to point the gun at it, watching for any movement. Annie held the light steady, still in her sleeping bag.

Annie finally spoke "Here, hold the flashlight for me. I need to get out of this sleeping bag."

He reached in from the well deck and took the flashlight.

Out on deck, he started to shiver. He was not sure if it was the chill of the evening or the surging adrenaline running through him with all the excitement of the cat's encounter.

Within seconds, Annie was standing next to him, looking at the cat. She said, "Big one, don't you think?"

"Miss Annie, he wasn't going to take 'no' for an answer. Here, hold the flashlight. I want to get him off the boat, so he doesn't get blood everywhere."

Logan leaned the gun up against the cabin. He found a piece of line and slipped it over the animal's head, then picked it up and threw the carcass overboard with a splash.

"I'll get dressed, then drag it up on the beach. Tomorrow, in the daylight, we can bury it."

Annie hugged Logan. "Thank you for protecting us the way you did." Logan only smiled.

Once dressed, Logan stepped on deck, taking the line with the dead cat at the other end. He climbed into the skiff, then up onto the boom log, all the time pulling on the carcass. Once on the beach, he pulled the body above the tide line.

Annie started the small cabin stove, got dressed, and put the teapot on.

Logan untied the skiff from the boom log and tied it alongside Points North for the night. Now there was no bridge for uninvited visitors.

Points North was tending easy on the anchor. *The rest of the night should be a quiet one.*

Logan pulled out an extra board he had in the engine room and made a temporary repair on the doors. They were secure in the little cabin again. Sitting in the galley seat, they shared a steaming hot cup of tea.

Annie sat close to Logan, feeling his warmth. "Now that was exciting. Is it lying on the beach?"

"Yes, above the tide line. And with a little luck, the critters of the forest should have it cleaned up by morning."

"I heard you bring up the skiff."

"Yep, no more visitors for us tonight. I want to get a good night's sleep, please."

"That sounds perfect to me. Kawatsi tomorrow?"

"Yes, I want to see if there is any color in the gold pan up at the waterfall."

By morning, a thin fog shrouded the bay. Logan thought it would burn off sometime after breakfast.

Annie fixed a big breakfast to get them going for the day. Logan went ashore and found an empty spot where the cat had been. Something had drug the cat into the forest.

After pulling the anchor up by hand, Logan had Annie run the boat. On the way out of Watson Cove, they stopped to watch the vast waterfall with the water sliding across smooth rocks and falling into the channel below.

"I think I remember the name of the falls. It's Lucy or Lacey falls. Dad said it was worth the time to stop and enjoy," Annie purred, mesmerized by its unique beauty.

Soon, they turned and continued up Tribune Channel, then rounded the corner into beautiful Kawatsi Bay. Sheer granite cliffs loomed skyward on both sides, the water below them flat calm, reflecting the fluffy clouds and deep blue sky.

Putt-Putt was singing her song as the bow of Points North parted the water. A small wake came off the stern, closing the water behind them.

"One word comes to mind, Miss Annie, 'smooth.' No wind, no swell, the sun warm on our backs. There are no sharp edges today, just smooth."

Annie smiled.

# CHAPTER 24

Passing a tiny island on their port side, Logan and Annie could see good anchorage behind it. "Cutter said the falls were there on the left, and if you listened closely, you could hear it. The loudest was where it hit the pool, a hundred feet below."

"We have time to explore?" Annie asked, excitement in her voice.

"Yes, let's go now and then have a late lunch. You pull up the boat, and I'll get the shotgun."

Within minutes, they were heading to the beach. "Can you hear that?" Annie was excited. "It's the waterfall!" They landed the boat and hiked up the wide beach into the edge of the forest. The air was cool and smelled of moss and fir needles.

Annie was in the lead. "Come on, Logan. This way, it's louder this way."

*She is her father's daughter.* She loved the forest with all its natural beauty wrapped around her.

"Come on! Would you stop gawking!" she said for the second time. They walked deeper into the shadow of the forest, climbing the hill to find the stream at the end of a faint trail. There it was, the glorious waterfall plunging one hundred feet down the face of the granite cliff as it had done for centuries, slowly carving out the stone basin to form a beautiful pool, then making its final journey to the bay in a narrow, crooked stream.

"Oh my, this is so beautiful, we need to share this. I want to bring my journal back, and then I can write while you pan our fortune in gold."

"Afraid not," said Logan. "There won't be any fortune here. Your dad is right, Annie. Wherever you go, most likely, someone has been there before you."

"Yes, he could be right. But I don't think that should keep us from dreaming about it. Do you?"

"No, panning gold is like going fishing. There's more to fishing than catching fish."

Logan had a chance to compare their trip with living in Vancouver, so he took it. "Look at our adventure. It gives us the chance to see and share in such a beautiful place. You would never see this in Vancouver."

Annie smiled thoughtfully. "All right, I'll agree with you on that. You do realize there wouldn't be a mountain lion knocking at your condo door if you were in Vancouver?"

"Right again, my friend. But you don't have the chance of a lifetime to kill a big cat in the dark of night that wants to eat you. Adventure, Miss Annie, that's what it's all about. Adventure. I love it. It's what helps me get up in the morning—not knowing what's out there waiting for me. Adventure, everyone should have a couple in their lives."

"You realize we've had two in the last two days," Annie reminded him.

"Yes, and may there be many more before we see the lights of Scott Cove again!"

"Oh brother, you won't quit, will you?"

"No, ma'am. Let's go get some lunch, your journal, and my pan, then get right back up here."

After a quick lunch, they hurried back up to the falls to spend the afternoon. As the sun fell behind the mountain, Annie closed her journal. "No gold, huh? Too bad! I was hoping."

"Don't fret, pretty lady. We found peace, and that is golden. You wrote in your journal, and I answered my question of 'gold in them thar hills,' to quote the old-timers."

On the stern of Points North that evening, Annie asked, "What are you thinking for tomorrow?"

"I was going to suggest we put out the shrimp pots. Then while the pots are fishing, we could explore the rest of the bay."

"This is such a beautiful place, with all the green trees and granite cliffs." Annie purred.

"Yes, it is."

"I was noticing today that once we got past the shoreline, the undergrowth was minimal. Would that be because the trees are so close together?"

"I do believe so. I've heard that called the canopy. Did you see the sheer granite walls coming in?"

"Yes, I've been writing about them in my journal."

As Annie crawled into her sleeping bag for the night, she said, "Goodnight, Logan. Thank you for pointing out the value of our adventures."

"Thank you for sharing them with me, Miss Annie." Logan reached over and put his hand on her arm to acknowledge their closeness.

The next day went by lightning fast with catching shrimp and exploring the rest of the bay. Back at Points North, they cleaned, cooked shrimp, and fried more salmon for dinner. The evening arrived, and they needed to do their planning for the next day.

"You know," Logan started. "We see fishing boats here and there. I'm thinking they might be fishing for the schools of salmon that go into Bond Sound for spawning."

"That sounds interesting. How far is it?"

"Only around the corner to the east, three hours of run-time away. The chart shows there might be an anchorage over by the river with a stern tie."

She gave him a questioning look, remembering what happened the last time they tied to shore. Logan smiled, "No, we will be using a line for the stern tie, not the boat. If something wants to visit us in the night, it'll have to swim."

"Good, that was my first question. My second question is, will we pick up our shrimp pots and move them to Bond Sound?"

"Yes, and, it might be fun to catch a fish or two on the way."

"I thought we hadn't caught any fish in the last couple of days." Annie was the fishing person of the two of them. Logan smiled.

The sun was up and warm in the eastern morning sky, waiting for them to get going. Right after breakfast, they headed straight for their pots on the south side of the island.

"Auntie will be so pleased with these huge prawns," Annie said, smiling thoughtfully.

Logan could feel her genuine care for others. She put others before herself, and this was one of the many things he respected in her.

Passing the waterfalls on their east side, they departed Kawatsi Bay, rounded Miller's point and worked their way toward Bond Sound, fishing lines in the water.

Annie caught two nice Coho and could hardly contain her excitement.

"Logan, tell me what it's like to be a commercial fisherman."

"It's fun and a lot of hard work. I like to catch lots of fish, and big ones too. You're always thinking of ways to catch more fish. That helps you make more money. It is a very greed-motivated type of work."

"You never talk about losing your dad to fishing. Do you think you'll ever go fishing where he did?"

"I don't know. Guess I need to take small steps first. I'll hand-troll with Points North up in Southeast Alaska. If the money's there, I could get a better boat."

"Does that ever make you think you could go like your dad?"

"No, he taught me good. But Grandpa also taught me that if your number is up, it's your time to go."

"Is it all that simple? What if you had a family like your dad did? What about them?"

They were getting close to the head of the bay and would be anchoring up soon.

Logan wasn't sure where this conversation was going, so he decided to play it out to see what she had in mind.

"Dad had that job to support his family. It's like your dad, where he works in the woods. How about Barney lying in the hospital in town? Did that make sense?"

"Well, my question is, why do men have to work such dangerous jobs?"

"Whoa there, let me answer a question with a question. What would you do if your dad got killed in the woods?"

"That's not fair."

"Yes, it is. You would be sad. Then you would pull yourself together the best you could and move on. Annie, our will to live and be happy is one of the strongest gifts we have from our creator."

"Why are you always right?"

"I've been there, losing a dad. You also, losing your mom so young like you were."

"Hey, I'm not so young. We'll both be sixteen soon."

"Right, well, back to the question. I had to scrape all the loose pieces up and move on as you did. Now back to my answer, if you want to live safe, get your job and condo in Vancouver." Logan paused to think.

"You be careful, and don't let some idiot mow you down while you're walking across the street in the crosswalk. You see, you're never completely out of danger, even in your big, beautiful city."

Annie kept pressing Logan "What about the loved ones? Don't you owe it to them by not working a dangerous job?"

"I'm not sure where this is going. If I want to be a fisherman, a logger, or a racecar driver, I will be that. If I weren't happy with my job, I'd be a miserable person to live with."

"Yes, you would be." She reached over and put her arm inside of his and pulled him to her with a smile.

"For what it's worth," Logan said, "you would make one heck of a lady salmon-troller-skipper." She smiled and squeezed his arm a second time.

They sat close until it was time to anchor up. Annie steered while Logan went forward to the anchor. It was becoming a routine now.

# CHAPTER 25

"It must be Sunday law," Logan said, "because there are no boats here. They've all gone home for time off. Let's take our light fishing poles and gear and see if we could scare up a cutthroat trout."

"We should take our boots and rain gear. It might rain."

"I'll wrap up the shotgun in plastic for going on the fishing exploration."

"You think there'll be bears?"

"Yeah, if the salmon are running, the bears are running for dinner. If we see them, we'll go the other way."

"That is a good plan. Here's your rain gear."

Logan and Annie loaded up into the skiff. Annie asked to drive, of course. "Okay," Logan said, glad that Annie was willing to learn so much. "Don't drag the prop in the rocks. Shut down early and lift the motor up, please."

She smiled, "Yes, Captain."

Logan was sitting in the bow of the skiff as Annie drove the boat. He watched the clouds crawling over the granite-gray skies, getting darker by the minute.

Logan shouted over the gas outboard motor noise. "You're right, and it'll be raining in an hour. Still, want to go?"

"Oh, yes. If it pours, we can go back. Could we put the tarp over the boom and read for the afternoon?"

Logan motioned Annie to beach the skiff on shore and nodded as he stepped out onto the beach and pulled the boat up.

"You know it's flooding, Logan. Do you want me to drive us upriver further?"

"Sure, but we need to keep a sharp eye out for bears. As I said, it's the season for them too."

He pushed the boat off and climbed back in. Annie cranked up the motor, swinging the bow to stem the current. Yelling over the motor noise, she asked, "How far should we go?"

"No more than an hour, I'd guess. We don't want to run out of water up there when the tide changes."

She nodded and kept the bow upstream, watching the current closely.

Not fifteen minutes later, Annie spotted a small black bear walking along the waterline. He was sniffing and rolling a few rocks over, looking underneath them for something to eat.

They continued up the river until the evergreen trees were close to the shoreline. Looking at the tideline on the shore, they could see there was still six inches of tide to come in.

"Would you like to stop and do some fishing with the motor off?" He hollered.

"Yes, let's see if there are any of those cutthroat trout you were talking about."

Handing her a fishing pole, Logan said, "Now there is a special custom lure on that pole put there just for you."

"Thank you, kind sir. I'm going to leave the motor down in case we need to move back out into the middle of the river."

"It's ok. I'll use the oars, and we can drift fish our way back downriver." Logan didn't like the idea of leaving the outboard down.

"No, please. I like running the motor when we need it." Annie replied with a smile.

Logan knew there was no point arguing with the captain.

He handed her the hooded raincoat as the rain gently started. As they fished, they enjoyed the shower and the closeness that the Alto River gave them.

Logan figured Annie would want to land the first fish in the boat. They both had a bite, but neither one caught anything.

They drifted down with the flow of the river. Suddenly, the motor snagged on something hard. The boat quickly spun around before Annie could lift the motor, putting the stern of the boat upstream. The outboard motor was locked solid on the bottom of the river.

Annie had dropped her fishing pole in the bottom of the boat and was trying to get the motor release to let go and tilt it up. "It is not budging, Logan," Annie said, panic creeping into her voice.

There was too much pressure on the flat of the boat's stern as the bow was facing downstream. With the strong river runoff, water started pouring over the stern next to the outboard motor and into the boat.

Annie cried out, "Come help me, quick."

Logan had already put his pole in the bottom of the boat and checked to make sure the shotgun was still securely wedged in place. If the skiff rolled over, he didn't want to lose the gun.

As he worked toward the stern, he had Annie go forward to ballast the boat and to keep the stern from going under more.

"I want you to hang onto the gun in case the skiff rolls over, okay?"

"Okay." Annie knew this could be bad. She sat in the bow of the boat with the gun across her knees, watching every move Logan made.

Logan had his head over the stern, trying to see what the motor had hung on.

Annie said, "I'm so sorry I didn't pull it up when you told me to." Logan had his body half over the stern, his arms in the water, feeling around the motor shaft.

"Don't worry about it. Do you have your life vest on?"

"No."

"Well, put it on and throw me mine. We need to have the vests on now."

Minutes had ticked by ever so slowly. It was like hours to Annie, watching the river hitting against the boat's stern, always pushing.

The boat was taking water on, slow at first, but as it came in, it made the stern heavier and lower in the water, which made water pour into the boat faster. And the motor was not budging.

Logan couldn't quite see what was holding onto the motor. It was terrible with the tide still coming in as the rising tide would sink the boat if the river flow didn't do it first.

"I think it's some old logging wire left out here a long time ago," Logan yelled as he started unscrewing the transom clamps that held the motor to the stern of the skiff. He needed to let the outboard motor go, and now.

He yelled, "Start bailing if you can, and don't lose that gun if she rolls over."

Frantically, Logan kept loosening the clamps to free up the motor and let it go to the bottom of the river.

Annie grabbed a small bucket they had for that very purpose. She was quiet, realizing how much danger they were in out here in the middle of nowhere.

The motor was almost loose as Annie got on her knees in the bottom of the boat and started wildly bailing the water out.

Logan was also down on his knees, pulling up on the motor which pushed the stern lower into the river. Finally, it came loose from the stern of the boat. Once clear, he let the outboard motor go and dropped it to the bottom of the river.

On its way down, the gas tank flew to the back of the boat and went overboard, nearly hitting Logan as it went by with the hose still hooked on the motor.

Logan gave a quick thank you to the universe. The boat was free at last, and the water stopped pouring in over the stern. The skiff was immediately carried downstream by the current and as they looked back, they could see the red gas can, half full of gas, bobbing in the stream, telling them where the motor laid.

"Wow, that was a close one! Are you okay?" Logan asked, the stress still in his voice.

"That happened so fast! I never would've thought. . ." Annie replied.

"No problem," Logan said. "Now we need to get out the oars and keep the boat mid-channel for now. You want to bail or row?"

"Bailing would be best for me right now. Besides, you're our expert rower."

Logan mounted the oars on the gunnels in their oarlocks and sat in the middle seat to row. He watched Annie closely, noticing she was shaking like she had the chills.

"Did you soak your jeans under your rain pants?" he asked, concerned.

She nodded yes, looking down at the bottom of the boat, seeing that most of the water was gone.

"Here, sit across from me and tuck your knees between mine. I can keep you warm. When we get back to the boat, you'll get warmed up like you need to be."

"What about the motor? Should we go back and get it? I feel so bad. That was stupid of me."

"Don't worry about it. We can buy a new motor. I didn't want to roll the boat over or swamp it with us and the gun in it," Logan said, smiling. "You sit tight, and we'll be back at the boat before you know it."

"Now that it's raining, we may as well go back to the boat anyway."

He could see Annie was fighting back the chattering of her teeth. Her lips were blue by the time they got to Points North.

Logan didn't tell her, but this was the hardest he had ever rowed in his life.

Annie had a hard time standing up and balancing herself in the skiff, her hands numb and legs stiff. Logan guided her on board and had her sit on the aft seat, then peeled off her wet rain gear. Her clothes were soaked, and her skin white with cold. She slipped into the cabin to dry and layout clothes, severely shaking all the time.

Logan followed her in and fired up the little stove, keeping his back to her for privacy. "Call me when you're changed," he said as he went back outside.

Ten minutes later, she called out to Logan as he was rigging the boom cover.

Logan opened the door, took her wet clothes, and hung them under the tarp. He had rigged up a makeshift clothesline under the sail boom and tarp that made the shelter.

As he climbed down into the boat, Annie was sitting on the V-berth wrapped in a blanket. Her lips were not so blue, and the shaking was slowing.

"You need to get into your sleeping bag. I'll cover you with mine."

She gave a thankful smile, "Do you think you could rub my legs to help get the circulation back into them?"

"Sure. Let me get out of my rain gear and boots."

Logan put the water kettle on for hot cocoa as the little stove heated up. He sat in the seat across from the stove and made cocoa when the kettle whistled. Annie, still wrapped in a blanket, stretched her legs out across Logan's lap.

He rubbed her dry jeans in the dim light of the cabin, feeling the coldness of her legs through her jeans. It took time, but she finally started to warm up, all the time sipping on her hot drink.

Annie's face was more relaxed now, her cold blue lips turning to warm pink. They sat there silent, for almost an hour, as he continued rubbing her legs.

"Are you hungry?" he asked.

"Yes. I suppose we should eat something." Dazing off into the distance, Annie looked exhausted.

"Good. You slide into your bag, I'll cover you with mine, and I can start dinner."

Annie nodded, turned around, and crawled into her sleeping bag, pulling it up to her chin. She laid her head on the small pillow and closed her eyes.

Logan reached forward by her feet and pulled on the bag zipper, zipping it up to her chin. Then put his bag over her, tucking it in around her slender body.

As he opened the door to get yesterday's fresh-caught salmon, Annie spoke in a half-asleep voice.

"Thank you for always making me feel safe. That was scary, and I knew you could make things right, not letting the skiff swamp. Thank you, Logan."

Logan stepped back, placed his hand over hers, and kissed her forehead as he would his little sister.

"You're welcome. I like holding up that end of our friendship," smiling as he brushed her cheek with the back of his hand.

Annie heard Logan go out on deck as she drifted away to slumberland. She thought, *This could be the one. Logan's sweet, always a kind word, and so respectful. This is his home. A city is a different place. He is always saying, "You are a product of your environment." He repeats that a lot. What a wonderful man, I will never forget this day.*

Logan pulled out the salmon to fillet and went back into the cabin. Annie was sound asleep.

Soon, salmon, rice, and potato were sliced up and gently simmering in the skillet.

Annie woke up to all the delicious aromas coming from their tiny galley. She smiled as she asked herself, *where did the word "their" galley come from? It's Logan's galley and Logan's alone. He doesn't mind sharing, that's for sure, and it's my job to cook. Okay, it's "our" galley. I need to talk to Logan about this more sometime.*

She thought about the motor on the bottom of the river. It was her fault. She would pay Dad for it if they couldn't get it back tomorrow. *We need to talk about that over dinner too.*

"Rise and shine, Princess of the North. Points North that is." Logan laughed, putting his hand on her back to help wake her. He could see a slight smile on her lips in the dim light of the cabin lamp.

Annie crawled out, swung around, and sat on the bunk. "That smells good, fried potatoes too. Yum!"

"Come and get it, or the evening cook is throwing it out."

"No problem here." Annie moved down to the small double cabin seat as Logan kneeled in front of the stove, dishing her a heaping plate of hot food.

"Thank you again, Logan. You're a good man, and you know that, don't you?"

Logan grinned. "Born to serve ma'am, now you eat up and go back to bed."

Big fat raindrops hit the cabin roof as they ate. Then the wind started, blowing hard, making the mast rigging whistle them a tune.

Annie asked, "You think we should go up and retrieve the motor tomorrow?"

"No, not worth it," Logan replied.

"And why not? You said it was only three feet under during high water. When the tide is out, we should be able to walk up to it, untangle it, and put it in the boat." She watched his face as he gathered up the dinner dishes. There was no expression.

"Logan, what is it? Tell me why you can't do it."

"No." He answered.

She sat up straight in the galley seat, "Why not?"

"Yes, I can tell you, 'no,' Annie. We should not press our luck."

# CHAPTER 26

"Well then, tell me, Captain. Why not?"

Logan could see Annie was not happy. He knew it was the word 'no' she didn't like.

"Okay, my shipmate, this decision is simple. We had a scrape with the mountain lion over at Watson Cove. That was not good thinking on my part. I knew better, listening to your dad and the loggers tell stories. I don't want to repeat bad judgment."

Before he could finish his explanation, Annie piped up. "That is not a bad idea to go get our motor."

When she stopped to take a breath, he jumped back into the conversation.

"Yes, it is. The bears are out and feeding on the salmon. We saw so much sign up that stream today. They might be farther up the river when it's high water. The fish would be in the shallow water further upstream. Besides, all we have is a popgun to keep 'them thar bears' off us. Would you think about it, please?"

"Well, Mister 'Not Scared of Anything,' I'll go by myself. I may as well, I put it there, so I'll go back and get it."

"No, your dad and Ida would never forgive me if I let you go alone. Let me cut a few cords of wood, and I can pay for it. Your dad would understand."

*Yep, she was not happy with me.*

Annie was sure Logan knew they needed to get the motor.

"Fine, let's agree to disagree," Logan said. "I don't want our last words of the evening to be in an argument."

Annie paused to think if she wanted to pursue the discussion more, knowing that to push would probably be a bad idea.

And Logan knew this conversation was not over with her. If that outboard motor were lying on the bottom of that river, they would resume the talk in the morning.

"Fine." She said with a smile. "We can agree to disagree." Annie knew she couldn't be unhappy with this guy for long.

Heavy rain announced the arrival of dawn, thundering down on the cabin roof. The wind swung the boat back and forth on the anchor, the swells slapping on the tin hull.

Logan and Annie agreed it would be miserable being stuck inside the boat all day. After breakfast, they decided to row to the beach and stretch their legs, storm or no storm.

Logan packed a small backpack in case they got stuck on the beach and needed a fire, as well as their cutthroat trout poles. The shotgun and extra shells went too. Bundled up with rain gear and boots, they climbed into the boat.

"You don't look worse for wear after freezing your legs off yesterday," Logan remarked as Annie climbed into the boat.

She peeked out from under the bill of her raincoat hood. "When you hang out with the logger's daughter, you're with some sturdy stock." Logan enjoyed watching her beautiful smile.

He rowed the boat up to the mouth of the river and Annie noticed the water was at the bottom of the low tide line, and she thought up a plan. She knew that Logan would rear back like an old mule if she told him what to do. If she suggested something to him, then gave him time to think it over, he would come back with the correct answer.

Pulling the boat onto the beach, they took their poles and started spin casting. The wind was coming up again and would blow their line the wrong way as they cast.

"Okay, you win," Logan said out of nowhere. "Let's row up the river a bit to get out of this wind." Annie smiled and nodded.

They rowed up the river as the tide helped push them along.

As yesterday, Logan rowed, and Annie sat in the stern, casting out her lure. Shortly, they had four nice fat trout in the boat.

Logan kept rowing. He knew what she was doing. The motor was laying on the bottom a mile up the river, waiting for them.

No bears so far. Logan kept reminding Annie to watch for them. The area didn't feel comfortable to him, that old gut feeling he knew so well was churning his stomach.

"Logan . . ." When she started a sentence with his first name, he knew a question was coming. *Yes, we can get the motor.*

"Yes, my lady Annie?"

She smiled, "You know we are so far up here. Let's swing by and pick up the motor, ok?"

"All right. You should take a course in political science and negotiations. You would make an awesome politician. Don't worry about being a skipper on a salmon troller."

She smiled, thinking it better not to go where the conversation could take them. She didn't like last night's disagreement. They both didn't want anything coming between their peaceful friendship.

"Look! I see the gas can, it's floating, and it's still hooked to the motor. I almost think I can see the handle on the motor. How are we going to do this, Captain?" Annie knew he probably already had it figured out.

"We'll anchor upstream from the motor, then I can let slack out until the bow is abeam of it. I packed some tools in the backpack, and maybe I can free it from the wire."

"You knew all the time we were coming here to get it didn't you?" Annie said, mildly shocked.

Logan smiled. "Wasn't sure things would work out. You sit in the stern where you are and take the gun out of the plastic bag. Keep a sharp eye out for those pesky bears. They might be looking for a picnic basket."

Logan rowed them a little past the motor. The gas can bumped on the hull as they went by. Logan jumped forward and threw out the anchor. They were in less than three feet of water and only five feet from the riverbank.

The bow of the boat was lying in the stream with little strain on the anchor line. Not like yesterday with the stern being pushed under by the fast-moving stream.

Logan looked over the side of the boat with a pair of pliers in his hand. "I'll stay forward and reach in to get it."

"Okay," Annie replied from the stern seat. "Looks good here, no varmint sightings yet."

He leaned his knees against the side of the boat and reached into the water as far as he could. "It's too deep. Hand me the gaff hook, please."

Annie handed it to him, handle first, and went back to watching, the gun across her knees.

Logan hooked the motor with the gaff and was able to partially pull it up. He hung the outboard motor on the side of the boat by pinning the gaff with his knee, then reached down, and using the pliers, cleared the propeller from the wire. Just then, Annie yelled.

"Look!" She was pointing to a coyote running as hard as it could straight for them. The grass was only 12 inches tall, so it was easy to see it and what was chasing it.

It was a big old brown bear, down on all fours. It wasn't black, but brown, and chasing dinner. The bear was also at full gallop, totally focused on the coyote. Logan could see the coyote was on a straight line for them.

He jerked the motor up and threw it in the bottom of the boat. Then he jumped forward again to pull the anchor line while standing in the bow of the boat.

He yelled to Annie, "Don't shoot unless you have to. We can't afford to wound it."

Right then, the coyote jumped five feet from the bank into the middle of the boat.

It laid cowering in the bottom of the boat, next to the outboard motor, teeth bared and snarling.

A half a second later, the bear launched its massive frame from the bank, flying over the five feet of water, and landed square in the middle of the boat, pinning the coyote with his huge crushing claws. Then he opened his mouth and, with terrifying jaws, snapped the coyote's neck. The coyote was dead.

The impact of the 800-pound bear landing in the middle of the boat threw Logan off his feet, catapulting him into the water. He landed on his side, hard, in three feet of water. The bear's weight had bent the skiff's keel, loosening the rivets holding the boat seams together and water started seeping rapidly into the boat.

Annie screamed again, pulling up the gun and taking aim, holding her breath to see what the bear would do next.

*Logan was right,* she thought, *we don't want to wound it, or we'll have bigger problems.* As if they didn't have enough as it was.

The bear acted like he hadn't even seen the humans. He lumbered out of the boat then stood up to his full height in the water, the dead coyote hanging from his mouth.

At that moment, the bear saw Logan, also in the water, now standing next to the boat's bow. Logan stood very still, water up to his knees, and slowly reached through his rain gear for the fishing knife on his belt.

Annie had the gun aimed at the bear, looking down the barrel, the safety off. The three of them seemed frozen in time, staring at each other. For Annie, it was like an eternity.

Logan couldn't fight his fishing knife out of his rain gear.

The bear, still on his hind legs, sniffed the air, the dead coyote hanging from its mouth.

It was apparent the bear hadn't noticed Annie. It was Logan moving around in his green rain suit that had the bear's interest.

Still on his hind legs, not wanting to drop the dead coyote, the bear started working its way toward Logan.

"He is coming toward you! Can I shoot?" Annie asked, her voice low, not wanting to alert the bear.

Logan didn't take his eyes off the bear. "No, not yet. If you do have to shoot, put two slugs under his left front, for the heart. I want to see if I can spook it off first."

Logan had finally freed his knife and thrust his arms into the air, wildly waving them, and shouted as loud as he could. "No, no bear, go away. You're not wanted around here."

It was as if the bear didn't hear Logan. He continued moving slowly toward him.

Logan's hands were still raised above his shoulders, his fishing knife gripped in his right hand.

Annie yelled, "It is not stopping." Logan finally screamed, "Shoot, Annie, Shoot."

Before the words left his mouth, an earsplitting boom was immediately followed by the unmistakable sound of racking back the pump on the shotgun. In less than a second, the gun cut loose with another resounding boom.

Logan looked hard, but he couldn't see a hole in the bear. He couldn't tell if Annie had got him or not.

Annie pumped in another shell but didn't fire. The bear turned and looked at Annie as if to ask, "What did you do to me?"

He then dropped down on all four legs and ran to the riverbank. As he left the water, he kept going for the taller grass, then disappeared into the timber.

Logan climbed back into the boat. "Nice shooting, Miss Annie, you drilled him both times."

She smiled, her voice shaking from the excitement. "Did you see any blood in the water?"

"Yep, he sprung a leak. I hope he enjoys his dinner after bashing in the boat. I'll start rowing as fast as I can for Points North. Could you bail, please?"

Annie replied, "He sure did some damage, didn't he?"

Logan leaned into the oars as hard as he could. "Guess you could say that's what happens when you drop 800 pounds out of the sky in the middle of an aluminum skiff."

He continued to row as Annie bailed, knowing her life depended on it. She felt it very much did.

Her dad had taught her that a wounded bear is meaner than ever. That was why they needed to kill them on the first shot.

As Logan and Annie made it to the first bend Annie said, "I don't think I'm keeping up with the water. It is pouring in through the seams awful fast."

There was silence except for the plop, plop of the oars followed by the extra slap of water flung out of the bailing bucket.

"Logan, did you hear me? We're sinking. I can't keep up." She sobbed.

"That's okay. We have bigger fish to fry." He was gazing far away to the forest line.

"What are you looking at? It's . . . it's still there, isn't it?"

"Yeah, he's stalking us. Might be waiting to make his move. I don't know why those two slugs didn't do him more damage."

"What will we do? The boat is sinking." Annie moaned, thinking that their only safe place would soon be gone.

"Easy does it. We'll row for the far bank. Once there, we'll pull the bow up on the bank. Water will run back to the stern. I can bail the boat out there. Now, if the bear stays away, I'll shove pieces of my shirt into the leaking seams. That'll slow the water down enough to get back to Points North."

Logan stopped rowing and quickly tore off his raincoat, then ripped his flannel shirt open, tearing the buttons off and tossed it to Annie, then handed her his fishing knife. "I need it cut into four-inch strips for caulking."

She nodded and got to work. Logan quickly sat down and pulled on the oars with all his strength, aiming for the far shore.

By the time they hit the far riverbank, the bear had moved across from them on the other bank.

They both jumped out of the boat, setting the gun and backpack on the bank as the rain started.

The water in the boat made it quite heavy. Both took a side of the bow and, with straining muscles, pulled the boat's bow up onto the bank as far as they could.

Logan grabbed the bailing bucket and ran back to the stern, wading into the river up to his knees. He started throwing water everywhere, mostly out of the boat.

Annie kept cutting up Logan's shirt into strips. With bailing completed in record time, Logan ran to Annie. "I need the screwdriver out of the backpack. We'll need to stuff the biggest dent first in case the bear shows up early."

She nodded. "Logan, you're freezing! Put on your raincoat to keep the wind off you." She scooped his raincoat out of the bottom of the boat and gave it a shake to clear as much water off as she could. Then she held it open so he could slide his arms into the wet sleeves.

Annie gave a little moan when she saw how he was shivering and shaking so hard from the cold.

They both heard the roar from the far bank. The bear was on its hind legs, mouth open and teeth glistening. They could see it was one mad bear.

"Will he swim over here?" Annie asked.

"Not sure. I guess it could try. That wouldn't buy much time being the strong swimmers they are. Keep an eye on him, please."

Logan squatted down, half in the water, and started pushing strips from his shirt into the boat's leaky seams using the screwdriver.

Five minutes passed in the shivering cold and pouring rain.

Annie stood next to Logan, holding the shotgun, and wearing the backpack. She watched the bear, reporting blow-by-blow what the bear was doing.

The bear looked madder yet, knowing where they were, even with his poor eyesight. Annie said, "He sat down. Logan, he's tearing the coyote to pieces and eating it."

"Good, I only need another minute. Now when we go downriver, the bear will smell us because the wind is in our face. That will keep him right behind us."

"What about when we get to where the river and the bay meet? Won't the water be rough with this wind?"

"Yes, you're right. It's blowing harder now. Been thinking about that too. There's a chance we'll have to pull in, beach the boat, build a fire, and dry us out."

"Hold on there, Captain. We have a half-crazed wounded bear chasing us!"

"That's the best we can do until the wind goes down. And that should be when the evening comes. We'll be able to make it out to Points North then."

Logan put the tools in the backpack Annie still had on her back. He pointed for her to go to the other side of the bow.

The boat was much lighter now and floated completely. Water was still seeping in, but no longer pouring in.

"Get in quick. We got to go," Logan said, tension rising in his voice. Shoving off fast, they were in the mainstream of the river again, and Logan started rowing as hard and fast as he could.

Annie went back to bailing, but only a third as much water. Luck was with them. The tide and the runoff of the river sped them along.

As they rounded the point, the wind created waves that pounded head on to the bow of the boat. Logan knew this was bad as the old boat wouldn't hold together for long, taking that kind of a beating.

And yes, the bear was still there, working his way down the far bank. Occasionally, he would stop, raise on his hind legs, sniff the air, then continue his walk on all fours.

They both agreed he was moving a lot slower as they went farther down the river.

Rowing for the shore away from the bear, Logan aimed for a spot where an eddy current washed out a small cove. He nosed the boat into the cove, giving them some shelter from the wind and rain. He hoped the storm was at its peak now. They needed to build a fire and lay low for the weather to calm down.

"What do we do when the bear shows up?" Annie asked, searching Logan's face for the correct answer.

"Look behind you. There's a nice tree with big branches. We'll climb and hold out there."

"The bear will try and get us up in the tree, won't it?"

"That's what I'm hoping. There will be nowhere to go when I rain lead down on its head at close range."

She frowned, "I should've figured. You want me to climb up the tree first?"

"Yes, ma'am, with the backpack. You'll need to keep the hatchet and flashlight handy. I threw a box of slugs in the backpack for the shotgun, and we should be okay."

She shook her head ever so slightly with disagreement. "I trust that is a plan, and it sounds better than no plan."

Logan nodded in agreement, his face grim. He knew they had few choices, and this one was better than fighting the bear on flat land.

Annie thought, *this guy melts my heart even when we could be dead by morning.*

They started gathering wood for the fire. It was summertime, and even with the recent rain, there was plenty of dry wood close by to get the fire burning good before dark.

The rain was still coming down hard, and they both had the shakes from the cold.

Logan removed the backpack from Annie's back and took it up the tree for safekeeping. He then returned to Annie next to the fire. "Now, you will know where to go from the light of the fire."

They cuddled next to the burning bonfire sharing each other's warmth. The wind-swept waves kept coming across the bay. Looking over the top of the sand berm, he could see Points North was riding well at her anchor in the lee of the bite.

Dark was closing in. The wind had let up some, but not enough for them to row out to Points North. It was giving them a shred of hope.

Annie looked at Logan, "Do you . . .?" They heard something.

"Yes, it is." They both strained to look toward the near dark horizon.

"Quick! Up in the tree. Hang on to the flashlight."

Logan stood up, shoving the hatchet into his raingear belt, then slinging the shotgun over his shoulder.

Annie was already scurrying up the tree. Logan stood, listening. He could hear the bear grunting and growling but couldn't tell which direction it was coming. With the wind still blowing, the noise had been vague, and he couldn't quite make it out.

"I'm up," Annie called to Logan. "Would you come on? Please hurry!"

Logan suddenly spun around and ran for the tree. Out of the corner of his eye, he had caught a glimpse of the bear, just outside the light of the fire.

He jumped for the first branch. Annie screamed, "Logan!"

He reached out and caught the branch, swinging himself upon it.

Logan's right leg was a little slow. That was when he felt the burning tearing force of the bear's claw at the boot of his right foot.

Logan could feel panic coming over him. There was no time. He had to hurry up more branches, then clear the gun from his shoulder to shoot.

Too late! The bear had his leg. Logan screamed, "Annie, here's the gun, take it," as he hung on with only one arm. He swung the shotgun off his shoulder with his other hand, hefting it up to Annie.

"Shoot it! It has my boot." Annie reached down and caught the gun barrel, trying to keep her balance on the branch. She flipped the gun around, aiming the barrel straight down toward the bear's head. She slowed for a second to steady herself.

A foot away from Logan's head, he heard Boom! Slam, slam. Boom! Slam, slam. Boom!

With his ears ringing, time stopped. Then the hatchet was in his free hand, and he was swinging it down toward his foot as hard as he could.

The bear pulled hard, his teeth buried in Logan's boot. The bear fell backwards as he pulled Logan out of the tree. Logan grabbed for another branch, but there were none.

Both he and the bear went sprawling on the ground, next to the roaring bonfire. There was only a distance of four feet between them.

Both Logan and the bear were on their backs. Boom! Slam, slam. Boom! Slam, slam again.

"Save the shells!" Logan yelled.

He rolled over and up onto his knees, the hatchet still in his hand. He drew his arm high above his head, aiming for the bear's heart under all that fur. It was an easy target as there were two holes right where he would plant the hatchet.

Logan's mind raced as the hatchet descended upon the bear. "Why didn't that kill him?"

The hatchet drove in with a loud thud, followed by the snapping of bone.

The pain must've aroused the bear. Still laying on his back, its paw swung around and raked across Logan's raincoat-covered right shoulder.

The bear's paw fell to the ground as Logan tried to rip the hatchet out of its chest for another swing. The blasted hatchet had stuck in the bear's chest. Logan struggled up to his knees, still pulling on the hatchet.

In the light of the fire, he could see the life drain out of the bear's eyes. The fight was over. The bear would never move again.

Logan slumped back, his eyes not leaving the bear's face. "Come on down. It's all over. We're safe now, and he's dead."

Logan looked up the tree as Annie climbed down, leaning the shotgun up against the tree's trunk.

"I need to go back up and get the backpack," she said, climbing up one more time. In the dim firelight, Logan reached over to take the gun, still on his knees with exhaustion.

*That was one fierce bear.*

Annie swung off the last branch and touched his shoulder. "Are you okay?"

"Yeah," he replied. "How about you?"

"My shoulder is a little sore from all the shooting I had to do today." They both gave a silly little laugh as the tension drained from their bodies.

"Logan . . ."

He thought, *Uh-oh. Here we go.*

"I'm sorry I called you 'Mr. Not Scared of Anything.' You know you're my 'Mr. Not Scared of Anything.'"

"Thank you for that. I thought I had a lecture coming or something." He smiled, glad she was safe.

Together, they loaded all the gear into the boat, safe and secure. Logan carved off the two front claws in case someone thought this didn't happen. Annie held the flashlight as the fire burned down and Logan used their bailing bucket to douse the embers.

The wind had all but stopped blowing as Logan rowed them out to Points North, a welcome safe and dry haven for the night.

Logan stayed in the boat, steading it, while Annie got up on the forward deck and tied off the bowline. Then aft for the stern line. He handed all the gear up, including the claws, then hefted up the motor onto the deck of Points North. "Our skiff might sink tonight, and I don't want to lose anything else."

# CHAPTER 27

Annie was first to get into the cabin and lit the lamp. It was such a comforting feeling to be in their little safe, dry place.

She started pulling out dry clothes for both of them and called out to Logan, "Get that wet gear off and get in here."

"Yes, ma'am. Whatever you say."

Logan sat outside in the stern of Points North, taking a moment to think about the events of the day. He finally peeled off his boots and socks and saw two gashes on his right foot where the bear had clawed him. Most of the bleeding had already stopped, but he knew the injury would need to be cleaned and dressed.

His shoulder was a different story. He could feel the burning and the warmth from the blood oozing down his back. He pulled his T-shirt off, winching from the pain and stiffness settling into his muscles. He couldn't see where the skin was laid open from the bear's claws.

"Annie, I think we have a problem."

The rain had started again, and Logan could hear it pelting the tarp that made the shelter over the well deck.

Annie stuck her head out of the cabin door while buttoning her shirt. "What's that?" she replied, speaking up over the groan of the wind that had started up with the rain.

He was down to his skivvies, slumped over in the stern seat.

"Your leg? At least it isn't pouring blood anymore."

"No, but my shoulder is. That would be when the bear took the last swipe at me."

"Turn around, let me see."

Logan was bent over under the boom tarp. He kneeled, groaning with the effort and pain, then tried to straighten his back.

Annie gasped. The wounds were deep with blood still oozing out, running down Logan's side. He said, "I have an old dry shirt at the foot of my bunk."

"Let me get it, then you come in and lay on your front on the bunk." Annie ducked back into the cabin.

"Logan, why didn't you tell me earlier? I could have rowed us out."

Logan smiled. "When you start with my first name, I know I'm in trouble. I wanted to get us out to the boat as fast as possible. I'm so darned cold, I'm sure it slowed the blood loss. And the truth is, I'm so numb I can hardly feel a thing."

"Oh, Logan!"

Crawling into the foot space of the v-berth, Annie found his shirt. "Okay, come in and lay your stomach on the bunk for me, please. I need to clean you up."

As he crawled into the bunk, Annie noticed his face had flushed out to a pale white color. Annie thought that was the loss of blood.

Logan couldn't help but give some directions. "There are some butterfly bandages in the first aid box. When you dress the wound, pull the cut edges together, then the butterfly should hold it together. Hopefully, I won't need stitches."

"Thank you, and I will do that." She worked with speed, not making it hurt any more than she had to.

"Don't worry about hurting me. I'm still numb. I couldn't feel it if I wanted to."

She had to fight back tears, seeing the gashes the bear tore into his back. Logan started shaking from cold. Annie had to reposition two bandages to get them right. He was shaking so hard she couldn't get them right the first time.

"In the net next to my bunk is a one-piece union suit."

"I'll get it."

He tried to move to put it on. No, he didn't have the steam to do it.

"Can I help?"

"Thank you."

Once they got him dressed, Annie helped him crawl into his sleeping bag, then started fixing dinner. Later on, she would check the bleeding to make sure it slowed.

"You need to eat something to help replenish the loss of blood."

"Salmon, please, some big chunks, and I should drink water to replace fluids."

She handed him the chunks of cooked salmon and water. He slid over, facing the hull, and ate quickly. Annie slid into her sleeping bag next to him. They both were still shaking from being so cold.

"Logan?"

"Are you asleep?"

"No. What can I do for you?"

"Do you think we should head out for Scott Cove and get you medical attention?"

"I am cared for by the best there is already. Besides, I don't want to deal with Tribune Channel in the dark. I don't have the steam in my boiler to do it tonight."

"Are you sure? You know I can run the boat, can't I?"

"Yes, you can, and very well at that. And here is 'the but,' you don't have the nighttime experience. We need to sleep and let our bodies get warm. Sweet, sweet, warmth with as much sleep as we can get."

"Alright, I'm here if you need anything at all during the night. You call me. Even if you only want to talk, okay?"

"Yes ma'am. But you're the one that usually wants to talk." Logan was so tired he could hardly answer.

Annie smiled in the dark. "I know. You're my best friend, and best friends talk. Thank you for everything today."

"You killed the bear, not me. I want to thank you for that."

"You're welcome," she said, smiling, caressing his temple. "Goodnight." No answer. He was sound asleep.

Logan woke during the night as the boat swung on her anchor with the gusting wind. His mind was going over everything that had happened the day before. Yes, the wind went down when they rowed out to the boat, and now it was blowing hard again. What was it Annie had told him? They always have a summer storm to remind everyone how pleasant summers are.

Laying in his sleeping bag, Logan listened to her breathing, and she felt so good sleeping next to his backside.

*That right shoulder will be sore for a while.* Logan drifted back to sleep, his last thought being, *we're lucky to be alive.*

The light was streaming through the two tiny portholes when Logan woke the next morning. He pulled his arm out of the bag, wincing with pain and patted the bunk where Annie was sleeping. She was gone. "Are you here?"

"Yes, right here, over in the seat reading. Can I get you something?"

"No. I thought maybe you took off for the beach to find yourself another bear."

She laughed out loud. "No, thank you! I have had my fill of bears, as you would say."

"Just checking." Logan fell back to sleep.

Annie woke him a few hours later to eat and drink more fluids. She already had the stove lit, with salmon and soup warmed up. "It's been blowing hard all day. I don't think we should run for home today. You sleep. I can feed you when you wake."

"Sounds good to me. A guy sure has to go through a lot to get a day off around here."

Annie laughed and served up lunch. She thought today was a good day to hunker down and listen to the wind and rain on the cabin roof.

*Tomorrow we'll go home*, Annie thought. *It's time anyway.*

Logan was okay with resting more. He was on his boat and with his girl.

By the next morning, the weather had improved with broken clouds, a light breeze, and a fair tide to help them on their way back to camp.

Logan managed to crawl out of bed and, with Annie's help, get dressed. After breakfast, he bailed out the skiff, then they fired up Putt-Putt and pulled anchor.

Logan noticed that Annie had slid naturally into the driver seat. *Come to think of it*, he thought, *she's been driving every chance she could.*

The run back to camp was fast with the tide. By noon, they tied up across from Burney and Allison's. They both came out to greet the "kids" as they called them. Alison notice Logan was limping and favoring his shoulder. "All right, did you outrun someone again?"

"Yes, you could say that." Logan nodded with a smile.

Annie shot him a look of disbelief. "Yes! We had to outrun a bear."

Logan joined in, "Once he got us cornered, Annie sent him to the 'happy berry-picking patch.'"

Annie spoke up, "Let's find Dad and Ida. Then we can come back and have a visit with you both. We'll tell you what happened and see how Burney here is doing."

It was Sunday, and the crew was lying around for their one day off for the week.

Oley and Ida were sitting at their table when Logan and Annie came in. Ida jumped up to hug Annie as she took her coat off.

Oley smiled and waited for his hug next.

Ida hugged Logan and noticed his grimace. "I'm so happy to have my two-fishing people back. Why are you sore?"

Oley held out his hand and shook Logan's. "Velcome back, Logan. Good trip?"

# CHAPTER 28

"Well, sir, you could say it was a good trip. We made it back."

"Dad let's all sit down," Annie said, moving toward the kitchen. "I want to feed Logan first. He's lost a lot of blood, so his eating is first."

Aunt Ida spoke up. "Blood? Who lost blood? Logan, now how did you do dat?"

Logan smiled at Auntie. "Let's let Annie tell the story. Then we have large prawns on the boat for you, and yes, some fish too."

"Yaw sure, you come to sit down, Logan. Everyone come sit, ve vant to hear what happened."

Everyone had a seat as well as some of the crew that had followed them up to the kitchen.

Annie came back with a massive plate of food for Logan and one for herself.

No one spoke. The crew would hush up others as they came in, making too much noise.

Annie talked them through it all, from leaving Scott Cove until they got back. When she had finished, Logan raised his hand.

"We owe you a boat and motor. It will be the first fishing boat that we'll buy together."

They all clapped, and Annie blushed, making her cheeks red. She told her dad how bad she felt as it all started by not wanting to tip the motor up.

Oley laughed loudly. "This is perfect. I'll need the two of you working for the next two summers to pay it off!"

Annie said, loud enough for him to hear her, and shaking her head, "Dad!"

Oley got his composure back. "Logan, how is your hand?"

"It's good. Is Irvine flying out soon?"

"Yaw, he flew out yesterday after work. You good to go to work tomorrow morning on the log bronc?"

Annie spoke up, "Hey, you two, wait a minute. Logan got his shoulder tore open, and he might still need stitches."

Logan looked at Annie. "Annie, you got to drive the boat all you wanted. Do you need to drive me too?"

She leaned back in her chair. "I'm sorry you lost so much blood." She took his hand, looking into his sky-blue eyes like there wasn't another person in the room.

"Logan, you have to promise me I can check it twice a day. If it bothers you, we'll take you to town and get it stitched up. Promise me now."

"I promise." The whole room went back to breathing. They were so proud of their little Annie.

"All right then," Oley announced. "Tomorrow, Logan will be our new temporary log bronc driver. Now, let's put Points North back where she belongs so that Logan can get a good night's sleep for tomorrow."

By early afternoon, Points North was back on her blocks behind the bachelor quarters. Logan and Annie had unpacked the fish and prawns and delivered them to Auntie. That out of the way, they packed Annie's gear and her dad's gun to the house.

The rain had finally stopped, and the sky was clearing.

"I want to check your shoulder dressing."

Sitting at Oley's kitchen table, Annie had Logan's shirt off when Oley walked in. He walked over and looked at the gashes. "No red, no infection, you vill live."

"Thank you, sir. I'll be ready to go first thing in the morning. Will Burney be off for a while?"

"Ya, a veek or so, you and I vill do yust fine at the log dump."

"Yes, sir, I'm looking forward to it."

Annie spoke up, "All right, Logan, you're good to go. Dad, we're going to go to Burney and Allison's for a short visit."

"Ya, you come in early. The day starts early." He laughed. "You both have been on holiday for a vhile and forgot vhat time we go to work around here." Then he started laughing again.

They held hands, walking over to the houseboat. Auntie came out of the kitchen as they passed by. "And where are my two favorite fisher people headed to this night?"

"We want to check in on Burney."

"Yaw dis is good. You tell him I said for him to get vell real soon now."

"We'll see you back at the house soon. 4 AM comes early around here."

"Yaw, it does. I vill be so happy to have you back working vith me in the kitchen." Auntie smiled and walked on for the house.

Annie squeezed Logan's hand. "You know, for only being gone for a week, everyone is happy to have us back."

Logan smiled. "I do feel like I'm part of the camp family."

"We would hope you feel the same for us. That is Dad, Auntie, and me."

"Oh, yes! I don't ever want you to feel like I was assuming I had a place."

"Well, you do. You have a place in all our hearts."

He didn't ask about her Aunt Sam's feelings. By now, they were at the boathouse. Allison met them at the door before they had a chance to knock.

"Come. Come in, you two, we were hoping you would stop by."

"We thought about Burney a lot. How was he doing?" Logan blurted out, stepping through the door.

Burney was in his comfortable chair, his feet propped up. There was a paperback book lying on the blanket covering his legs.

"I'm good. Allison doesn't want me to go back to work for two weeks. I can only sit around for another week. Then it's time to be working again."

"Ah, that's why Oley said a week or two." They all were laughing when Allison walked back into the room with tea. The boys didn't say a word as she gave them a look. Annie came clean and filled her in. Allison shook her head no, with a smile on her face. "I want to hear about your week. I know with you two, there was some adventuring going on."

Logan spoke first, "I think Annie should tell it from start to finish, except I will tell you upfront. We have to work for Oley the next two summers to pay for the aluminum boat and outboard motor we destroyed."

Annie cleared her throat and started talking. Halfway through, Burney held up his hand. "Two things, more tea, please, and I want to know how you destroyed a boat and motor?"

Annie smiled to Burney. "It's not 'how' but 'what' destroyed the boat."

She continued to tell the story and finally brought them back home again.

Allison commented, "You two are fortunate to be alive."

"Oh no," Annie said. "Logan says he has an angel on his shoulder to bring him through scrapes."

Burney nodded in agreement. "That could be. He sure had one on his shoulder dragging me out of that yarder. Thank you, Logan, you saved my life."

Allison chimed in. "Yes, we both thank you for what you did."

Logan said, "That's what friends are for."

A round of good nights were exchanged, and the young couple made their way to the house.

Before they reached the front porch steps, Annie turned and faced Logan. "I have been thinking about this for a long time."

"I knew something was on your mind. What is it my dear?"

"Do you realize that we haven't shared our first kiss?"

"Yes, it seems to me I offered once. That was about when Bobby came around. Wasn't that when your Aunt Sam was here too?"

"Yes, I remember. You were working on a chainsaw, and I had come from a marathon lecture from my aunt."

"I will remind you that there is always a kiss waiting for you. You only need to give me the nod."

"All right. Oh my, this sounds so stupid."

Before she could say another word, Logan wrapped his arms around her waist. He gave her the warmest, unencumbered soft kiss he could muster.

It was apparent Annie had something altogether different in mind.

When he started to pull away, Annie put both hands to the back of his head and pulled his lips to hers.

She didn't let go right away, savoring the moment they were sharing. She wanted Logan to know she was not allowing the moment to slip by. Locked in the embrace, they enjoyed the warmth of each other's tenderness.

Logan pulled her tighter to him. When the time came to come up for air, she relaxed in his embrace. Pulling away from his lips, she buried her head into his shoulder.

The excitement had taken her breath away. She slid her hands down to rest on Logan's shoulders. He could feel a shiver go through her body as she whispered, "I never would've thought."

"Me too. That was wonderful." Logan whispered into her soft hair. "I've never felt like this before."

They stood holding each other in the late evening light for a long while.

Logan spoke first. "We need to get you in for the night. Neither one of us wants your dad to see us like this."

"You're right." Walking up the steps, she whispered, "That was wonderful. We'll have to do that again sometime . . . soon."

"Thank you, Annie, I don't think it will hurt our friendship."

"Neither do I, but it did take us to another level."

"You're right again."

They walked to the front door. Logan opened it for her as she reached for his hand. "Wait." She turned to face him and stole a kiss from his lips.

Logan smiled. "That was good. See you in the morning." He finished opening the door so she could step into the house.

Annie turned, still smiling. "See you in the morning, for sure."

"Goodnight, Annie. Thank you for sharing a great holiday." He gave a little wave as she did, and closed the door.

Standing inside the door, Annie paused for a moment then turned, and said, "Goodnight, Dad, and Auntie."

She drifted off for her bedroom, her voice trailing off like she was a million miles away. "See you in the morning."

After Annie's bedroom door closed, Auntie looked up from her book to her brother, "Vat vas that all about?"

"Not sure. I guess the vall Aunt Sam tried to build caved in, and good for them."

"Brother, he might not be the one, but they vill grow together. Being kind to one another, that's what matters."

The next morning Annie was up early, happy, and giggly. Auntie asked, "How was your evening?"

Annie smiled. "The best I could ever ask for."

# CHAPTER 29

Over breakfast, Annie was almost giggly to Logan. He wondered what brought it on, but there wasn't time to worry about it. Maybe they could discuss it over lunch.

Logan headed for the log bronc, as promised. The bronc had a steering wheel with a suicide knob, and he could operate it with his right hand. With his left hand still wrapped, he would work the pike pole to pull up the boom chains.

Logan had watched what was going on with the bronc while he was cutting cordwood. That gave him a good idea of what he had to do. So, he knew how to operate the log bronc and building the tows with the log bundles.

Annie came down to the log boom for lunch and was already talking before climbing into the old Dodge to share their meal. Logan waited her out.

At last, it was his chance, "Why so giggly over breakfast this morning?"

Annie stopped for a moment, thinking, "Well. After saying goodnight the way we did, it was like I had the biggest of all secrets bottled up in me, and I could only share it with you. The whole experience was one of the greatest I have shared with anyone."

"Do you mean kissing?"

Annie, "Yes, and more. That one kiss will be etched in my mind forever. I'm still confused about the rest of my life, but that one kiss is crystal clear in my mind. It is hard with you being my best friend and the one that kissed me last night."

"So, I guess I shouldn't ask you where we stand even after one of the hottest kisses either one of us has ever experienced?"

"Yes. Like I said in the shop that night, check back with me every so often, and I'll let you know where I'm at."

"All right, Miss Annie, I promise to check back with you as I am waiting you out. You see, I can do that. You do know why, don't you?"

"Not sure."

"I'm sure. You're worth the wait."

They so enjoyed sitting in the old truck and spending their lunchtime together. It could rain all it wanted. Both were dry and enjoying each other's company. Nothing else mattered.

They both knew that too soon, it would be over, and they would have to go back to school.

Salmon were running in the rivers, and they spent the evenings in the boat.

The more time they spent together, the happier they were.

Friday morning over breakfast, Oley asked, "Logan, ve need to run the crew into Alert Bay for a Saturday night on the town. Vould you and Annie mind doing dat for me?"

"How about it, Annie? I'm game if you are." She gave a big smile and nodded yes.

"Good," said Oley. "You can start loading dem up at noon and head for Alert Bay. You might vant to check the boat, but I tink it is all ready to go.

"Now, you be sure to get them collected up by noon on Sunday and bring them home no matter what condition they're in. If there are any missing or stragglers, you need to come home without them. They can get a floatplane back to Scott Cove."

Oley paused. "Are you good going into town vith Logan for a night, Annie?"

"Yes, Dad, I'm fine. I couldn't be safer."

"Logan, you up to it?"

"Yes, sir, it will be fun for us. What a great break. Thank you for trusting me with Annie and the crew."

"Good. You get a mooring slip for the night at the Shell dock. Tell the crew the rules, you're in charge, and you enforce them."

"One question. Auntie Ida, would you like to go with us?"

Ida smiled, "Not on your life, I'd get in trouble. Besides, I need to feed my family here. You two go have a good time."

Logan immediately started thinking about the mileage, the route, and where to tie up.

Oley asked, "Anything else Logan?"

"I can't think of anything else to do besides staying here and hauling garbage Sunday morning."

Oley gave a big laugh. "Logan, garbage vill be here vaiting for you vhen you get back Sunday afternoon."

"That's okay, boss, I got the best help in the camp." Logan patted Annie's hand.

Saturday morning arrived. Logan planned on he and Annie staying on the crew boat. They had straightened up the forward cabin, with its V-birth, small stove, and a little porta-potty between the berths.

"You could say all the comforts of home." Logan smiled.

He took a cash draw, so they could eat uptown in a real-live restaurant, then walk around and enjoy the sights.

He thought Annie was more excited than him. Logan knew the responsibility was big. Most of all, he was to see that Annie was safe.

By noon, the crew started showing up at the crew boat.

Oley was standing off to the side, not saying a word. This was Logan's show.

Logan stood by the outside boat controls. The crew was joking and laughing as they came on board, ready for time off in town.

As they stood in the stern of the boat, Logan announced, "Welcome to the Alert Bay Express." He laughed and went over the rules. "Be back on time. I will pull the pin when we need to leave for camp. You all know the rest of the drill, so with that, we won't waste our time."

Logan nodded to let the lines go. With the two engines rumbling at an idle, he backed the boat, sliding away from the log boom dock.

He figured they would be in town in a couple of hours as fast as the crew boat was.

As the boat pulled into the marina, everyone was standing at the rails, waiting to hit the town.

Logan maneuvered the boat to the public dock and hollered over the rumble of the engines. "Noon tomorrow, boys! Be here. The boat will be in the harbor, and you're welcome to sleep on the boat. Just keep it quiet."

They all gave a cheer of thanks and jumped off the boat.

"Annie, I guess it's you and me, girl."

She smiled, "I like it like that."

They walked to the harbor office and arranged moorage for the boat amongst the other crew and fishing boats.

"Let's go uptown for a walk. It's been a long summer for us both, don't you agree?" Annie smiled, taking Logan's hand.

"I agree it has been a long summer."

They walked toward town, stopping at the post office so Logan could drop off a letter for his mother, letting her know he would be home soon.

Both he and Annie knew their summer would soon be over.

Stopping to rest on a bench in front of the courthouse, Annie said, "Thank you for taking my hand, Logan. It was good to walk through town, holding hands."

"That was the only way I could keep all the crazies at arm's length. You are a beautiful woman that can turn any man's head."

"Thank you. You do know you're the one I want to be with for now."

Logan didn't say anything. It hurt too much. He wanted to know what would happen when he was not sitting on the bench next to her.

"What are you thinking, Logan?"

"Do you want to know, or are we making conversation?"

Keeping her hand in his, she leaned back and looked at him. "You have never said anything like that before."

"Yes, you're right. The clock is ticking on our time together. I'm not blind to it, and I know it will be here soon. You are so beautiful in so many ways to me. It will hurt to say goodbye when it's time. My heart will ache when you are only 90 miles away."

Annie took Logan's other hand in hers. "I know, it's the same for me. You're such a gift in my life. There is so much to do with school, then University after that. You understand, don't you?"

"Yeah, I'll never be a Bobby, and the fact is I don't want to be. It will be your choice if you ever decide to keep me around, down the road."

Annie didn't want to have this conversation right now. "Let's enjoy the moment. I don't want the future to get in the way of the present. We don't want to ruin our evening in town, agreed?"

Logan knew she was putting him off. "You're right, and we need to find some dinner and enjoy the night."

They found a nice table for two in the hotel on Main street. The previous conversation was still going on in Logan's mind. It was hard to ease up, but he did manage to give it a rest over dinner.

As they walked toward the boat, the evening sky was turning red, getting ready to bring out the stars. Not only were the stars coming out, but the drunks were coming out as well.

Logan guided them to the quiet side of town, where the crew boat was. Walking back together and holding hands, was like a dream come true for both of them.

Logan continued their earlier conversation. "Thank you for showing up in my life. It is such a pleasure to be your friend. If you choose life in Vancouver, I will understand."

Annie could tell he was thinking out what he was going to say. Logan continued, "I disagree but, I understand. You have so much more there and deserve the life you choose."

Annie tried to keep the conversation light. "So, are you saying you're not much of the city kind of guy?"

"Well, I grew up in a small fishing town. A big city like Vancouver doesn't sound like my kind of place."

"I see what you're saying. We both come from different places."

"I am not quite sure that I understand the pleasure you find in a place with so many people surrounding you."

She was thinking about what he had said, so he continued, "I know your mom and dad raised you in a logging camp. That's where I see your roots. Your Aunt Samantha has been working on you, and it's obvious she is trying to take that out of you."

Annie paused in her stride. "You're right, and she showed me the place to be."

Logan tugged slightly, getting Annie to keep walking. "You won't catch any Coho salmon in Vancouver. You know that don't you? Annie, I am not trying to sway you one way or the other. Pick your path when it's time and stick with it. That's what Grandpa used to tell me all the time."

"I know, Logan. You and I are too young to pick a path, don't you think?"

Logan shook his head. "I know what I like. That makes my path a little easier to pick, okay?"

"You come from a different place than me."

"No, Annie, we come from the same place. I come from the old country through my heritage, like you.

"You lost your mother like I lost my dad. Where do we differ? Could it be your overbearing aunt in Vancouver?"

Annie was quiet but didn't let go of Logan's hand. Finally, with a deep sigh, she said, "I am so confused. Logan, you're fighting a battle inside, and you know it."

"Yep, you're right. I hate losing. Don't you? This battle is a matter of the heart."

"You're right. It is a matter of the heart. Where will we be two years from now?"

"I think I will be out of your life," Logan said quietly.

They got back to the crew boat just before dark.

Opening the forward cabin, Logan said, "Think I'll sit outside for a while. You're welcome to join me if you like."

Annie smiled. "That sounds good. Can we quit tormenting ourselves that our summer will be over in two weeks?"

"Yes, I promise. I will keep my emotions in check, as hard as it is."

"Good, I was hoping you would say that. Let's enjoy the rest of the evening."

Annie settled in next to Logan on the bench seat, unable to put the unfinished conversation to rest. "Does it frustrate you that I've never told you what I want?"

"I was hoping you would want to drop the other shoe someday."

"You could say I don't have the other shoe to drop. You know this is crazy, two young people to commit to one another. We both have years of school to complete, and we live so far apart. It would be hard not seeing one another for long periods."

"You're right. Life is just beginning for both of us. We have all these new experiences coming at us."

"Like this summer spending our off time together," Annie said, smiling as the memories cascaded across her mind.

"How about now? Your dad trusted us alone together, again."

"He's smart as a fox. There is a reason he trusts us together."

"Oh yeah? What would that be?" Logan wondered where the conversation was going.

Annie gazed up at the stars. "He likes you a whole lot more than Bobby or anyone like him. Look at you two. You come from the same cut of cloth. Face it, you respect each other."

"Well, yes, you're right there. I would like to think your dad would want us to have some time together in town."

Annie snuggled up close as the evening cool settled in the marina. He put his arm around her as they watched the stars and she melted into his side. They sat there for an hour before tiredness prompted them into the little cabin.

Annie headed in, and Logan said, "You go first and hop into your bunk. I'll check the lines and be along." A few minutes later, he slipped into the cabin then into his sleeping bag. Putting his feet to the bottom of the bag, he bumped Annie's feet in the V berth, pulling away not to bother her.

"No, don't move your feet. I like feeling them there. Then I know you're close."

All night, Logan could feel Annie's feet against his. He liked knowing she was close to him.

Logan got up at daylight, counting five of the crew on the boat's back deck. Annie was still sound asleep in the cabin. He went for a walk up the dock, looking at boats and thinking about what they had talked of last night.

She was right. They have so much ahead of them. Logan knew he would miss their friendship in a few days. Looking up the dock, he saw Annie watching him as he wandered along.

"Hi there," he said as he returned to the crew boat. "Let me buy you breakfast." She nodded and smiled as she took his offered hand and stepped on the dock and didn't let go as they headed into town.

There was no more talk about being apart. They couldn't stop the clock.

# CHAPTER 30

Logan started up the crew boat and putted from the overnight mooring to the government dock with Annie tending lines. Big black clouds were filling the sky, pushed along by a gusty wind. *It appears a storm is brewing*, Logan thought.

The five crew members who slept on the boat last night were awake and eating snacks Ida had packed. The rest were standing at the government dock, ready to go back to camp.

Everyone knew the weather was deteriorating and the run back to camp would be a rough one. The forty-foot boat had two Detroit diesel engines and with the boat's hard chine and flat bottom, they could make good speed.

Logan planned to stay north of Pers Islands. It would help him avoid the afternoon Queen Charlotte winds.

Most of the crew fell asleep, wedged into the small cabin down below, trying to heal the pain of last night's party.

Annie stood next to Logan as he drove the boat, and Cutter came up to keep them company.

Logan decided to go east more, keeping above Hansen Island, to take Blackney Passage instead of cutting across Blackfish Sound.

It all was good planning, but that didn't mean it was going to work out that way.

As they rounded Gordon Bluff on their port side, they could see the winds had come early today.

Logan said, to no one in particular, "Could be 25 to 30 knots already."

The farther they got out into Pers Passage, the bigger the seas got. Strong buffeting winds swept around Cormorant Island. Logan had to reduce speed to control the boat's rocking and rolling.

Once they reached the lee side of Pers Island, the wind was blocked, and the seas eased.

Logan wanted to go back to full cruising speed. As he pushed the throttles back up to full power, the port engine didn't respond. He could tell by the sound and vibration it was not running right.

"Annie, take the wheel," Logan said as he slowed both motors then pulled the port engine back to an idle.

"Come with me, Cutter. We need to open the engine hatches so I can see what's going on."

With the hatches off, Logan climbed down between the two engines. The port engine had died at a dead idle, and the starboard engine started running rough. Logan followed his training, which was always to inspect the fuel filters' glass bowl first. Yep, there was dirt, sediment, and water in it.

"Throw me that bucket and rags. Tell Annie to turn us around and head for the southeast end of Pers Island. I'm going to try and get the port engine running again."

"Okay. Anything else?"

"Yeah, find me some new filters. Check under the seats in the cabin. I need them right away."

A moment after Cutter went to relay Logan's message, he could feel the boat swing around and buck the building seas. Annie was doing exactly what he had asked her to do, which was to head into the wind and take the waves head on. And by heading to the closest land, he hoped to find a sheltered cove in time. The ride would be rougher, but the boat would be safe.

He knew he didn't have much time before the starboard engine would die as well. If that happened, the boat would turn sideways to the seas, and the rolling would start.

There were two filters, one mounted on the engine and one on the engine room bulkhead. The engine filter was a spin on. He grabbed a filter spanner, spun it off, and dumped it in a bucket. He saw 50% water, as he emptied it the best he could. He immediately filled it with fuel and spun it back onto the engine fitting.

Logan dumped the second filter glass bowl in the bucket and pulled the filter element out of the top. He hollered up for Cutter, "You find any filters yet?"

In the cabin, crew and equipment were being tossed around so bad they could hardly hang on.

Cutter hollered back, "We can't find ourselves! It's like being in a washing machine down here."

"No luck," Annie relayed.

"Okay, guess we'll make do."

Logan beat the second filter on the side of the bucket, knowing that might do the trick by knocking out dirt and water. He put the filter back together again, remembering to fill it up to the top with fuel.

He reached over and pushed the remote starter button next to the engine room gauges. The port engine sputtered and died. "Damn!" he cursed. "Air in the lines."

He pulled on the engine throttle cable and rolled the starter for a full thirty seconds. The starboard engine coughed and was going down for the count.

Logan tried the port engine remote start two more times. On the third try, the port engine caught and started. He jumped out of the engine room, up next to Annie.

Looking forward, he could make out the southeast corner of the island. He had spent part of a night there earlier in the summer.

Taking the wheel, he shoved the port engine throttle to the dash. The engine sputtered a couple of times and woke up with a loud roar.

A cheer came up to the steering station from below deck. Logan smiled at Annie, but he knew their luck might not last long.

The starboard engine was spitting and sputtering.

He could only hope the engines would keep running. They needed to get into the first little bay, the one he had used to hide from the RCMP in the fog.

As the boat finally approached the protection of the cove, the water calmed. All the crew came out on deck to see what was going on.

One of them spoke up, "You going to take us into that small narrow slot? Are you sure there's enough water there, Logan?"

"Oh yea, I've been here before, so just hang on. Cutter, could you get a line ready? We'll tie up to the rock wall over there," he said, pointing to the sheer cliff of granite and the kelp bed that lay next to it.

"Sure. You want that from the bow?"

"Right. There is an overhanging root, throw a bite over that, then make it off on the bow cleat."

Cutter moved forward, "Whatever you say, Captain."

Logan brought the throttle back, idling along the last 20 feet. He worked the boat into the bull kelp, then to the sheer rock wall. High above was a sturdy tree root hanging out from the edge of the rock wall.

Cutter threw the line, caught the root, then made it fast to the cleat.

Logan looked over to Annie and smiled. "We will be safe here, and now I can finish my work down below."

She smiled, nodded, and patted his arm in acknowledgment.

He could hear the crew on deck talking. "Good job, kid, that could have been a miserable ride."

Logan went into the cabin and found fuel filters under the v-berth he and Annie had slept on the night before. He passed them out on deck to Annie and Cutter and they took them to the engine room.

By the end of the hour, Logan had all the fuel filters changed out, and proceeded to tap the fuel tank drains. *That should take care of the water in the fuel problem.*

Logan started both engines to test run them, shut them off quickly to make sure they didn't suck up any kelp in the sea-suction.

Annie insisted Logan use hand cleaner and wash all the diesel off himself. The crew was sitting in the small cabin watching him. As he wiped his hands dry, a voice asked, "What now, Capt?"

Logan said, "Well, boys and girl," smiling at Annie. "Here's the deal. The ebb tide is blasting out of Johnston Straits right now, until later this afternoon. Queen Charlotte's are blowing hard enough to make things stack up in the swell department. That would make a miserable ride of it if we went right now."

He paused long enough for his words to sink in.

"And that could create a repeat performance of what we went through in the last hour. Now we could stay cozied up here next to this granite wall for about three hours to let some of that weather and tide cool off, then take the back way through Blackney Pass and be home before dinner."

Everyone was quiet. Cutter spoke up, "We sure don't want to repeat what we just went through."

"Good. We got a couple of poles on here. If I remember right, they're a bunch of fat cod that live in this here kelp bed under our feet."

For the next three hours, half the crew caught, and the other half cleaned cod. It made a bag full of perfect fillets for fish and chips when they got back to camp. And Annie was having the best time, now that she was doing most of the catching.

As Logan watched Annie, she would catch him out of the corner of her eye. Their eyes would meet and smile at each other. The crew noticed it too and knew there was something special going on between those two.

Logan drained the fuel tanks for water one more time, after giving any water time to settle before they headed home.

"Okay, Cutter, untie us. I want to drift out away from the kelp before I startup."

Both engines came to life, ready to run for home. They ran east for two hours with the wind square on their stern, passing the south side of Hansen Island, then cutting through Blackney Pass.

By slipping through White Beach Pass, they were on the inside of the islands, which put them in protected waters the rest of the way back to camp.

Once clear of the pass, Annie wanted to drive which was good for Logan. He could study the charts and focus on the sounder for the depth of water they were traveling over.

When they arrived back at camp, Annie wanted to land the boat while Logan stood beside her. He gave her pointers for the tricky maneuvering of twin engines.

The crew was happy to tie the boat up and headed up to their rooms. As they passed Oley, they told him with quick comments that the kid knew his stuff.

As Logan and Annie shut down and closed up the boat, Oley came by, smiling from ear to ear with Auntie right beside him.

Aunt Ida already had dinner in mind, "I hear you have some nice cod for me, my two fisher people."

Annie smiled. "Yes, Logan knew he couldn't come home empty-handed, or you might send him right back out to catch you something for dinner." Aunt Ida nodded in agreement.

Oley looked over to Logan. "Problems?"

"Yeah, water in the fuel, it could be from the last load of fuel we got. Unless it's getting in at the tank somehow?"

"Ve'll watch that. Let's go up for dinner. Then Annie can tell us all about it. I know she can hardly vait, after running the boat in here and tying it up as she did."

Dinner was fun at the family table. Annie had to tell all that went on in town followed by all the details of their near-disastrous afternoon.

She saved the best for last, telling how much fun it was to drive the crew boat the rest of the way home.

As the family listened to Annie spinning her yarn, crewmembers would walk up to Logan, pat him on the back and say, "Good job, kid."

He would return the compliment with a humble "Thanks."

When Annie finally slowed down to take a breath, Oley asked, "Logan, I know you are saving the day and everything. Could we bother you with one more chore?"

"I'm on it boss, the garbage run is as good as done."

They all laughed. "Are you coming, Annie?"

"I wouldn't miss the bear show with you for anything."

They were still laughing while putting on their coats. "I'll get the truck and pick you up out back of the kitchen."

That all sounded harmless, but it was precious time they spent together. Both enjoyed watching the bears, and time was slipping away faster and faster.

They were hanging onto every moment as time ticked past them, like sand falling through an hourglass.

With the day done, Logan walked Annie home. Stopping on the front porch, she pulled on the hand she was holding. He turned in mid-step coming face to face with her.

"You did a great job today," Annie said. "I want to thank you for it." She leaned into him and placed a sweet, gentle kiss on his lips, then put her face next to his as they held one another close.

"Goodnight, Logan." Annie turned to the door and slipped through without a glance back. Logan turned and headed for Points North.

*Where do I stand with this beautiful girl?* That thought mulled around his mind all night.

# CHAPTER 31

There was minimal talk over breakfast. Annie seemed to have gone to another planet after they said goodnight last night.

At noon, Logan saw Annie coming down to the log boom. Logan drove over to the dock to tie up, she took his line and waited for him to shut off the noisy motor.

"Already time for lunch?" Logan asked, trying to guess why Annie was so quiet.

"Logan, your sister called. Dad and Allison talked to her on the radio through the marine operator. She needs you to call her as soon as you can."

"Okay, they can calm down. I'm not late coming home, am I?" He smiled at Annie's sad but still beautiful face.

He noticed a small tear working its way down her cheek.

"No, Logan, it's your mother. I'm so sorry. She is undergoing treatment for cancer, and they want you to come home to be with her."

Logan's jaw set with grim determination. "Alright, let's get up to the office, and I'll make the call."

"Logan, wait. I understand this is a terrible thing for your mother. You need to go to be with her. I remember when this happened to my mother. It was hard, but we needed to be there for her."

"You're right. I better call Carrie and let her know I'll be along as soon as I can."

They walked to the office, a heavy silence between them.

Logan made the call through the marine operator. "Thank you, Operator. Hello Carrie, this is Logan. How is Mom? Over."

Carrie's voice sounded much older than when he left home only a few months ago. "Mom is going through treatment now, and it doesn't look good. Logan, can you come home, please? Over."

"Yes, I have four more days, then I can come home. I need to finish my job here. Okay? Over."

"I knew you would say that. I'll tell Mother you're coming home, but it will be a few days. Over."

"I need to finish my job here, Sis. First, I need to talk to the boss. I can keep you posted when I leave the camp for home. Take care. I love you, tell Mom also for me, please. Over."

"Yes, I will. Love you too. See you soon. Over."

"See you soon. Out."

Standing beside him, Annie's hand pressed the inside of his arm.

"Come on, Annie. I'll buy you lunch. Thank you, Allison."

Lunch was as quiet as breakfast but with a new feeling of dread in the air. Logan got back to work on the little log bronc, finding it hard to concentrate on the job at hand. When it was time for him to knock off, Annie was there.

"I wanted to come down to be with you. Ida is thinking of you also. If you need anything, please let her know."

"She has done all she can do. She sent you to me. Annie, you are the best. I can never thank you enough for the time we spent together this summer."

"It has been the best summer ever."

At the supper table, Oley spoke up. "Logan, vhen you finish up here, come to the house. Ve'll need to talk."

"Yes, sir."

At the house, Oley was sitting at the kitchen table. Auntie Ida, Annie, and Logan came in, taking off their coats in the late summer evening chill, and sat at the table.

"I heard your mother is in for cancer treatments?"

"Yes, sir. I want to work until Irving gets back. That should be in four days, well three now, then put my boat in the water to go home."

"Annie and I have talked about that, and she has a better idea. How about you take one of the heavy equipment tarps in the shop, and vith all the rough lumber we have, you and Annie can build a frame around your boat den cover it with the tarp."

He paused, watching Logan for his reaction.

"I'll vatch it for you through the vinter. It vill be yust fine there, vaiting for you in the spring, vhen you come back to vork for the summer."

"That would give me more time with Mother. It doesn't sound like there is a lot of that left."

"Ya, good. You and Annie can take off on the floatplane to Vancouver together. Then ve'll get you on a train to Mount Vernon, Washington."

"That would be great, sir. I'd be thrilled to go out with Annie."

"I thought you vould be. Then this is good, vhen Irving arrives, you vill go out for home."

Ida smiled, and Annie reached under the table and took Logan's hand.

Oley continued. "Logan, you came here as a brave youngster, now I say goodbye to one of my top hands, and a young man. You've done a good job for all of us."

Oley took a deep breath and glanced to Annie for agreement.

"You be sure and keep in touch vith Ida and me. Ve want you back next summer now, Yaw."

Ida smiled. "Yaw, we do. You need to fill my freezer vith fish, you and Annie here."

Annie squeezed Logan's hand again.

"Thank you for trusting me and letting me sit at the family table. That means a lot to me."

He stared at the table, feeling his emotions well up in his chest.

"Would you excuse me? I need to check the battery switch on the log bronc."

"Yes, of course."

Logan got up, reaching for his coat. Annie stood up as well.

He said, "You don't have to go. It's raining."

"Now, when did a little rain stop me from going with you?"

"Not lately, that's for sure."

Walking down to the log boom, Logan said, "Thanks for coming with me. I had to get outside. I can breathe easier out here."

"I know. You still have the cover on Points North. Can we sit in the stern?"

"Sure do, that's perfect. I'm not cold at all. I don't want to get wet unless we have to. It has been a wet summer, aye?"

She started laughing.

"What's so funny?"

"You."

"Why?

"You're starting to sound more and more like a Canadian."

"Oh no! I'm one of you. Oh well, relax and enjoy it, aye?"

She chuckled again. Logan lifted the corner of the tarp-covered roof he had made over the stern of Points North and they sat on the seat across from the tiller. Annie scooted up close to Logan. He put his arm around her so that they could share the warmth and closeness of each other.

She held his hand in hers. "You know your mother could be fine after treatment. We have a different medical system up here. Your mother has a better chance than mine. you'll see."

"From what I understand, it depends if they catch it soon enough."

They were quiet, then they both fell asleep listening to the rhythm of the rain on the canvas roof over their heads. The next thing they knew, there was a flashlight shining in on them. It was Oley.

"You two vake up. I knew I'd find you here. Come on home, Annie. It is time for bed."

"I'm sorry, sir, we fell asleep. I didn't mean to."

"I know Logan. You are yust fine. You sleep vell tonight now."

"Annie, I'll valk you to the house."

"Thanks, Dad, you don't have to wait. Logan will walk me to the house."

"All right then, I'll see you there."

They walked hand in hand to the house, saying goodnight with the gut-wrenching, ever-present feeling of time slipping away.

# CHAPTER 32

Irving came in late Thursday afternoon. Up at the kitchen, everyone knew Annie and Logan would be flying to Vancouver the next morning.

The entire log camp crew stopped by their table, one by one, to say goodbye and tell Logan how good it was working with him. They all hoped to see him next summer.

After dinner, Logan and Annie went for a walk at Annie's insistence. "Come on, Logan, let's walk by Points North. I want to look at the shed we built. It should work for the winter, shouldn't it?"

"Yeah, your dad said he would keep an eye on it for me."

Logan asked, "Will you come back up for the holidays?"

"Not sure. Sometimes, Aunt Samantha likes to spend Christmas in Cabo San Lucas, in Mexico."

"That would be nice."

"How about you, will you stay at home?"

"There was not much money to go around in a fisherman's house. Now that Dad came up missing, I'm sure a chunk of my wages will go to Mom to support the house and help feed us."

He paused to think about what he had said, feeling the heavy weight of responsibility. Annie squeezed his hand to acknowledge she understood.

"I'm okay with that," Logan continued. "She needs support. This winter, I can dig up some woodcutting jobs. You never know, huh?"

"Are you always so optimistic?"

"Sure. Why not? I don't know how successful I'll be. All I want is to be happy with my life and work. How about you?"

"When we first met, I was sure that life for me was the city. Then University and after that, my work would afford me the things I wanted."

She paused, deep in thought. "Now, I'm not sure. I like your idea of being happy with life. You make me laugh when you keep everything so easy-going and simple."

Annie took a deep breath. "Logan, you don't let a lot of drama come crashing through the door on you. If you don't mind me quoting you, that tells me a lot. You will have a much happier life than me living life my way."

"So, what are you saying? We're not right for one another?"

"No. It's that we're different in some ways and so much alike in other ways. I'm not making sense again, am I?"

"Yes you are. I think you see the other side of things. You are not like your city aunt. You are your own person Annie. Don't ever let someone else pull your levers."

He gave a little smile. "Not even me, as much as I'd like to."

"You've got a deal, mister. I won't let anyone do that, 'pull my levers,' that is."

She turned to look at him and his ever-present smile.

"We should go back to the house. I'll fix us a cup of cocoa. Dad might still be up. He's fun to listen to. I'll get him to tell us a story about his childhood. His was a lot like yours, Logan."

Oley was still up. They all had a cup of cocoa at the kitchen table and listened to oft'-told stories. As Oley said goodnight, he reminded them he would see them at 4 AM.

Annie chided, "Dad, don't I get to sleep in my last morning?"

Oley shook his head. "You are part of our table, and you vould be missed too much, both of you."

"Alright then, I'll walk you to the door Logan."

As Annie opened the door for Logan, he thought, *no kiss tonight, and it was our last chance. Guess I didn't make the cut, Coach.*

The next morning blew by. Each of their bags were at the office by 9:30 AM, waiting for the plane. Annie was deep in thought about something. She wasn't talking and that wasn't normal.

Even Auntie Ida was there. Logan asked if she was giving up some of her precious nap time.

"I yust want to see my two favorite fishing people off. Now you vrite to me, both of you. I vant to keep track of how your lives at school are going."

It was time to be out on the dock and Annie hugged everyone.

Ida made Logan give her a hug. Then she reminded him again to write and keep them informed on what he was doing. He might not be in the camp, but that didn't mean he wasn't in their thoughts and hearts.

Logan shook Oley's hand, thanking him for giving him a chance.

Oley nodded. He always knew Logan would make it. "You keep in touch, you hear? I vant you back next summer now. You're a fine hand, and ve'll miss you."

"Yes, sir, I'll keep in touch."

Logan and Annie climbed into the plane. Being the last passengers, they were in the air in no time, heading straight for Vancouver, their next destination.

Logan watched Annie. She was still not talking or even giving Logan a slight glance across the seaplane's crowded cabin. She stared out the passenger window, rubbing her hand on her knee.

Logan wanted to scream out over the roar of the loud seaplane engine,

*Annie, this is it. What can I do to tell you that I love and care for you?*

The conversation in his head continued. *I know we are too young, but I have these feelings, and if you don't feel the same way, there is nothing I can do.* As he sat there, a million thoughts raced through his head.

The plane touched down at the downtown seaplane airport.

Climbing out of the bobbing seaplane, they waited quietly for their bags on the dock.

Logan could see Annie's aunt waiting at the head of the ramp. He had dreaded this moment. Annie headed up the sloped ramp, like she didn't even know Logan. Aunt Samantha her gave a warm, welcoming hug.

Logan didn't get a glance. As far as Samantha was concerned, he could have been a bag handler.

Samantha had already started pulling Annie away from Logan.

Annie stopped. "No, Auntie. I need time to talk to Logan and tell him what I've been thinking about."

Her aunt stood back, her mouth in a permanent frown with a look that asked why. Annie spoke up again firmly. "Because I have to, I owe it to him. We've grown close this summer, and I need to tell him what I'm thinking."

As Logan reached the top of the ramp, Annie reached out for Logan's hand, and he did the same. They walked over to sit in two of the airport's waiting chairs.

Her aunt had a sour look on her face. Annie had been so firm on what she needed to do that the aunt kept silent and stood there, fuming.

Logan liked it when Annie stood up to her.

Annie turned to Logan. "Logan, I told you once in the middle of the summer that on occasion, I would let you know what was going through my head."

She paused, putting the words together for the most important statement of her life.

"Yes, I'm ready to pick my path. That path would be with you if I can quote you. I want to drop the other shoe now."

She started sniffing, her eyes misty. "I want you in my life. I will wait for you and you only. I know you will be there for me because, Logan, I trust you."

Logan stayed quiet and waited. He did not want to break the moment of her sharing what she was thinking.

She cleared her throat and started again. "Yes, I will stay with you. I will go with you wherever your next adventure will take us. All I ask is for you to be you, and I can be me, like we were this summer. That's how it should be."

Annie couldn't stop herself, "You are so kind and patient with me. You are a wonderful man, waiting for me as you have. I know you will be fine with us apart. Our relationship will be stronger and better, and we will appreciate our time together."

She stopped, studying his eyes. "Am I clear on what's on my mind?"

He snapped out of his thousand-mile gaze.

"Yes. Oh, yes." A feeling of relief flowed over him. "We have the rest of our lives, and it will be happy, together."

Annie was glad she finally made the decision and knew his commitment was strong.

"Logan, I want you to call me as soon as you get home, please. I want to know how your mother is doing. I want to hear it all. You're mine now, and let's keep it that way, forever please?"

She hesitated, then reached up and brushed a tear from her eye. Logan was sure that was a tear of happiness.

They stood up from their chairs. It was time to go.

"Annie, I never had any other thought. I never knew how to say it without hurting your feelings. I never want to hurt you, and you are the one for me. Most of all, you can count on me. I will be there for you."

"Thank you, Logan."

Annie wrapped her warm arms around his shoulders. Leaning back and looking intently into his eyes one more time, she said, "You know I've always loved you. From the first day we met."

Logan slid his strong arms around her slim waist and embraced her. "You may not believe this, but I was in love with you when your Aunt Ida told me all about you, before you even arrived in camp."

She leaned into his firm, but gentle, embrace and they shared a long, lingering kiss that seemed to go on forever.

## THE END